LINE OF
DARKNESS

LINE OF
DARKNESS

A COLLEEN HAYES MYSTERY

MAX TOMLINSON

OCEANVIEW ⊙ PUBLISHING
SARASOTA, FLORIDA

ISBN 978-1-60809-564-3

Published in the United States of America by Oceanview Publishing

Sarasota, Florida

www.oceanviewpub.com

10 9 8 7 6 5 4 3 2

PRINTED IN THE UNITED STATES OF AMERICA

In memory of my mother, Catherine Jeanne Tomlinson

LINE OF
DARKNESS

PROLOGUE

He'd been following the German all day.

Now he was down by the Boca where he shadowed the older man along the river, the sun going down. The German was beer-gut heavy, in his Bermuda shorts and tourist T-shirt, with a crew cut and sunburn to set him further apart from the locals, making him easy to follow through the Paris of South America. Like tracking an aging rhinoceros. Still lethal.

But no whip or club now.

No gas chamber now.

He watched the sixty-seven-year-old plod over the garish multi-colored stones, eating his ice cream in the pleasant spring evening, stopping at the mouth of El Caminito as the barkers outside the bars and clubs tried to lure him in with cut-rate Flamenco shows, cheap steins of beer, girls in split skirts and heavy eye makeup who pouted from doorways. Their desperation was evident as the tinny music wafted out of this place, that place.

The German waddled down El Caminito, the children coming up to him, begging for change. He swatted a small hand away. An old woman approached, hands in prayer, pleading. He pushed past her. The soldiers, machine guns over shoulders, watched everyone. The generals had been in power for several years.

The man continued to track the German. Unlike the German, he was fit, in his forties, dark, more than ready for what was about to come.

It was all about patience.

He had waited since 1942. He could wait a little longer.

He felt in his jacket pocket. The ID card was all set. The switch-blade knife was ready. He had one more weapon in his other pocket, the *pièce de résistance*.

In the middle of the narrow street, old colonial Spanish houses contrasted with the kitschy primary colors that had been slapped on all over the Boca. A woman in stacked high heels and a tight red skirt, her gleaming hair pinned back, danced out from a bar on the cobblestones to meet the German. Her blood-red lips puckered as she took his arm, pulling him into the dark club. The German laughed as he shoved the last of his ice cream cone into his mouth, licking a drop off his thumb. The man watched the German stumble in past the doorman, whose well-worn pin-striped suit hung on him in the heat.

The man followed the German inside.

It was dark in here, the Flamenco music echoing. Cane-backed chairs hung from the ceiling. A few other tourists sat at small tables, where Chianti bottles with melted wax candles served as decoration. The smell of beer saturated the floorboards. Another woman danced on a low stage, the hems of her frilly skirt swirling as she clacked castanets. Behind her a bored combo played dutifully with forced smiles.

The man stood at the bar, anonymous in his cap and sunglasses, black roomy jacket, jeans and sneaks. Just another tourist on the prowl.

He watched the German sit down at a table with the woman in the red skirt.

The barman appeared, smiling around his mustache.

"Espresso," the man said.

The barman nodding *si, si,* turned to a fancy chrome machine. Already the waitress for the German was at the counter, ordering a liter of beer and a champagne. The woman in red at the table had her hand on the German's pink pudgy knee.

The barman set his coffee down in front of the man with a flourish and a smile.

"Deutsche?" he asked.

"Americano," the man lied.

"No, no . . ." The barman grinned as he shook his head, thumbing his white-shirted chest. "*We* are the Americanos. You are the *norte* Americanos!"

The man smiled at the quip, sipped his coffee, held it up to compliment the barman. The barman grinned back, turned to the counter to pour a frothy stein of beer for the German and a fizzy drink of some sort from an unlabeled bottle into a champagne flute.

The man would bide his time. He had waited thirty-seven years.

After another liter of beer and another "champagne," the woman in red was practically in the fat man's lap. Then he pushed her away, struggled to get up, chair squeaking over the music.

A worried look crossed her face. That he might leave.

"Toilet!" the German shouted.

Ah. She pointed back past the stage with a long red-nailed finger, a fresh smile plastered on her face. As soon as he turned away from her, the smile faded.

The German staggered across the tiny floor, past the stage where the dancing was reaching a climax. Down a dark hallway.

Time. It was time.

The man paid for his coffee, tipped the barman well, but not so well that he'd be remembered.

Headed back to the restroom.

Pushed open the blue door marked *Gauchos*. The sharp smell of urine.

The German stood at the only urinal, his back to him, head tilted up as he relieved himself.

The man slid the bolt lock on the door. Turned to the German. He slipped his hands in his pockets, ready.

The German turned his head halfway as he finished up.

"Just waiting for a piss," the man said in German to the fat man. "You don't buy beer; you only rent it."

The German laughed, big belly jiggling as he zipped himself up. "Where are you from, friend? Do I hear Berlin? That's my town."

"Sachsenhausen," the man said darkly.

The German's eyes narrowed as he turned around, face dropping. "*Where?*"

"You know where," he said. "The concentration camp."

"What the hell are you talking about?"

"Don't pretend. Thirty-five kilometers north of Berlin. The shoe-testing track? Where my mother walked twelve hours a day over gravel and rocks, while you bastards tested out the latest in military footwear? You thought it was funny when she collapsed. Before you shot her."

The German's drunken face grew brutal. "You're living in a fantasy, pal. I was never in the army."

The man brought out the thirty-seven-year-old SS ID, held it up.

"Really?" he said, feigning confusion. He looked at the card, then at the German. "Is this not you? Rottenführer Kruger? It certainly looks like you. Admittedly, quite a few kilos ago." He smiled. "It's a constant battle, isn't it—keeping the weight off? Not for me, though. I learned how to do with almost nothing back in the camps. It's a habit that stuck."

The German looked at the card, bleary at first, then ignored it with a fleshy scowl.

"Out of my way, Yid." He moved to push past.

The man brought the switchblade out, pressed the button, a long stiletto of steel ejecting with a smooth *shick*.

The German stood back, blinking in fear. "What the hell? What do you want?"

He held out the ID card. "Want to get rid of this?"

There was a pause. A cagey squint. "How much?"

"No charge."

"What?"

"All you have to do is eat it."

"What?"

"You obviously like to eat. So eat this. Hide the evidence. Like you did with my mother's body in the lime pit behind Sachsenhausen."

"You're fucking crazy!"

He nodded in agreement. "Yes." He held the ID out further. "Chomp chomp, eh?" He held the knife up in the other hand. "Or, take your pick."

The German blinked frantically. Out in the bar, the syrupy music played.

The German gave a gasp, took the ID, shoved it in his mouth, started chewing, the old paper dry, the photograph crumpling with difficulty between his teeth. Grunting a painful mouthful.

"Mach Schnell, Rottenführer." The man poked him gently in the gut with the tip of the knife blade, so as not to break skin. The German flinched. "Almost done."

The German fought it down, swallowing with a grimace.

When he was done, he said, "Satisfied, punk?"

The man pulled the garrote from his other pocket. Didn't smile. There was nothing to smile about anymore.

"Remember the gallows? Where you hung prisoners with piano wire while we stood in line at roll call? I was only six at the time but it's not something you forget."

The German's face turned to tears. "*Halt! Bitte!*"

"On your knees, Rottenführer."

The German's mouth opened in a shout for help. But the man had anticipated that. A swift butt of his forehead into his face, crunching his nose, knocked him back into the cubicle wall with a bang. Several more blows had him down on the filthy tiles. Flipped him over. The garrote around his neck now. Caught one of the German's fingers in it as he tightened it, slicing deep as the German fought for his life. Blood spurted.

*   *   *

Moments later, the man left the bar, head down. The woman in the red skirt was sitting at the same table, smoking a cigarette, looking bored, waiting for her German to return. Onstage, the music and dancing continued.

CHAPTER ONE

Colleen was slipping a file folder into a cabinet in her new office when she heard footsteps approaching the end of Pier 26. Light footsteps. A woman's. They echoed along the cavernous deck of the huge covered pier beyond the wall of her office—once a marine workshop—off the high ceiling of the warehouse that sat out on the water, a structure last refurbished during World War II. With the demise of the shipyards, cheap office space was to be had. And Colleen was having it, despite the cold, drafty, dark room. A sweater took care of the chill. The fresh sea air was welcome, despite the hint of diesel and the sounds of ships. And through her window, albeit to one side and partially obstructed by the huge cement tower of the bridge on Treasure Island, the lights of Oakland twinkled on the bay. High above the roof, the white noise of post-rush-hour traffic whirred on the Bay Bridge.

Business was picking up. And an office at home was no longer doable, not with her daughter eight months pregnant. Pam needed the flat to herself.

And Colleen needed her sanity.

The nimble footsteps stopped at her open door.

Colleen looked up, two days into moving in, empty boxes here and there, her old beat-up metal desk facing the door, the phone not hooked up yet. The banker's lamp cast a pall of light across the dark walls and empty space, across old shipping charts long forgotten.

A woman of medium height stood at the open door. She was middle-aged, not slim or overweight, with a serious dark oval face, her brown hair up in a businesslike do. Her dark-framed glasses accented a blue skirt suit that screamed European designer. Sensible black heels with squarish toes and a slight platform made her look like she had just stepped out of a board meeting. In one hand she carried a slender black briefcase. Colleen's friend Alex spent a small fortune on clothes, and this woman could be serious competition. By contrast Colleen felt down-home, her chestnut hair pulled back in a loose ponytail come undone on one side, her turtleneck over wide denim bell-bottoms, treasured Pony Topstars with the red stripes to top it off. "Can I help you?" she asked, standing up, slapping dust from her hands, then straightening her hair.

The woman looked at the frosted glass panel stenciled "Maintenance," then at Colleen quizzically.

"Still moving in," Colleen said. "It should read 'Hayes Confidential.'"

"Ah," the woman said. "Then I have the right place." She spoke perfect English but with the hint of a German accent.

Colleen went to the wall where two high-backed guest chairs were stacked against a slanted I-beam, grabbed one, dusted it off with a handkerchief from her back pocket, walked around, set the chair in front of the desk.

The woman thanked her, came in, smoothed her skirt out as she sat down. She kept her briefcase on her lap. Colleen shut the door.

"My coffee machine is still packed," she said, going back around to sit in her squeaky roller desk chair. "But I can scare up some chewing gum."

"No thank you," the woman said, returning a polite smile.

Colleen asked how she could help.

"Before I continue," the woman said, "I need assurance that any business we might conduct is completely private."

"Hayes *Confidential*," Colleen said, sitting back, folding her hands over her stomach.

"Very well," the woman said, opening her briefcase, coming out with a photo and a business card. She placed both on the desk. "I'm looking for my nephew."

Colleen reached over, picked up the business card first. Ingrid Richter, Senior Vice President, First Trust of Zurich. An address in Berlin. Next Colleen picked up the photo.

A photo of Ingrid Richter in casual clothes and a man in his early forties, if that, trim, in good shape. They were sitting at a table outdoors somewhere green, a restaurant, a beer garden perhaps. Two large beer steins sat on the table in front of them. Even though the man wore sunglasses, his eyes were intense. He had tight-cropped dark hair, a receding hairline, and needed a shave. He wore a loose summer shirt open over a black tank top. Lean but muscular. Both of them were smiling in a reserved manner although the man had a somewhat threatening look. Hard.

Colleen set the photo down. "When someone says 'nephew,' I tend to think of a six-year-old with missing front teeth and a cowlick."

Ingrid Richter gave another polite smile. "Erich is forty-two."

"A grown man. But you're concerned about him."

"Erich tends to . . . ah . . . favor having a good time over almost anything else. Including his safety."

"He's got plenty of company. Does he have any other family?"

"Just me."

"Is he in any trouble that you know of?"

"No, but Erich is what they call 'manic-depressive.' Which doesn't help matters."

Colleen picked up the photo again, looked at Erich. Confident smile but too taut. Forced. She could see the tension in him now.

"So he goes off on jaunts," Colleen said.

Ingrid Richter returned a single nod. Not very forthcoming.

"And he came to San Francisco for this one?" Colleen asked.

"Yes."

"Some would say he picked the right place to party," Colleen said. "Is he gay?"

Ingrid sat up, obviously taken aback.

"It's not a judgement," Colleen said. "I have to ask these questions so that, if you hire me, I know where to start looking. For a small city, San Francisco is a pretty big place."

"Erich is not 'gay.' But who knows what he fails to divulge to his aunt?"

Colleen pressed the button on her Pulsar watch. Past seven o'clock. "I can keep playing twenty questions, Ms. Richter, or you can tell me what you know about Erich's disappearance and we can see if it makes sense for us to work together."

Ingrid Richter dug into her briefcase, came out with a sheet of paper, neatly typed, and handed it to Colleen. "Erich's itinerary, from Berlin to San Francisco in the last week. With a stop in Buenos Aires."

"What was your nephew doing in South America?"

"Sampling the abundant nightlife and cheap wine. One can live like a prince on a shoestring there."

"And you're sure he made it to San Francisco?"

"Erich called me from San Francisco International last Friday night. Out of the blue. He's like that: impulsive."

"How did he know to find you here?"

"We stay in touch. I'm here for a conference, which has since turned into a long-term assignment. He had just arrived when he called. We made plans to get together, last Saturday, for dinner."

It was Tuesday. Four nights ago. "And Erich never showed up."

Ingrid Richter nodded. "Erich never showed up."

"Where were you supposed to meet?"

"At the Fairmont, where I'm staying."

"You say he has no family apart from you? What happened there?"

"The war," was all Ingrid Richter said. "I'm the only relative he has left."

"I'm sorry to hear that. Lucky for Erich he has an aunt who cares so much about him." Ingrid Richter wasn't that much older than Erich, maybe a decade or so.

Ingrid Richter smiled courteously. "My immediate family died during the war as well. I handled my father's affairs. Erich became one of them—one I didn't mind at all. He's all I have left as well."

Ingrid came from an affluent family by the sounds of things. Even so, she hadn't escaped the brutality of war. "What happened to your family?"

"My father was shot by the Gestapo," she said as if she might be telling you what she had for breakfast. "1942. My mother died the year before. I had just turned seventeen when my father died. Now, do you need to know anything else about me, or shall we get on with Erich?"

Defensive. But Colleen felt an affinity. At seventeen, she had been arrested for killing her husband. Sentenced to fourteen years, served ten. One really didn't have a choice about growing up once that was set in motion. It was sink or swim.

"I apologize if it sounds intrusive," she said. "I'm just trying to get a handle on things."

"It was a long time ago," Ingrid Richter said.

"What does Erich do when he's not jet-setting?"

"He lives on investments. Enough to support his vagabond life-style. He also borrows. From me."

"Is Erich in any danger that you're aware of? Enemies?"

Ingrid Richter shook her head.

Colleen drummed her fingers. "Bottom line, Ms. Richter, Erich is a grown man. From what you've told me, missing dinner with you shouldn't be a huge surprise. He came in on a Friday night. Maybe he was diverted by the city's many distractions."

"But we hadn't seen each other in two years. And, as I say, Erich came out to San Francisco specifically to visit me. I'm worried he might have hurt himself. One time, in Algeria, he wound up penniless, living with an Arab family who were essentially 'keeping' him until I paid his 'expenses.' I had to arrange for him to be brought back to Germany. "

"Have you called San Francisco Police? Filed a Missing Persons report?"

Ingrid Richter shook her head. "Erich is not an American. Nor am I. Neither one of us needs the publicity. With my position, I can't afford to wind up in a police file. And, as you say, Erich is a grown man. How many resources would the police allocate looking for a party boy who is far too old to be getting into scrapes?"

Colleen understood Ms. Richter's situation but wondered why the exposure would really matter so much to Erich. "How did you get my name, Ms. Richter?"

"A man at the Fairmont. The security manager."

Colleen knew the one. "Well, I can put a day or two into looking for Erich but I wouldn't suggest too much more at this point. He's just as likely to show up out of nowhere since that seems to be his way."

Ingrid Richter already had her purse out, a sleek black thing. "Fine."

"You haven't heard my rate yet," Colleen said.

"I'm sure it's acceptable. I'm told you are very qualified."

Colleen told her anyway. "Plus expenses."

Ingrid Richter peeled off numerous hundred-dollar bills, set them delicately on the desk blotter. She didn't need a receipt. "You can contact me at the Fairmont if you need more."

Cash in advance. A lot of it. That didn't happen every day.

But it could also be a red flag.

Colleen thanked her. Held up the photo of the two of them in a beer garden or wherever. "Is this mine?"

"Yes."

"Do you have one of just your nephew?"

"Nothing recent, I'm afraid."

The itinerary Ms. Richter had given her said Erich's last name was Hahn.

"Does he go by any other names?" Colleen asked.

"Not that I know of."

Colleen wondered about that. But aunties didn't know everything.

"I'm obviously quite concerned to know where Erich is," Ingrid Richter said.

"I'll start on it tonight," Colleen said.

CHAPTER TWO

One of the plusses of the new office on Pier 26 was how close it was to downtown. After Ingrid Richter left, Colleen got out her scissors, cut the photo of Ingrid and Erich down the middle, separating the two halves. When looking for one person, it was best not to cloud the issue with two.

She called her daughter at home, told her she'd be late.

"We're out of milk," Pam said.

Right, Colleen thought, curious as to how a twenty-year-old, even eight months pregnant, was suddenly incapacitated.

She got into her Torino, parked on the deck of the pier inside the voluminous covered warehouse, and motored out onto Embarcadero, the spring night crisp and clear along the water. At the Ferry Building, she turned on Market, stopped at the Hyatt Regency. With its high open interior reminiscent of the inside of a futuristic pyramid, and its exposed Plexiglas elevator and revolving bar, it was a natural place for an errant, past-his-prime thrill-seeker to bed down.

No luck. No one at registration had seen Erich, let alone had a record of his stay. The night security man, one of Colleen's contacts, said he would ask around. Colleen made up a quick flyer with Erich Hahn's half-photo, with her phone numbers, travel info, and the eye-catching "Reward for Information" underneath. The security man Xeroxed off several dozen copies. Black-and-white, blurry with photocopying, the picture wasn't the best, but it worked. He kept one to put up in the Hyatt's employee break room. Colleen promised to take him to lunch next time they had a free afternoon.

The rest of the evening went the same way, Colleen hitting the big hotels, the tourist motels along Lombard, the girlie bars in North Beach where she started with the Condor Club, with its flashing red nipples on the story-high likeness of Carol Doda in her black bikini.

By the time the bars were shutting down, she headed to the Yellow Cab depot on Bayshore where she spoke to the dispatcher who told her to go ahead and pin her flyer up in the break room. She did the same with Desoto and Veteran's.

No one had seen Erich Hahn.

She'd done as much as she could for one night. Around two a.m. Colleen parked the Torino behind her building on Vermont Street, trudged up three flights of exterior switchback stairwell to the porch of her Edwardian flat, the purr of the elevated freeway in the distance soothing at the end of a long day. She let herself quietly into her kitchen, so as not to wake Pamela.

But she could hear the television in the living room, the latest acquisition she wasn't crazy about. But Pamela had pushed.

She could also smell cigarette smoke. She had quit when she learned Pam was pregnant. Pam had, too. For a while.

Through the kitchen off the porch, into the living room, she found Pamela sitting on the black leather sofa, feet up on the glass coffee table, in the same white velour bathrobe she had been wearing that morning. By the looks of things, her pretty red hair had not been brushed. Her freckled face was tired and drawn. Her pregnant belly distorted her normally shapely figure like a funhouse mirror. And like that mirror, pregnancy was not suiting her. Not long ago, Colleen had rescued her daughter from a religious cult. And now this. But she reminded herself that *this* was still a definite improvement.

The coffee table was littered with cups, a glass, a half-eaten bowl of cereal. A pack of Pall Malls lay open next to an ashtray that held several dead butts. Not what Colleen wanted to see.

Pamela looked up, clearly annoyed at being silently judged, changed the channel with the remote.

"You're late," she said.

"Work," Colleen said, peeling off her leather car coat. She headed into the hall to hang it up.

"I thought you might have stopped over at Matt's," Pamela said.

"No," Colleen said, hanging up her coat, straightening the shoulders. "Just work."

"I bet you didn't remember milk."

No, she hadn't.

Colleen drew a deep breath for the patience that was in it, went back to the living room, holding the doorframe on either side, leaning in. "I'll pick some up tomorrow. Or, you can. I have a pretty busy day."

Pamela sighed audibly. "I don't have a car."

"The store is literally two blocks away."

"Down a hill."

Colleen refrained from shaking her head. Pam never failed to try her patience, especially after a long day. But at least she wasn't hanging out with the latest cult du jour. "I'm going to bed," she said. "Don't stay up too late."

Pamela thumbed the remote. An old war movie came on and Colleen was reminded of Ingrid Richter telling her that Erich's parents had been killed during the war. Ingrid Richter's too.

Tomorrow she'd hit the airport, make the rounds of the lesser-known hotels and clubs. Someone like Erich Hahn, if he were a libertine worth his salt, might like his accommodation and entertainment a little more on the edgier side. There were also the many gay bars and clubs, despite what Ingrid Richter seemed to think about her nephew. Nephews didn't always tell their aunties what they got up to. And aunties didn't always want to know.

But something about this particular auntie made Colleen wonder. Ingrid Richter didn't fit the mold. But well-paying gigs were not to be sniffed at, especially with Pamela's situation. And this one shouldn't take long.

CHAPTER THREE

Seven o'clock next evening, Matt Dwight slid next to Colleen sitting on a stool at the window of The Buena Vista, with its vantage point overlooking Aquatic Park. The late spring weather was holding and Angel Island was fading nicely into twilight.

She turned to look at him.

Matt wore a brown leisure jacket with white stitching and a striped shirt with long lapels and a blue tie with a big knot. His ash brown hair touched his collar, bold for a cop, even a San Francisco cop. His trimmed mustache was filling in nicely, setting off sculpted cheekbones. His steely blue eyes shone. As usual he was something to look at. He was glad to see her too she could tell. They hadn't seen each other all week. They clicked in the most basic of ways, although Colleen was doing her best not to let things get out of hand.

"Sorry I'm late," Matt said, giving her a soft peck on the cheek.

She finished her Irish coffee, savoring the sweet whiskey burn after a day of tramping around second- and third-rate hotels, bars, and the like. She was pleasantly weary but otherwise frustrated. No trace of Erich Hahn. She had thought this was going to be a quick gig.

"As it turns out, you're just in time," she said, sliding her empty glass mug in front of Matt.

He smiled, signaled the waitress for two Irish coffees.

His pager went off. He pulled it from his belt, looked at it, then frowned.

Not again, she thought.

"I'll be right back," he said.

Colleen suppressed a sigh while Matt went to use the payphone, ran a brush through her hair, getting longer and fluffier, giving Farrah a run for her money. She reapplied pastel peach lipstick. A couple more years and makeup might have to be part of the equation but she was getting away without it now. The waitress gave her a knowing smile as she set the drinks down. Matt attracted attention. Colleen slipped her things away in her shoulder bag, set it down by her feet. In her oversized black leather coat over a bright yellow baggy peekaboo top, wide-leg flares with Frye boots, she might have been a little overdressed for tramping around all day, but she knew she was seeing Matt tonight. She just hoped it wasn't going to be another rain check.

Matt returned, the smile on his face long gone.

"Let me guess," she said. "Problems at 850." 850 Bryant. SFPD Headquarters.

"I'm sorry," he said, clinking mugs. They drank together before he looked at his watch. She wasn't too surprised. This happened more often than not.

"Guess number two," she said, setting her Irish coffee down. "Dr. Lange."

"Dr. Lange," he said, nodding. "It's getting close."

Dr. Lange was the reputed leader of Aryan Alliance, a local neo-Nazi faction with shadowy connections to the KKK and other extremist groups. Colleen had run into Lange on a case she had worked last year when the mayor had been assassinated. Lange was well dressed, well educated, and well practiced at lurking in the background where he couldn't be implicated.

"That's big," she said. "This has been brewing the better part of a year."

Matt's face was tense.

"Well," she said, "if you pull him in, make sure you smack his head on the car door a couple of times for me."

Matt frowned at first, then rectified it with a smile. "I'll make it up to you."

"Damn right you will," she said. "I'm wearing the black lace underwear you seem to like so much."

"Jesus," Matt said, running his hand through his hair. "Why did I become a cop?"

"Because you're misguided?"

"Possibly," he said, draining his Irish coffee, pulling a twenty-dollar bill from his wallet, leaving it on the table. "I can drop by later if I get done early."

She shook her head. "It would be you and me and the pregnant princess in the other room," she said. "And I'd hate to subject you to that."

He dug in his pocket, came out with a house key, held it up. "Want to wait at my place? The freezer compartment is freshly stocked with TV dinners."

"Pretty tempting," she said. "But who knows when you might be finished? And I might eat them all. But call me if you're done before midnight and I'll burn rubber."

"Deal." He set the key down on the counter. "Take it just in case." He squinted with a sly smile. "You never know when you might need it."

She didn't know how she felt about that. But she didn't want to hurt his feelings. She took the key.

"Since you're going back to work," she said. "Can you look something up for me?"

"Who is it *this* time, Coll?" Matt sighed.

She had planned to make the request postcoital, where it was likely to be agreed to without question. She didn't like to ask for work favors. And Matt had been under pressure of late on the Lange case.

"A German tourist named Erich Hahn," she said. "Missing since last Friday."

It was Thursday. "Almost a week. Did you call Missing Persons?"

"My client doesn't want that. And he's nowhere to be found."

"I'll try," he said, reaching over, giving her a kiss on the lips, which lingered for a moment. "God, I hate to walk away from you and your black lace underwear."

"Eat your heart out," she said, winking. "But call me even if it's after midnight. You might get lucky."

CHAPTER FOUR

1979

"I think your nephew might have moved on, Ms. Richter," Colleen said into the phone, which Pacific Bell had finally hooked up in her new office. She was sitting with her back to her beat-up green metal desk, facing the partial view of the bay. Early Friday morning fog blew across the surface of the water. A sailboat nosed out from behind the concrete tower base, its jib catching wind as it cleared the bridge. The boat leaned over, picking up speed.

The third day looking for Erich Hahn meant it was time to stop and evaluate. A normal search usually turned up something by now.

Perhaps this wasn't a normal search. It was starting to look that way.

"Erich and I may have a tenuous relationship," Ingrid Richter said in clipped English on her end of the phone from the Fairmont Hotel. "But it's a strong one. When Erich knew I was coming to San Francisco on business, he flew in specifically to visit me. Visiting San Francisco would save Erich a duty trip to Europe to see his aunt. He was overdue. He also wanted to talk to me. Which usually means he needs an advance on his remittance. He wasn't likely to let that drop."

"A remittance at forty-two?"

"Trust fund with strict conditions. I saw how irresponsible Erich was with money early on. So I keep the purse strings tight. Plus, from a selfish aspect, it means he has to visit me from time to time. He's my only real family too."

"It's not really any of my business, Ms. Richter, but some might say you're very generous to keep the purse strings available at all at his age."

"I have a responsibility to him," was all she said.

Now it made less sense that Erich was nowhere to be found.

Unless something had happened to him.

"I'll keep going for another day or two," Colleen said. "I'll check in with you end of day."

Ingrid Richter thanked her.

Colleen spun in her roller chair around to her desk, hung up the phone, finished taping her greeting on her new Record-a-Call 80A answering machine. It had a decoder she could use to call remotely and pick up messages. If all worked out, she'd cancel her answering service. Right now they were forwarding calls to her new office number.

She set the answering machine up for six rings, got up, pulled her leather coat on over her blue skirt suit, went out onto the Embarcadero where the wind blew her hair to one side. She headed down to Red's Java House for breakfast. She was spending less time at home and felt guilty enough about it, but Pam was going through the terrible twos at twenty and both of them needed their space.

By the time Colleen returned to her office, the red light of the machine was blinking. Modern technology.

The caller was a cabbie with Veteran's. He'd seen her flyer with Erich Hahn's picture on it in the depot break room.

"How much for information leading to this person you're looking for?" he asked.

"Fifty," Colleen said. "If it checks out."

"I drove him to his hotel from SFO. Last week."

"When?"

"Friday night. International terminal."

"Which hotel?"

There was a pause. He didn't answer.

"I wouldn't stay in business if I didn't pay for info," Colleen said. "Ask your dispatcher."

"I can pick you up," he said. "Take you there." He was going to make sure he got his cash.

"Sure," she said with a sigh, gathering her leather shoulder bag full of tricks. Ten minutes later, a red, white, and green cab arrived in front of Pier 26. A lanky black man in a floppy denim newsboy cap drove Colleen six blocks, south of Market, with KDIA pumping out Chaka Khan on the car radio. He pulled up in front of the Metro, a flop hotel near Sixth and Howard that had once been beige with blue trim. Now it was blackened with bus exhaust soot, further marred by handbills and graffiti. A crack in the glass door had been repaired with duct tape. A couple of lost characters hung around out front, hands in their pockets. One guy was a man with a long face and a comb-over who looked like he'd just lost a huge bet. All that was missing from the Metro was a plaque over the door that read "Abandon All Hope Ye Who Enter Here."

"You brought my guy *here*?" Colleen asked the cabbie, more than surprised.

He clicked the meter. "Like I said, SFO International Terminal. Last Friday night."

She got out her half photo of Erich Hahn, held it up over the bench seat. "*This* guy?"

He scrutinized the photo and nodded. "*That* guy."

"Was he alone?"

Another nod.

"Luggage?"

"Small bag as I recall."

"Did he talk?"

"Didn't even leave a tip."

"Okay," she said, handing over two twenties and a ten, folded up. "Thanks."

He took the money, counted it as she started to open the door.

"Whoa!" he said.

"Whoa what?"

He pointed at the meter.

"Wow. I get to pay a reward *and* a cab fare for six lousy blocks?"

He shrugged.

She threw him a five-dollar bill.

"Want me to wait for you?" he asked. "Drive you back to your office?"

"I think I can walk," she said, getting out.

"Thank you for choosing Veteran's."

The lobby of the Metro was a small affair reeking of Lysol. A swarthy woman in a faded print dress sat behind a sliding glass window with notices taped up here and there across from a tattered love seat that barely contained a big man in a sleeveless tank top reading the *National Enquirer*. The headline concerned a head transplant for Elvis, who had died a couple of years back.

Colleen asked for Erich Hahn.

The woman looked at her coolly.

Colleen had a folded twenty ready. She slipped it through the slot. It disappeared.

"He is here," the woman confirmed.

"Room?"

"Twenty," the woman said.

"Is he in his room now?"

"Yes."

"I'm just going to go up and say 'Hi,'" Colleen said.

"No 'guests.'" The way she emphasized the word made Colleen realize she thought Colleen might be soliciting. And Colleen had paid a pretty penny for this suit too.

"Can you call his room then?" she asked. "Tell him he has a visitor at reception?"

"Phone in twenty is out of whack."

"Didn't I just pay you twenty bucks?"

The woman gave a heavy sigh and looked over Colleen's shoulder. "Walter?"

The love seat behind Colleen creaked. She turned.

The big guy was looking at Colleen over the top of his tabloid. Hotel security came in all shapes and sizes. "Can I help you?" he said in a semi-threatening tone.

"Room twenty?" she said.

"Room twenty specifically asked not to be disturbed." He flipped a page.

Interesting.

"Well, he's going to want to see this visitor." Colleen dug into her shoulder bag, came out with an envelope with the name Erich Hahn typed on it. Inside was a coupon for a free order of McDonald's fries. She held up the envelope. "I have a check for him."

"Leave it at the desk," Walter said, flicking another page, rubbing his bulbous nose.

"He needs to sign."

Walter grunted, set his paper to one side, raised himself from the love seat with some effort.

"Wait here." He lumbered off to a miniscule elevator, racked the scissor gate open, wedged himself in, pulled the gate shut. The elevator rattled upstairs.

Several minutes later, Walter returned.

"No answer. The shower's running."

"I'll wait."

"No. You're going to have to leave."

Colleen snorted her displeasure, left. Bleeding money and not even ten a.m. But she *had* found her mark. Most likely. She just needed to verify that Erich Hahn was indeed the man in room twenty. Then she could call Ingrid Richter and call it a day. She wished she had her car now. She went across the street to the corner liquor store, picked up a pack of Juicy Fruit and a *Chronicle*, thought about a pack of Virginia Slims. But she'd quit smoking for Pam's sake. Who had started up again.

Outside the store, she treated herself to not one but two sticks of gum, got her camera out, readied it, hung it over her shoulder, leaned against the brick wall. Opened the paper to Herb Caen. Everybody was in love with Dianne Feinstein, the first female mayor of San Francisco, who had taken over when her predecessor had been shot and killed last year.

Colleen was down to the want ads by the time she saw Erich Hahn walk out the door of the Metro Hotel. He wore a Giants ball cap, sunglasses—even though it was overcast—a brown leather jacket over a blue shirt, gray work pants, and tan lace-up work boots. All the gear looked new, straight from Sears. It certainly didn't look like the outfit of an international playboy about to slay Baghdad by the Bay. But it was him, all right. She had her camera ready. Newspaper up in one hand like a curtain, she shot a pic of him. And another.

Colleen put her camera away, eyed the payphone on the wall outside the liquor store. She thought about calling Ingrid Richter, telling her where she could find her nephew. Her work was done. Technically.

But something wasn't right. Erich not contacting his aunt, all of two miles away at the Fairmont. Staying in a dive hotel, telling security to keep the world at bay, dressing incognito. And Ingrid Richter wasn't your auntie from central casting either. Why was she really looking for Erich Hahn? Colleen had put too much time into this to just walk away at this point.

She tossed the paper in the trash, wandered back across Sixth to the Metro. One of the two characters who had been hanging out earlier when she had arrived was there, alone. He was the one with the comb-over and the long face. He was other side of forty, with intelligent brown eyes and his hands in the pockets of a beat-up brown warehouseman's jacket. She gave him a smile he didn't return but he seemed approachable enough.

She walked past him, went down to the first side street, Tehama, nosed around. A fire escape. She wasn't climbing a fire escape in broad daylight in her new suit, even if she could get up there, although there was a trash dumpster on the sidewalk. She checked further, saw a back door with a metal gate on it, spray-painted DOA. She tried the gate gently. Locked, of course. By law, the hotel would need a second exit, but she doubted if it was used much. Probably trash night and deliveries only.

She went back to the guy with the long face. They traded cautious looks.

"You live here?" she said.

He looked at her for a while before he spoke. "If you're with General Assistance, I've been looking for work. Every day. There isn't any."

"Nothing like that," she said, getting out her fake investigator's badge. Sacramento still hadn't come through. Detective licenses for felons were not rush orders. She gave him one of her business cards, with the old answering service number crossed out and her new office number written in in ballpoint.

He took her business card, read it. "A female detective?"

"As number two, I try harder," she said, putting her badge away. "That guy who came out of here just now? In the Giants cap?"

He nodded.

"Know him?"

Shook his head *no.*

"I was hired to find him. Nothing serious, just a family member who's worried, wants to make sure he's okay. Wonders why he hasn't called home."

"Maybe he has his reasons."

"I'm sure he does. I kinda need to know what they are so his mother can rest easy. The people at the desk won't let me in. Walter is a tad grumpy, but I bet you knew that. I just want a quick look at his room, get an idea what he's up to, see if he might have plans to stay or whatever. Maybe he's working. Room twenty. It'll take two minutes."

He squinted at her.

"It's not nearly as bad as it sounds," Colleen said. "You can watch me, make sure I don't swipe anything."

"You were hired to find him, you say?"

"Indeedy. His name is Erich Hahn. What's yours?"

"Nathan."

"Colleen." She put her hand out. They shook.

"So how would this work?" Nathan said, rubbing his chin.

She got her roll of money out. It was getting a workout today. It caught Nathan's eye.

"Looks like there's a back way into this building," she said. "Door by the dumpster. But it's locked." She looked Nathan in the face. "But for someone who lives here, it could be unlocked for just a minute, I bet."

He eyed the money. "Possibly."

She peeled off a twenty. "Another one of these bad boys when I'm done. Like I say, we'll be super quick."

He thought about it.

"Can you make it two more of those bad boys?"

Why stop now? Ingrid Richter was going to be billed for extra miscellaneous expenses, but money didn't seem like a problem for her.

"Sure," Colleen said. "But when we're done, I'll go wait by the back door, by the dumpster."

CHAPTER FIVE

The lock to Erich Hahn's room was so old and loose Colleen didn't need her mini torque wrench. She selected a basic lock pick from her set in its handy leatherette case and was in room 20 in no time, much to Nathan's surprise. He stood in the dingy narrow hall, covering her while she worked the door.

"And that's why you don't leave anything of value in your room," she whispered, slipping her tools back into the case, dropping it back into her shoulder bag.

Nathan followed her in, pulling the door shut quietly behind him.

Erich Hahn's room was garden variety flophouse, down to the stained rugs, wallpaper, and disinfected urine odor. But it was neat. He'd made the bed. No clutter. A worn copy of the Tanakh lay on the tattered armchair. Erich was Jewish. A closet held a single gray suit, a white shirt, a blue tie, a pair of good shoes. Nothing in the pockets. The dresser contained socks, underwear, T-shirts. All neatly folded and organized. Erich Hahn wasn't your typical vagabond party boy. Not by a long shot.

Nothing of value, even under the sagging mattress. But a man like Erich Hahn would know better than to leave anything he wanted to keep in a hotel like this.

An air duct ran through the room from the bathroom, the wall-paper peeling off of it.

The cramped bathroom contained a shaving kit, toothbrush, a tube of Colgate in Spanish. He'd just been to Argentina.

And an air vent cover over the sink to the duct.

"Seen enough?" Nathan asked nervously, standing at the door to the bathroom.

"I just need to use the ladies' room real quick," Colleen said.

"Are you serious?"

"I've been standing across the street all morning. Watch the hall, will you? I'll be out in a jif."

"Jesus." Nathan went out into the hall. "Hurry up."

She shut the door, put the lid down on the commode, something Erich didn't do, stepped out of her heels, got up on the lid, bag over her shoulder. The bolts to the heating vent weren't tight. She got them off with her fingers.

And voila. Something wrapped in a blue handkerchief. Something the size of a gun. If it wasn't a gun, she'd eat the stylish black cloche hat in her bag.

Still standing on the pot, she removed the item from the vent, carefully opened the bundle.

A Hungarian FEG 40RZ .40 caliber semiautomatic. A Smith and Wesson copy. An old gun, much of the bluing faded, discoloration, and plenty of scratches, in particular the serial numbers, which had been gouged off both the frame and below the bolt.

Where did Erich get this? She seriously doubted he brought it in on an international flight. He must have acquired it here.

"You said 'a jif,'" she heard Nathan whisper on the other side of the bathroom door.

"A little privacy, please?" Colleen whispered, wrapping the gun back up the way she'd found it. "Back out in the hallway, Nathan."

I'll be right out." She stepped on the toilet handle with her big toe and the toilet flushed. She heard Nathan step back out into the hall. She was about to slide the gun in its handkerchief back into the vent when the edge of a small manila envelope caught her eye. It was behind where the gun had been.

She pulled it toward her, picked it up.

"Come on, already!" Nathan said out in the hall.

"Almost done." She kicked the faucet in the sink with her bare foot. Water ran. She clutched the gun under her armpit so she could open the envelope for a quick look-see.

Inside the envelope she found the right half of a very old white banknote, which had been torn down the middle by the looks of it, but still large compared to today's money.

The note was part of a white Bank of England five-pound note, dated March 16, 1936. The serial number was 57903.

There was a card inside the envelope too.

A cracked ID card, yellowed with the years, in German.

Ausweis. No. 370. Sachsenhausen.

A photo of a stern-looking young man in a peaked SS officer's cap. Square-jawed, blond, a dour professional smile. Werner Beckmann. SS Sturmbannführer. Sounded high-ranking. The photo was stamped with a Nazi Eagle and the word *Sachsenhausen* again in an embossed circle with lettering around it. She could make out the year: 1942.

If that didn't send a chill through her. She dearly wanted a picture. Her Polaroid camera was in her shoulder bag.

She heard the scissor gates clank downstairs.

"Someone's coming up!" Nathan hissed. "Now!"

"On my way!"

With Nathan out in the hall, she put everything back in the vent, twisted the bolts back in swiftly. Got down from the pot. Faucet off. Heard the elevator clutch into gear. Stepped into her shoes. Lights out, back into the room, when she remembered she'd left the lid down. With a flutter of nerves, she dashed back into the bathroom and lifted the lid and seat.

"Hurry up!" Nathan whispered frantically. "What if it's him?"

Heart thumping, she was soon back out in the hall, pulling the door shut behind her. The elevator was arriving.

Nathan was hovering in the hall, chewing his lip.

She peeled off bills, handed them over without delay. "I'll see myself out."

Nathan grabbed the money, headed down the other end of the hall to a room where he fumbled a key out of his jacket as the scissor gates of the elevator flexed open. Colleen was already heading downstairs, pulling the hat from her shoulder bag down low on her head.

"Nathan?" she heard Walter say to Nathan upstairs. "You don't have a guest up here, do you? You know the rules."

"I know the rules, Walter. I know the rules. Check my room, if you want."

Head down, one hand up to hide her face, Colleen dashed by the woman behind the glass on her way to the front door.

"Excuse me?" she called after Colleen.

Colleen pushed open the front door, headed down Sixth.

CHAPTER SIX

1979

Afternoon light filtered in through the sheer curtains of the lobby bar at the Fairmont, on top of Nob Hill, bringing out the blues of the pastel landscape murals and the beige of the painted stone columns, casting soft rays on the central mini-forest artistically arranged around a splashing fountain. A pianist was playing "Feelings" with extra embellishment, punctuating a subdued mood that prevailed among the few patrons scattered across the large room. Colleen found Ingrid Richter at a round table with a heavy crisp white tablecloth, dressed in a dark business pantsuit, going over papers and a green-and-white computer printout full of numbers, a glass of water by her side. She wore dark-framed reading glasses.

Colleen sat down and got out a folder containing a single sheet she had just typed up at her used IBM Selectric, thirty words a minute and getting faster every day, thank you. Attached to the report were two photos of Erich Hahn leaving the Metro Hotel. The report contained the address and phone number of the hotel, Erich's room number, and a note that Erich was not accepting visitors. There was a paragraph on Colleen's other efforts to locate Erich. Colleen wasn't sure she was going to tell Ingrid Richter about the pistol, half banknote, and Nazi ID found in Erich's air duct. She had been paid to find Erich Hahn and she had done that. But something wasn't adding up.

Ingrid read the report quickly. Looked up in surprise.

"Erich's been there all this time? It's been over a week."

"The cabbie says he took him there from SFO International Terminal last Friday. About the time Erich called you."

"What has he been up to?"

"Good question."

"What kind of hotel is it?"

"Unlike the Fairmont—which has a five-star rating—the Metro has five stars less. It should probably have negative stars."

Ingrid Richter nodded, took her glasses off, set them down on her papers. "I see."

"Does Erich make it a habit to stay in dive hotels?"

"Erich normally prefers something more chic, but bohemian is just fine. He could also be broke. He did want to see me. That usually means he needs an advance on his trust fund payment."

"But he didn't see you—did he?"

Ingrid Richter gave a slight nod. She seemed to be more relaxed knowing where her nephew was. "I'll get in touch with him." She picked up a sleek black handbag, got her checkbook out. "May I write you a check for the balance of what I must owe? If not, I can see how much cash they have at the front desk. I can also go to the bank tomorrow as well. I can't get away today—I have a presentation."

"A check is fine," Colleen said, getting her invoice out, also hot off her IBM Selectric. It listed the hours spent—quite a few—and miscellaneous expenses.

"That's not necessary," Ingrid Richter said, waving her invoice away. "Just tell me, please. My presentation is in twenty minutes."

Colleen told her the amount. Ingrid Richter slipped her glasses back on, made out the check, signed it, tore it off, handed it to Colleen. "Thank you. You're very thorough."

She returned to her paperwork, seemingly unaffected.

"I found something else," Colleen said.

Ingrid looked up, blinking through her glasses with a questioning look.

"I didn't mention it on the report. It's information you may want to keep confidential."

Ingrid took off her glasses again, tossed them on the papers, sat back, placed her hands on the arms of her chair, tapping one finger impatiently. "Yes?"

Ingrid Richter might be up to something. But if she was going to venture over to the Metro, she deserved to know about the pistol. Because Erich might be up to no good too.

And maybe they weren't aunt and nephew.

So she told Ingrid Richter about the pistol.

"I see." Ingrid exhaled a heavy sigh. "Thank you."

"Ms. Richter, is your nephew possibly looking for someone else besides you?" Nazi hunters were nothing new. Neither was revenge. Erich had lived through the war. Lost his parents. He might well have an ax to grind.

"And why does that concern you?"

Colleen narrowed her gaze. "My work is confidential, but I won't be a party to someone getting shot."

Ingrid Richter divulged a taut smile. "Erich is being Erich. Boys and their toys. But he does tend to associate with a mixed crew so perhaps a firearm isn't a bad thing to have."

Colleen smelled bullshit.

"Are you married, Ms. Richter?"

Ingrid Richter squinted. "Why on earth would you ask that? No, I'm not."

"Last name," Colleen said. Colleen mentioned the Tanakh she found in Erich's room. Richter was not a Jewish surname. But Ingrid Richter had a Jewish "nephew."

Ingrid returned a blank stare. "I didn't see what difference it made."

"It might have helped me find him sooner."

"Well, you've found him regardless. Thank you."

Colleen wasn't ready to be dismissed so easily. "If Erich is on a vendetta of some sort, the police should be notified."

Ingrid's face fell into a polite scowl. "Absolutely not. I'm a senior vice president with an international bank. I'm not an American citizen and can*not* afford to get involved with the U.S. authorities. It could affect the business significantly. I also paid you quite handsomely for your services—services I was assured were completely confidential."

"Of course," Colleen said, backing off. "But if you're planning on heading over to the Metro, you need to be careful. It's a rough part of town. I can go with you for protection. I also have someone who could go with you as well, if I'm not available." She was thinking of Boom, her part-time employee, Vietnam vet, and general badass.

"Thank you," Ingrid Richter said. "But it won't be necessary. I'll give Erich a call at the Metro and ask him to meet him here."

"Good idea."

"I have to get back to my presentation." Ingrid Richter consulted her watch, a small gold thing, and returned to her paperwork without looking at Colleen. "Thank you, again," she said icily.

Colleen thanked her as well, left.

Officially the case was done.

She should be relieved.

She wasn't.

*   *   *

When the American private investigator left, Ingrid Richter picked up the one-page report again, read it, frowning.

Erich was here. *Here.* In San Francisco. Hadn't her intuition told her he would be? Erich *had* been the one in Buenos Aires, after all.

Now she had to stop him. Before he learned she was here too. Before it was too late.

She summoned the waiter and asked him to bring her a telephone. He went off, returned with a black phone trailing a long cord. When he left, she dialed another number in the hotel.

"We have a problem," she said in German.

CHAPTER SEVEN

There were no air raid sirens the night the knock on the door came. That only made the harsh rapping seem to echo louder throughout the Richter mansion.

It was well past curfew.

Blinking with nerves, seventeen-year-old Ingrid looked up from her bowl of soup. She hoped it was Father at the door. Perhaps he'd forgotten his key. But Father never forgot his key. Where was he? Her grandmother and little brother were on their way to Paris—hopefully—if they hadn't been caught.

Ingrid had chosen to stay behind. Someone needed to keep an eye on Father. Her mother had left them a year ago, just about this time. A Christmas suicide. Ingrid was still trying to come to terms with that. Her father felt the same, she knew, although he was terrible at expressing himself and focused purely on his work. The time of year, one of her mother's favorites—or so she thought—only made the loss more jarring. She couldn't leave her father behind.

The knocking at the door resumed. Louder, more insistent.

"Herbert?" Ingrid called out. "See who that is, please." The paneled walls of the long dining room glowed in the soft sconce lights, down to two bulbs to save electricity. Even so, Christmas wreaths and decorations filled the edges of darkness, in honor primarily of her mother. The scent of fresh pine offered a small respite from war.

The butler's heels came clicking down the long hallway to the dining room. They stopped at the door, his bald head catching a scrap of light. His face was a mask of apprehension.

"It appears to be the police, Miss Ingrid," he whispered.

If there was a single word guaranteed to raise blood pressure, that was it.

"*Appears* to be, Herbert?"

"I haven't answered the door, Miss Ingrid," Herbert continued. "Just spied from the sitting room. Orpos." Uniformed Order Police. "And a man in a greatcoat. There are two cars outside—a sedan and a squad car. A Horch." His mouth twisted at the last word. A Horch was a long vehicle suggesting something more than a casual visit. The type of vehicle a number of officers would arrive in. And take a number of people away in as well.

The door knocker resounded down the hall. Ingrid heard men talking outside in firm tones.

She frowned, her face compressed in foreboding.

Herbert spoke. "The car is out back, Miss Ingrid," he said. "If we hurry, I can drive you to safety."

She shook her head. "They'll have the house covered, Herbert. I won't have you implicated. You've already done too much for us. You best answer it," she said. "Perhaps it's something trivial." And not about Oma and Dieter trying to cross the border into France.

Their eyes met. She had known Herbert since she was a little girl.

He gave a solemn nod. "As you wish, Miss Ingrid."

"If anything should happen to us, Herbert, there's a provision in Father's will for you." If the Nazis didn't confiscate it.

"I can't believe it has come to this," Herbert said, turning to head down the hallway.

She could. Her father's rhetoric had finally landed the family in real trouble. She had seen it coming and now it was here.

*   *   *

"Where, exactly, is my father?"

Ingrid stood in her family's considerable living room, surrounded by several Orpos in their green uniforms, opposite a youngish man in a smart double-breasted gray suit under his fine woolen coat. The looming Christmas tree that she, Grandma, and Dieter had trimmed only yesterday, laden with generations of ornaments and silver ribbons, and candles waiting to be lit Christmas Eve, towered by the walk-in fireplace, but its festive effect was eclipsed by the grim mood that prevailed.

"Your father is in protective custody," the man said. A sweep of blond hair was combed back over his trimmed short back and sides. His blue eyes were clear and focused. He had probably been a clerk before the war. Now he was riding high on a wave of National Socialism, with a self-assured air about him.

Protective custody. Her heart drummed.

"And who are you?" she asked as if she didn't know.

With an impatient sigh he produced his warrant disc, held it up briefly for Ingrid to inspect. She examined it: the Nazi Eagle on one side, on the other: the words "Staatliche Kriminalpolizei," with a four-digit number underneath. He was a *Kriminalrat*—plainclothes Gestapo. He wasn't required to give his name.

She committed the four-digit number to memory.

He tucked his warrant disc back in the pocket of his overcoat.

"Why is my father in 'protective custody'?" she asked, attempting to control herself with deep breaths through her nose.

"That is confidential, I'm afraid."

The Gestapo had no courts or judicial oversight to govern them. No formal process. One was arrested. Taken into protective custody. Even to one of the KZs—Konzentrationslager camps—her father had told her about.

Or shot.

Or hung with piano wire.

But her father was an important man. That afforded her some leverage. For a while possibly.

"I demand to speak to my lawyer."

"Where is the rest of your family, Fraulein Richter?" the Gestapo officer said.

"Skiing," she said, taking another deep breath, doing her best to control the lie.

"Skiing." He nodded slowly, obviously not believing her.

"Although Grandma doesn't ski anymore, of course," Ingrid said in a forced light tone. "And Dieter really just plays in the snow. He's far too young to ski."

"And where does all this festivity take place?"

They would get this information from her father as well, a story they had previously agreed upon.

"Füssen," she said.

"The Bavarian Alps."

"We have a ski cabin there."

"Address?"

She told him.

"Someone write that down," the Kriminalrat said, not taking his eyes off Ingrid. An officer produced a notebook and scribbled away.

By the time they checked, Grandma and Dieter would hopefully be in Paris.

She heard heavy footsteps coming down the broad stairwell. Two men who had been searching the house.

They appeared at the wide entrance to the living room, the garland hanging over the doorway. More uniforms. Heavy black boots on the polished floors.

"No one upstairs or downstairs, Sturmbannführer."

He focused his attention on Ingrid. "When did your grandmother and little brother leave for Füssen?"

"Earlier today." Such a lie would allow them to still be in transit. More time to escape.

"They had the proper travel documents?"

"Of course."

"You saw them off at Anhalter Bahnhof?"

She wasn't going to fall into that trap. Although the trains still ran, bombing by the Allies had canceled many and shipping Jews east diverted others.

"They took the bus."

"The *bus*?" He pursed his lips, eyed her. "But you have a driver. And a car."

"He is to drive my father and me to Füssen tomorrow. In time for Christmas."

The officer tapped his finger on his lips. "So an elderly woman and a child from a wealthy family take the bus to Füssen, while you and your father ride in comfort?" An air of incredulity crept into his voice.

She pushed a smile onto her face. Lying to the Gestapo wasn't easy and she suspected there were many more such conversations to go. "Father had a meeting at the university. Dieter was excited to play in the snow. And Oma likes to get the place ready. It hasn't been aired out since summer. It'll be a block of ice. So they left a day early."

The Kriminalrat consulted his watch. Looked up.

"You'll have to come with us," he said.

Her heart rocked in her chest. She had had her chance to escape with Dieter and Oma. Her father had no issue with paying the ultimate price for his convictions, but that would change if he knew she had been arrested as well. She had destroyed his goals. Thank God Oma and Dieter had gotten away.

They should all have fled Germany long ago. But her father had been blind in his mission to unearth the truth, perhaps thinking that somehow protected them.

*   *   *

The next day, Christmas Eve, after a night of questioning by the blond Gestapo officer, the weak bulb came on in her blackened cell at number 8 Reichssicherheitshauptamt—the Reich main security office. Two guards came in as Ingrid blinked away the harshness of the light. They pulled her from the wire cot on the wall. With no blanket or mattress, she had worn her green velvet coat in an attempt to keep warm. She was chilled, drained, starving, and if she was honest with herself, terrified. But weakness was not an option.

"Up!" The guards, one on each side, lifted her to her feet, even though she was perfectly capable.

They stood with her, facing the open door.

Shortly after, they heard a door open down the hall and multiple pairs of shoes marching toward her cell. "This way," a man said. It was the Kriminalrat.

They came into view.

Standing in front was the Kriminalrat, in suit, tie, and white shirt, his sweep of blond hair combed back, his blue eyes tired.

"Ah," he said, "here we are."

He stood to one side and Ingrid saw, held up by guards, her father. Her heart sank in her chest.

"Ingrid!" her father gasped.

The shock of seeing her father was returned by the look on his face, obviously more stunned than she. But he was alive. Something, she told herself, to be thankful for.

Her father was bedraggled, his gray hair and beard tousled, still wearing the shirt and vest and trousers he had worn when he left the house yesterday, but crumpled, his tie and collar askew. He still had his wire-framed glasses but they were lopsided on his face, which she eyed for signs of a beating but didn't see. Small mercies. But he was clearly exhausted and distressed. His look of determination was not so resolute, no doubt from seeing his daughter in custody.

Now she saw she should have fled for his sake. So he could stand strong. She sucked in a desolate breath, cold and damp.

The Kriminalrat turned to her father. "Do you understand the situation now, Professor Richter?"

Her father shook his head in resignation.

"Let her go," he said. "Let my daughter go. I will sign whatever confession you want." He looked away, as if in shame.

"A wise decision, Professor," the Kriminalrat said. "I understand that this is not easy."

Ingrid stood, looking at her father. Without her in custody, he would have remained steadfast in his beliefs, regardless of the consequences. Died for them—had it not been for his foolish daughter, herself on the brink of torture and death. She loved him even more for that, knowing how much he truly loved her, but now understood she had breached his love by betraying his cause, the thing he loved most.

"No, Father!" she shouted. "Don't do it!"

He shook his head. "No, Ingrid. It's done."

The guards led him away.

*   *   *

Two days later, on Boxing Day, the guards pulled Ingrid out of solitary confinement and down the cement hall of the basement of 8 Reichssicherheitshauptamt, upstairs, out back, where a covered green military truck rumbled. It was raining cold needles of sleet.

Through the slats in the side of the truck she saw the shapes of people, including a small pair of eyes, watching her. A child.

Along with soldiers stood the blond Kriminalrat. He wore a raincoat over his suit.

The guards grabbed Ingrid, led her up to him, stumbling over the cobbles.

"Am I going home now?" she asked. She had been in custody for more than two days.

"No."

"Where is my father?"

"Your father was executed at the orders of the Führer."

Her legs buckled. Her head felt light and dizzy. The guards held her up.

"But he signed the confession!" she said. "Made the speech! The Reichs-Rundfunk-Gesellschaft broadcast it. I heard the guards talk about it."

"It was too late to save him," the Kriminalrat said.

The Führer's rage had prevailed.

Ingrid shook her head. "So I'm going to a camp."

"How do you know about such things?"

"Because my father was trying to tell the world about them. And he was punished for his efforts."

"They are not what you think. You're going to a rehabilitation camp."

Rehabilitation. Some went for a few weeks. Others months. Some never returned.

"There is one possible way to send you home today, however," he said.

"They're in Füssen," Ingrid said, meaning her grandmother and little brother.

"No, they're not."

"Then I don't know where they are."

"I find that hard to believe," he said.

"They said they were going to Füssen."

He gave a frown. Shook his head. "No. They ran. Because of your father. And they left you behind."

Grandmother and Dieter's freedom was the only thing driving her now.

"I don't know where they are," she said again. Hopefully they were in Paris by now. But the Gestapo could still find them.

"There is still time," he said, while the truck rumbled, "to change your mind."

She actually laughed. "And trust *you*? Now?" And then she did something she had never thought herself capable of. She spit on his fine shoes. For that split second she didn't care if he had her shot. To hell with him.

His pupils flared. She saw his anger and wondered if he might strike her. But he didn't. She was still the daughter of a prominent man, but not for much longer.

"Take her," he snapped at the soldiers. He spun on his heels, walked across the gravel, back to the security building.

Ingrid was led around to the back by one of the guards.

Two soldiers sat in the back of the truck, one on either side. A sergeant stood by with a clipboard. One of the guards who had delivered Ingrid filled out something on the clipboard, handed it back, along with a document pouch.

On seeing Ingrid, one of the soldiers hopped out, flipped down the tail gate for her. The sergeant handed her an armband, with an upside-down red triangle on it. A political prisoner. He instructed her to wear it at all times, not take it off. To do so would be a serious transgression.

Then he held his gloved hand out to assist Ingrid up to the back of the truck.

She ignored his hand, climbed in unassisted.

In the truck she saw a Jewish family, two homosexuals in black tie, enemies of the Reich.

This was really happening. To her. To all of them. Her pulse quickened.

Three of the passengers had yellow Star of David *Jude* patches sewn into their coats: two women, one elderly, the other in her thirties, obviously mother and daughter, and a boy about six or seven with precise dark bangs and deep-set eyes, the ones who had been watching Ingrid through the slat. He reminded her of Dieter, her little brother. She sat next to him while he stood, looking through the slats.

The tailgate slammed back up and the sergeant climbed aboard and they set off.

"Your father was the professor?" the older woman said to Ingrid.

Was. Ingrid nodded, unable to speak. Rain pelted the canvas overhead.

"He was a brave man," the younger woman said. "No one believes that speech he made. He was coerced."

"A brave man," the older woman said.

"No talking!" the sergeant shouted, jumping up, lurching forward, looming over the two women. Ingrid wondered if he would strike one of them. "No talking!" The women flinched, then looked down, while the boy stood closer to Ingrid, calm on the outside but she could feel him shaking. He hung onto a slat, staring out the gap as the truck lumbered off, rocking back and forth. If she could be half as brave as he, perhaps she could survive.

The sergeant resumed his seat next to one of the soldiers.

"Five marks says Dresdner SC win the title next year," one soldier said to the other.

"No one is foolish enough to take that bet," the other soldier said.

Ingrid was going to a KZ—a Konzentrationslager. A camp. She shuddered.

She needed to save someone else. In order to save herself. That's what her father had told her once.

She turned to the boy. His face was frozen with fear but he was taking it like a grown man who wouldn't be thought a coward. Remarkable.

"I'm Ingrid," she said.

"No talking to the Jews, eh?" the sergeant said.

She obliged, gave the boy a sly smile and a wink. He returned a stoic glare.

Ingrid tried to rub some warmth into her velvet-clad arms. All the times she had seen the trucks around Berlin, the haunted eyes looking out, she had ignored them, if with a fleeting sense of shame. They'd had nothing to do with her. Now they did.

The truck boomed past Brandenburger Tor, the grand city gate festooned with Nazi flags and huge Christmas garlands.

The truck bounced and she felt the boy's breath in her ear as he leaned in.

"I'm Jakob," he whispered.

She turned her head slightly, speaking quietly out of the side of her mouth so she wouldn't be seen talking. "A pleasure to meet you, Jakob," she whispered back. She folded her arms, tucked one under the other, gave him a secret handshake.

If what her father had told her was true, the two women would not fare well. Put to work if they were lucky. But Jakob, the boy, he would be in real trouble.

"I'm going to keep an eye on you, Jakob," Ingrid whispered. "Think of me as the auntie you never knew you had."

CHAPTER EIGHT

"Dang!" Colleen gasped, leaning back on the padded headboard to light a postcoital cigarette, her first in a long time—both cigarette and otherwise. She brushed a hand through her hair, pleasantly exhausted.

She had been overdue. Matt's schedule, and hers, had pushed tonight's date off too many times.

Matt had padded off to the kitchen to make a batch of margaritas.

It was Saturday evening in Matt's bachelor apartment on Jackson, with a sundown view of downtown out the bay window. Lights off, the golden dusk caught the spire and twin towers of Grace Cathedral. Naked, warm, and glowing, Colleen had a black sheet draped around her waist while, off in the kitchen, the blender whirred through the 1920s apartment with a pleasant hum. *Bitches Brew* oozed from the stereo in the living room: Miles Davis at his cool discordant best.

Life was good.

Not a care in the world.

Well, that wasn't quite true. Colleen puffed on a Marlboro, one of Matt's.

There was always Pam, always a concern. But especially so at eight months pregnant.

The Fairmont, where Ingrid Richter was currently residing, lay just out of view.

But not out of mind.

Matt came into the bedroom in a pair of snug yellow low-rise briefs he had donned for decency's sake. Well built, he flushed with recent sex, tousled hair, looking even better holding two frosted margaritas in blue-rimmed glasses.

"Are you trying to get me drunk?" she said, tapping ash into an ashtray on the nightstand.

"No point in that anymore, is there?"

"Aren't you going to try for round two?"

He grinned. "Still want to go out for dinner? It's not too late—if we get dressed and leave now." He set her drink down on her side of the bed. Relationships were getting serious when you had a side of the bed. He walked over to the window with his drink, stood looking out over the city, downtown, Chinatown, the financial district. Colleen was more focused on his firm butt.

She took a sip of perfectly slushy margarita. "I'd settle for one of those frozen TV dinners," she said. "After round two."

"You're on." He turned, sipping his drink. "I thought you quit." Nodding at her smoking.

"I did," she said. "Until Pam started up again. Pretty feeble excuse, isn't it?" She smashed out the barely started cigarette.

"How is she?" he said, putting his drink down on his nightstand, climbing into bed next to her.

As a first-time grandmother under forty, Colleen had her work cut out for her. But she had Pam back with her and that's what counted. She had let Pam down when she went to prison when Pam was a girl. They rarely saw eye to eye. But now she would be there. She would make it work. Somehow.

"We're not talking about Pam."

"I see."

They sat, drinking, enjoying the moment.

"This is nice," he said.

"Uh-huh." She drank, hoping he wasn't going to bring up the *moving in* subject.

"Be nice if there was more of it," he said.

Brushing her foot against his muscular calf under the sheet, she whispered, "Don't spoil it."

"I'm not spoiling anything. It's just that we'd have more time together. And you hardly go home anymore as it is."

"Pam needs her space. We're working things out."

"So work them out from a distance. She can have your place. You stay here. Perfect."

"She's due next month. I'm not going to abandon her." Again.

"Even if you're never home?"

Colleen gave a deep sigh, set her drink down. "I don't know how I feel about being a cop's girlfriend." She didn't know how she felt being anybody's girlfriend.

"Not just any cop, sweetheart," he said in a pretty decent Bogart impression.

She smiled at that. "You have *no* idea of what you'd be getting yourself into."

He set his drink down, sat up Boy Scout style. "Then I guess a cop's wife is out of the question, huh?"

Her chest knocked. "Ay yi yi. You can stop right there."

"Something wrong with it?"

"You have read my priors, right?'

"I figure the odds of you killing two husbands in a row are pretty much in my favor."

"Good point," she said. "But, honestly, I'm not anywhere near ready."

"You're pushing forty."

"Thirty-six, asshole. And if it's kids you want, I've got news for you: my baby-making days stopped at Pam. She's more than enough."

"I don't want kids. I want you."

"What do you think tonight is?"

"More." He sipped his margarita. "I want more."

"Have you ever heard of the theory of diminishing marginal utility?"

"I'm a simple cop, lady. I don't know them big words."

"Boom explained it to me. He's an Econ major. It's basically: 'too much of a good thing' isn't so good."

"I don't want you to get away."

"A ring doesn't guarantee anything, Matt. Ask Owens." Inspector Owens, the other cop she could trust, had just gone through a nasty divorce.

"I'm not Owens."

"No, you are not. Look, I'm more than flattered. But I just got out of prison a little over a year ago. I'm finally getting my business together. Finally making a little money. Finally got my daughter back. I'm going to be a grandma. I got plenty going on. So please, *please* slow down."

"I know how I feel."

She gave him a soft smile, rubbed his cheek. "Me too. But right now I want to take things easy."

He took her hand, kissed it. "You sure don't seem like you're taking things easy these days."

"Touché," she said. "It's this frickin' case."

"I thought that German broad paid you off."

"She did. And no one says 'broad' anymore, dude. Not if they want to jump my bones."

"I got news for you: I just did. Don't you remember? Is it the age thing? Thirty-six?"

"No, it's just that it went by so quickly."

"Come on. I bet that was the best thirty seconds you ever had."

"It wasn't bad. And you're not done yet."

"So what's the problem with the German *woman?*"

Colleen drank some margarita. "She's got a past."

"Isn't that what your business is built on? People with pasts?"

"Yeah, sure. But ex-Nazis are kind of an exception."

"Whoa." Matt's mouth dropped in surprise. He set his drink down. "You forgot to mention *that* little detail." He squinted. "She's an ex-Nazi?"

"No proof." But who knew? "But something funky is going on."

"Come on: spit it out."

Colleen did. Erich's hotel room. Werner Beckmann's SS ID. The half-British banknote. The Hungarian pistol, serial numbers scratched off. The fact that Erich was Jewish. And Ingrid wasn't. And that she was looking for him.

"This Erich sounds like the opposite of a Nazi," Matt said.

"Sounds like he's looking for one, though. Werner Beckmann maybe—the guy in the SS ID I found in his air duct."

"And Ingrid Richter is involved *how?*" Matt said.

"Claims she's his 'aunt.'" Colleen sipped. "At first I thought she might be one of those 'aunts' looking for her missing 'nephew.'"

"I had an 'aunt' like that in college. She taught my English Lit class."

"Was her name Mrs. Robinson?"

"Not quite. She still broke my heart, though."

"A tough guy like you?"

"It's all an act, baby."

"Well, it's a pretty good one."

"I'm deep like that." Matt smiled. "But this aunt sounds like more than just another horny old broad—*woman*—hot and heavy for her missing boy."

"I don't want to pick up the *Chronicle* one morning and find Erich Hahn or someone else is found floating in the bay."

"Isn't this kind of violating the whole confidential thing? I thought you heartless PI types had a code: whatever happens, happens. *Laissez faire*. The client is on their own. As long as you get paid, right?"

"Yeah, but I'm still pretty new at this. So I can still pretend to be a human. Besides, I don't have a license."

"Sacramento hasn't issued that damn thing yet?"

"Something to do with being a felon," she said. "My lawyer's looking into it."

"Well that, madam, is pure bullshit."

"That's what I say," Colleen said. "Can you look into it for me?"

"What? You want me to threaten the people in Sacramento because they won't give you—a felon—a PI license? What happened to the modern woman doing things for herself? Won't that upset Virginia Slims and her liberated friends?"

"No," she said. "What I mean is: Can you look into Erich Hahn for me?"

"You already asked me, remember? The other night?"

"And I'm assuming you never did."

"Uh, something to do with Dr. Lange? Sorry if I didn't drop my biggest case to do a Missing Persons search."

"I know you're busy. That's why I let it go."

"Wow. That's big of you. Especially since you found him just fine on your own."

"Eventually. But, Matt, there's only so far I can go. This has gotten more serious. I don't trust him or his 'aunt' not to shoot someone. Maybe some innocent bystander. And you being a cop, with access to a mainframe and all . . ."

He eyed her. "You want me to violate my professional integrity to dig up dirt on your client's 'nephew'?"

"You're not just a pretty face."

Matt sighed. "We've been through this kind of thing."

"There might be a connection to your case," she said. "Nazis and fascists and all that. I wouldn't ask unless it was important." Colleen divulged a winsome smile. "Maybe an Interpol check? Can you get Ingrid Richter too while you're at it?"

"What's in it for me?"

Colleen batted her eyelashes. "I thought that was pretty obvious."

"You know they have rules about this sort of thing, don't you?"

Colleen shrugged her bare shoulders. "So what's the point of banging a cop unless I get something out of it?"

"Well, I'm glad I'm good for something."

"Two things," she said, pulling the sheet back.

CHAPTER NINE

Outside Oranienburg the military truck thumped down a country road to a large white institutional structure built over an entrance with a metal gate that proclaimed "Arbeit Macht Frei." *Work sets you free.* The clock informed them it was past two in the morning. A cinder-block wall about four meters high extended in both directions from either side of the building.

The passengers in the back of the truck were wet and cold from the trip. Fear had chilled them even more.

The truck passed through the metal gates and Ingrid and the occupants were struck by the stench of smoke from something putrid. A smell of death, tinged with a sweet sickly odor. The gate clattered shut as they drove past a trio of gallows placed by a parade ground near the entrance. A noose blew in the wet wind.

Big tires crunched across the barren roll-call area, paved with cinder and ash, in front of lines of barracks fanning out in the dark, save for a single harsh light over each building. Machine gun towers, lit up, overlooked the camp. The cement block wall stretched around the entire perimeter, forming a huge triangle, easy to guard, Ingrid assumed, with a section of no-man's-land fenced off by electrified barbed wire.

The soldiers in the back of the truck, wearing raincoats now, hopped out, unfastened the tailgate with a clatter.

"Where are we, Ingrid?" Jakob whispered, gripping her hand, although he maintained his composure better than his mother, who was now beside herself with tears. His grandmother was tending to her.

"A camp, Jakob," Ingrid whispered back.

"What kind of camp?"

"Not the kind you might be thinking of, Jakob. Now, I need you to be very quiet for me, to not say a word, and do exactly as you're told. This is very important. Can you do that for me?"

Jakob shook an affirmative, clinging onto Ingrid's hand.

"Silence!" a woman's voice screamed in accented German. "*Get out!*"

Ingrid climbed out of the truck, helped Jakob down. The winter wind was bitter as it swept across the roll-call area.

Several soldiers stood by, all in coats, others under the overhang of the entry gate to the main building.

Waiting by the truck stood two women: a tall *Aufseherin*—a female SS camp guard—in her thirties, wearing a side cap with an SS death's head badge, her blond hair pinned neatly back. A heavy cloak draped over a smart gray wool uniform with a tidy array of medals over her left breast. Black leather gloves matched her pistol belt and holster. She clearly took great pride in her appearance, even in the middle of the night, even in the rain, as she watched the prisoners unload with a cool gaze.

The sergeant handed her a clipboard, with a sheet of thin rubber covering the papers.

The other woman, who had done the shouting, was not much older than Ingrid, skinny, with an aquiline nose and sharp cheekbones, wearing a plain scarf over her dark hair and a tatty blue wool coat too big for her over a blue-and-white striped prison dress. Her armband read KAPO. She was a prisoner who worked as a guard. On the right breast of her coat was an upside-down red triangle, the same as Ingrid's armband. A political prisoner.

"Form a line!" she screamed, brandishing a short club. "Hurry up, ladies!" she yelled at the two homosexuals as they climbed down from the truck in their smart evening suits. Her German was rough but effective.

The Aufseherin read the clipboard, keeping the papers protected from the rain. Jakob's grandma was struggling to get down out of the truck with her daughter's help.

"Hurry up, Bubbe!" The kapo poked her with the club as she tumbled out. "We don't have all night!"

"There's been a misunderstanding," the old woman said as she stood up straight. "My son-in-law works for the DAF. He's a Methodist."

"Oh, a Methodist is he? How nice! And I thought I told you to be quiet!" The kapo reared back with her club, struck the old woman over the head. There was a crack of skull as the woman collapsed to the ground, followed by gulps and shrieks.

"Oma!" Jakob cried, pulling away from Ingrid. "Oma!"

Ingrid jerked him back to her side, shushing him. "Jakob—stop!"

The grandmother lay on the ground, moaning. Blood glistened under her head in the cinder and ash.

"Did you have something to say, boy?" the kapo snapped, striding over to Jakob standing in front of Ingrid. The club quivered in her hand.

Ingrid squeezed Jakob's hand with all her might, willing him to be silent.

"He has nothing to say," Ingrid said.

Jakob looked down at the ground, shook his head *no*.

"Good." The kapo eyed Ingrid. She pointed the tip of her club at Ingrid's red triangle armband.

"Looks like we're sisters, princess."

"She's the professor's daughter," the Aufseherin said in a clear voice, leafing through the paperwork, flipping the sheet of rubber back over.

"Is she?" the kapo said, observing Ingrid with possible respect. "I see."

The truck started up, gathering the soldiers who had transported them, and waited while the camp guards opened the main gate. The truck bounced through, the gates clanging shut again.

The standing prisoners, the stricken grandmother, the kapo and the Aufseherin, were left in the rain-wet wind whipping through the camp. Ingrid's velvet coat wasn't up to the task, soaking through, chilling her to the bone as she clutched it tight.

"I am Overseer Graf," the Aufseherin said quietly, standing before the line. "You are at Sachsenhausen for rehabilitation. It's a pity we got off to such a poor start." She nodded at the grandmother on the ground, whose foot was twitching. "Perhaps you will learn that it's important to listen and do exactly as you are told."

A beam of light swept by from a machine gun tower. "There is no one to process you now," Graf continued. "You will have to wait until morning." She turned to the kapo with the club. "Salak, take over."

The kapo stood at attention, head down, and spoke quietly. "Yes, Overseer."

The Aufseherin walked smartly back to the building, through a side gate that a soldier held for her. The gate clanked shut.

Kapo Salak sauntered up and down the line, smacking her club on her palm. She stopped at the dying woman.

"Looks like we might have one less to check in."

She continued to march up and down the line, stroking the club. "I am Salak. But they also call me *suka z Sachsenhausen*. Do any of you know what that means?"

Ingrid nodded.

Salak stopped at Ingrid, gave her raised eyebrows. "Speak Polish, princess?"

Ingrid spoke a number of languages. She hoped she hadn't incurred the kapo's wrath somehow. "Yes," she stammered.

"Come on, then. Don't keep the Jews and fairies in suspense."

Ingrid cleared her throat.

"It means: 'the bitch of Sachsenhausen.'"

"That is correct: *the bitch of Sachsenhausen.*" Salak nodded with satisfaction as she strode up and down the line, stroking the club in a suggestive manner. "I earn that title every day. It keeps me from the gas chamber, the firing squad, the gallows." She stopped. "And not one of you will change that for me—is that perfectly clear?" She glared at the prisoners. "There are many kapos here. Perhaps you will be lucky enough to become one yourself." She looked at the homosexuals. "Oh, don't get your hopes up, ladies." She smiled at her joke. "But I'm the kapo you will have to watch out for. Again, is that perfectly clear? Say *yes.*"

The prisoners confirmed.

"Good. Form a line, shoulder to shoulder."

They did, apart from the old woman on the ground. Jakob's mother stared off in shock, beyond distraction, unable to watch Jakob. Jakob moved next to Ingrid, grabbed her hand. Ingrid squeezed back. Salak smirked at Ingrid. "Looks like you've made a friend, princess."

Ingrid said nothing.

"Be careful, eh?" Salak pointed at Jakob's yellow *Jude* badge on his coat with her club. "Choose your friends wisely."

Ingrid nodded.

"Nobody moves until morning," Salak said. "You don't sit. You stand. Is that also perfectly clear? Answer *yes.*"

They answered.

"Enjoy the fresh air." Salak strolled over to the entrance, stood next to one of the guards in the shelter from the rain. The guard gave her a cigarette. They chatted and smoked while the prisoners stood in the light but persistent rain.

Ingrid squeezed Jakob's hand as he watched his grandmother on the ground. The woman's foot jerked and she gave a weak groan. Ingrid knew she must stifle her feelings, which were running wild. She could do nothing for her. She could not let the situation get the better of her. It would do her no good. It would do Jakob no good. And she had to watch out for him.

*   *   *

They stood all night in the light rain. Exhaustion drained them and they were not permitted to huddle although Ingrid held Jakob close and was not chastised for it. By the time morning came, their clothes were soaking wet and they shivered mightily in the piercing wind.

Then the rain stopped and gray clouds billowed. It was still dark.

Another truck arrived. This one had quite a few new prisoners, mostly men.

Jakob's grandmother's lifeless body was carried off by prisoners as Salak barked orders. She returned with the same prisoners, no body. Jakob's mother was beside herself with grief, weeping openly, paying no attention to Jakob. Ingrid stayed with him, hands on his small, tight shoulders, squeezing them from time to time. Jakob stood stoically through it all.

There was nothing to say. Ingrid held her fear at bay. Somehow she must get through this. And she must see that others did the same. Her father had said the only way to truly save yourself was to save someone else. Jakob needed her.

Rousing military music echoed out of the metal loudspeakers around the camp as the day began. The clock tower indicated four thirty a.m. The barracks that fanned out around the parade ground stirred. An authoritative voice instructed the barracks to file out by number and stand in the roll-call area. There were hundreds at a time. Prisoners wore striped uniforms, wooden clogs, and striped caps with numbers on them. Many were emaciated and browbeaten. They wore various badges with different colored triangles: pink, green, blue, purple, black, red, and, of course, the yellow six-pointed star, all designating enemies of the state: homosexual, criminal, emigrant, Jehovah's Witness, anti-social, political, and Jew, respectively. The Jews looked worse off than the others, and their barracks were more heavily populated judging by roll call, some several times the occupancy of the non-Jewish barracks. By the time the parade grounds were assembled, there were thousands of prisoners. It was a sea of misery and oppression. The ratio of men to women was about ten to one. Roll call was taken. Those that had died during the night were ticked off a list. Random beatings broke out as guards punished prisoners for not standing up straight. Ingrid was sapped from standing all night but fought any waver in her stance and kept an eye on Jakob.

Roll call took hours.

At the end of roll call, a prisoner was hanged for stealing 200 grams of bread. Over the speakers an officer gave a lecture on the importance of honesty.

Kapo Salak appeared with guards, club in hand, to help oversee the induction of the new prisoners. She gave Ingrid a tough smile.

"Have a nice night, princess?"

Among the new prisoners, men were separated from women and children. Jews were further separated and treated to additional

beatings. Ingrid steeled herself, and realized she would be parting
ways with Jakob and his mother.

"Jakob," she said. "What is your last name?"

"Rosenstein," his mother said, wiping tears from her red eyes.
"Sheila Rosenstein."

"Ingrid Richter," Ingrid said.

"You've got nothing to worry about," Sheila Rosenstein said to her.
"You'll be back in Berlin in no time."

Ingrid could hope. Many politicos did return after a few weeks
or months, their faces troubled and drawn, full of fear. But nothing
was guaranteed.

"I'm going to do my best to help you," she said.

"They'll be shipping us off to Auschwitz," Sheila Rosenstein said.
"I heard it from the others. Poland, isn't it?"

"You don't want that," Ingrid said. Her father had told her Auschwitz was a death camp. Half went straight from the train to the gas
chambers. "Sachsenhausen is primarily a camp for political prisoners
and a work camp. There are many factories nearby. They need workers. Find something you can do, even if you have to make it up, and
convince them you're good at it. Tell them you want to work and
serve the Fatherland."

"I used to work in a cobblers. Yes. Thank you."

"Good luck." Ingrid worried for Jakob. He was of no use to anyone.

"Over there!" an SS officer shouted at Sheila and Jakob, pointing
a swagger stick at a line of Jews disrobing out in the cold. Their white
bodies trembled in the approaching dawn light. Their clothes and effects
were being catalogued and they were being given striped uniforms and
dresses and clogs to wear. The uniforms were used and stained.

Ingrid waved silently to Jakob and his mother. He stared back.
Once again, she prayed she could be half as brave as he.

"Next!" an officer snapped at her. "Hurry up!"

"Come on, princess!" Kapo Salak shouted. "You're not out at brunch with your hoity-toity friends now."

Ingrid stepped up to the table.

Overseer Graf looked up. Her face was fresh, her hair perfectly groomed and pinned up under her gray garrison cap with its Totenkopf "death head" pin. She was in such contrast to the surroundings that she stood out like a studio photograph. But her heart was no different than the soldiers and officers around her.

"Richter," Graf said. "The professor's daughter."

"Yes, Overseer," Ingrid said, heart thumping.

Graf had a clipboard and began filling out Ingrid's sheet.

"Who do you want to be notified in the event that something happens to you?"

"The Red Cross," Ingrid said. Her father was dead and hopefully her Oma and little brother were in Paris by now. She wasn't about to implicate anyone.

"Languages?"

"French, Italian, Latin, Polish, Russian, English, and, of course, German."

Graf checked off boxes.

"Special talents?"

"Piano. Violin."

"Work skills?"

"Accounting. Bookkeeping. Sketching. Engraving. "

Graf looked up. "Engraving?"

"I'm enrolled to study Fine Arts at Bauhaus Weimar next year." Or she was. "Engraving is my area of study. I work—*worked*—for Universität der Künste Berlin over the last two summers assisting the arts department in that area as well."

"I see." Graf made a note. Then she filled out a slip of paper. Handed it to her. "Barracks 19."

Ingrid wasn't sure what that meant.

Graf looked over Ingrid's shoulder. "Salak!"

Kapo Salak appeared, in her oversized coat, big boots, striped dress, scarf, head down, submissive.

"Yes, Overseer."

"Check her in, get her photographed, and take her to Barracks 19. And look lively about it."

"Barracks 19, Overseer Graf?" Salak said with surprise.

"That's what I said. Try to pay attention. Move along! Next!"

Shortly afterwards, Kapo Salak and a soldier escorted Ingrid, now wearing a blue-striped dress of coarse scratchy wool and cotton, jacket, clogs, and a kerchief over her shaved head. With all else, losing her hair should have been the least of her worries but she felt cold and naked, reduced to barely human. Her red triangle armband identified her as a political prisoner. Down a muddy path between rows of single-story barracks they went, gaunt faces watching from dirty windows as they passed. She was new and it was easy to tell; her healthy countenance and unemaciated figure gave her away. Even Kapo Salak was lean, with a sallow complexion.

"Barracks 19," Salak said, stroking her club as they walked. "Very nice."

Ingrid didn't know about that. All she did know was that fear was going to be a steady companion from now on. Was she going to be interrogated, tortured, or shot? All three? Or, was she going to be. . . no, she couldn't even think about it.

"What is Barracks 19?" she asked Salak.

Salak switched to Polish, so the guard walking behind might not understand. "I can't tell you exactly, princess, because I don't know. Very few do. It's a new project." Salak eyed her sideways as they walked. "But I think you might have just won the lottery."

"Meaning?"

"Extra rations. Cigarettes. Music. Very nice."

Ingrid shook inside. "It's not a . . ." She couldn't bring herself to complete her sentence.

Salak grinned. "Do you mean a *brothel,* princess? What—can't you even say the word? Oh my, wherever did you come from?" Salak brayed with laughter, head back. "Cathouse! Knocking shop! Clam shack! But really—you, a *tart*? A woman of 'abilities'? Would you use a metronome?" She recovered, wiping a tear from her eye. "Oh dear. No, they closed the brothel, princess. Everyone is too tired. And, quite honestly, look around you. It's not exactly Saturday night at the Palais, is it?"

Ingrid reddened with embarrassment. "But you don't know what Barracks 19 is."

"No one sees the occupants after they go in, unless they leave the camp. And they're always under guard. Guards who are sworn to secrecy. If you're accepted, that is. And you better hope you are. Those who aren't don't fare well. They don't want people to know what goes on in there, eh?"

They walked along a section of camp southwest of the main camp, the small camp. One side of a barracks was painted with the word *Gehorsham*—Obedience. More military music reverberated out of the camp loudspeakers. Announcements were made for work crews to assemble to march to various local factories. Ingrid balked when she saw two prisoners squatting on their haunches by a hut, arms straight out ahead of them. They were trembling with fatigue, keeping the awkward stance. A guard shouted at them not to move until end of day or face death. Their faces were masks of agony and it was still early.

"The Sachsenhausen Salute," Salak said. She continued, unmoved by the spectacle. "You and I, princess, we will see each other again."

Ingrid's nerves roiled inside her. Her hope that she might return to Berlin in a few weeks seemed like a distant one now. "We will?"

"As I said, we're sisters. We even speak the same language. Your Polish is very good, by the way."

"We're hardly sisters," Ingrid said. "You killed that poor old woman." She could hear a man being whipped behind a wall. He was being forced to count off the lashes. He was up to thirty-nine. Each crack of the whip made Ingrid shudder.

"It's my job!" Salak said. "I have to do it."

Ingrid eyed her with veiled contempt.

"What do you mean?"

The prisoner being whipped was up to forty-one.

"It might not be tennis with your toffee-nosed friends," Salak said. "But it's the way things work around *here*. Some of us choose to survive."

"I still don't understand."

"'To manage expectations,' Graf says. One out of every new group of arrivals."

Ingrid shuddered.

"Admit it," Salak said. "That woman dying in front of you took you down a notch or two."

Ingrid couldn't deny it even as the evil of such a tactic filled her with rage.

"In my defense," Salak said, "I always pick one who has absolutely no chance of survival. I did you all a favor. You're free to enjoy another day of Sachsenhausen. Perhaps you should thank me."

They approached two barracks, 18 and 19, with a separate barbed-wire fence around them and more fence wire over the top. No escape. There were guards on the entrance between the barracks. The windows were whited out with paint. The pounding of machinery and opera music emanated from within one building.

"Here we are, princess: the 'chicken cage.' A new secret project. And your new home—if they like you. They better."

Ingrid's mind was burning with the evil that prevailed around her. But she must keep her composure. If she didn't make it in this Barracks 19, she wasn't going to live.

Salak grimaced. "Look, that old woman would have been down in the execution trench by now anyway—target practice to toughen up the new guards. She wouldn't have even been issued a uniform. Believe me, I know. I've been here over a year. That's a good thousand years from wherever you're from. And I'm still here." She thumbed her chest. "Salak the Bitch lives for a thousand years. I'm doing better than the Reich itself. How many Polack prisoners can say that?"

"What does that mean for Jakob?" Ingrid asked. "His mother?"

"That little boy hanging onto you?" Salak actually gave a somewhat sympathetic look. "What did I say about making friends, princess? They're Jews. Where have you been?"

"Just tell me."

She stroked her club. "The mother might get by for a while. The factories are all behind on their quotas. But the boy?" She shook her head. "Well, none of us have much to look forward to, do we? Just thank God you're not a Jew. And your father is a respected man, whatever Der Fuckhead thought of him."

"He *was*," Ingrid said.

Salak shrugged again. "At least he died quickly. Shot. That's the way to go. But gone all the same. So it's time to think of yourself now."

An idea came to Ingrid.

"From what you tell me, I won't be coming back out here."

"If you do, princess, it won't be to a red carpet. They'll probably take you into that exercise yard"—Salak indicated the area between the two barracks, behind barbed wire.

"If I get that job in there," Ingrid said, "I'll need a favor."

"A favor?" Salak laughed. "I already saved your life once."

"The boy and his mother: Jakob and Sheila Rosenstein. Make sure they are kept together. Make sure she gets a job of some sort. I bet you can do that." Ingrid raised her eyebrows. "I'll find a way to repay you."

Salak rubbed the tip of her club absentmindedly on her neck. "I know everyone worth knowing in this shithole and people are scared of me—even a few of the guards. And now I know you. So it's a deal. But don't try to screw me. I'll be watching you." She pointed her club at Barracks 19. "I'll be watching." She stroked her club again and squinted.

"Why would I do that?" Ingrid said. "We're sisters."

CHAPTER TEN

1979

On her way home from Matt's Sunday morning, Colleen swung by the Metro Hotel, parked across the street. Officially her work with Ingrid Richter might be complete, but nagging doubts told another story. With his drop gun and Nazi ID, Erich Hahn was up to something nefarious, and his "aunt" might well be after him as well. If it all turned out to be nothing, fine. If it didn't, then it was time to ramp things up before innocent people became collateral damage.

Being Sunday, it was slow. Even Nathan with the comb-over wasn't lurking outside the Metro. Colleen used the payphone outside the corner liquor store, called the hotel, asked for Erich Hahn.

"I'll have to take a message," the woman at the desk said.

"No," Colleen said. "That's fine." She knew what she needed to know: Erich Hahn hadn't moved on.

She wanted to get home, make sure Pam hadn't burnt the place down. She also had another job to begin, locating hidden assets in a divorce case. She was elated to have Pam back—whatever it might seem like at times—but her expenses had risen with Pam, and the baby coming. Even so, she'd put a little more time and effort into Ingrid Richter. She called Boom, her part-time assistant, a Vietnam vet who lived in the Fillmore projects with his grandmother.

"Hiya, Chief," he said. "Need any bad guys killed today?"

"Not today. Studying?" Boom was two years into a BA degree.

"Always."

"Can you get hold of a car?"

"I can borrow one."

"I'm wondering if you can stake out a place for me while you study."

"I'm there."

"South of Market. It's an easy gig. Just watch who comes and goes."

"Cool," Boom said. "Let me get Gram's lunch ready and I'll head over."

*   *   *

Boom flipped a page on *Probability and Statistics*, started Chapter 2. It was a good thing he'd had his coffee that morning because Chapter 2 was one long ass chapter. He was parked up Sixth Street, across Mission, with a good view of the Metro Hotel down and across.

Every time he finished a paragraph he looked up, checked the entrance. So far, nothing. Not even the sad sack character Colleen had mentioned, the guy who hung around out front, hands in his pockets, looking like the world had ended.

Colleen had given Boom copies of photos: one of this Erich Hahn coming out of the Metro in new work clothes, another with two halves of a picture pieced together showing Erich and a German woman named Ingrid Richter sitting in front of liters of beer. Colleen was looking for Ingrid Richter to stop by the Metro.

Somewhere around Chapter 4, "Continuous and Mixed Random Variables," Boom stifled a yawn, looked up, saw a woman turn on Mission down Sixth in the direction of the Metro, strutting like she meant business. He used his compact binoculars to get a better look. Skinny, in tight jeans tucked into black leather boots. A red beret held her dark hair in place, gathered up underneath. Sunglasses. As she

turned to enter the Metro. he saw her olive-skinned profile, a prominent nose and cheekbones. Not a beauty but striking, with plenty of
attitude. A woman not to be messed with. She had her hands in the
pockets of a big beat-up black leather jacket with zippers. She wasn't
Ingrid Richter.

She pushed open the glass door, walked into the Metro.

CHAPTER ELEVEN

1979

"Erich Hahn," the female visitor said to the big woman behind the glass window at the desk at the Metro Hotel.

"Your name?"

"Angelica," she said. "Angelica Czarny." She pronounced the last name: "Char. Knee."

The woman on the desk eyed her, started dialing.

"Want to sit down?" a big flabby man said, sitting on a yellow vinyl love seat across from the desk, taking up most of it. He wore a sleeveless white T-shirt and a flat cap. He gave her a big toothy grin.

"No," she said, turning back to the woman behind the glass, who was speaking quietly into the phone. She hung up.

"He'll be right down," she said.

"What room?" the visitor said. "I can go up."

"No," the woman at the counter said. "No guests."

The visitor huffed an impatient sigh. That only made things difficult. She felt in the right pocket of her jacket, gripped the ACP Baby Browning.

Moments later she heard a door slam upstairs, then someone pounding down the stairs.

A man appeared, wearing an SF Giants ball cap, hands in the pockets of a brown leather jacket.

It was him. Erich Hahn.

If he had a pistol on him, it was small. But he should trust her. The name she had given, Angelica Czarny—Black Angel—told him who she was.

He gave her the once-over.

"Let's go outside," he said.

They pushed through the glass front door, with its duct tape over the crack, stood to one side of the hotel. Sparse Sunday morning traffic reverberated on Sixth Street.

Erich Hahn was slightly shorter than she. He raised his eyebrows in question, waiting.

She pulled the banknote from her pocket. Held it up for him to read.

Half a banknote actually. An old English fiver, 1936.

"Good?" she said.

He leaned forward, studied it. Returned a single nod.

She put the half banknote back in her pocket.

"I showed you mine," she said with a risqué edge. "Now show me yours."

Erich didn't smile as he pulled his half-five-pound note from his pocket, showed her.

"Do I know you?" he said as he put his banknote away.

"There's no reason you should. But you've seen my banknote."

"No," he said, shaking his head. "It's not that."

He was a suspicious one. "What is it, then?"

"Why did Black Cross send you?"

"To tell you that the mission has been aborted."

"Aborted?" His face showed as much surprise as a man like him would ever reveal. "Why?"

"Because the target knows."

"So?" he said. "That's often the way. They spend their whole lives looking over their shoulder. It just means I wait for my time."

"It's not your responsibility to question orders. Or to make your own decisions. Your only decision was to join Black Cross. The rest is no longer up to you."

He grimaced. "I need further confirmation. I've been in place for almost a week."

"There's a communiqué from Kontrol confirming what I've just said. In the drop box."

He scrutinized her. He *was* a suspicious one. But a man like him didn't survive by being otherwise.

"In that case, why tell me in person?"

She gripped the ACP in her pocket. She couldn't very well shoot him here, on a busy street, in broad daylight. She needed to distract him.

"My orders were to contact you in person, in case you did not visit the drop box in time, before any more progress was made on the target."

He rubbed his face, blinking in thought. "We'll check the drop box."

She drew a breath. She'd get him on the way there. Before he found her out. "Very well."

"Let's walk." Hands still in his own pockets, he turned, headed up Sixth Street. She followed.

* * *

Boom watched the interaction from the car. Those two were not on any kind of date. That much was clear.

The man was wearing the same work clothes as in the photo taken the other day, with a Giants cap and sunglasses, and had the same hunkered down stance. Erich Hahn.

Both of them had their hands in their jacket pockets. They weren't touching. They weren't smiling. If Boom were any judge, they had just had an argument of some sort. They might even be packing.

They crossed Mission, headed up toward Market.

Follow on foot? Or drive? If they were taking a vehicle or going to hail a cab he could easily lose them.

Boom closed *Probability and Statistics,* set the heavy textbook on the passenger seat, started up the Trans Am, the big engine shaking the car. Slipped it into gear with a crunch—he wasn't used to driving and especially this beast of a car—and drove down Sixth and spun a Uey in the middle of the street, the fat tires giving up a hint of squeal before he eased off the gas. He came back up Sixth, followed the pair, staying half a block behind.

On Market Street they crossed over, turned right in front of the Warfield Theater, headed downtown. Boom kept up, rumbling along.

The two were walking on the other side of Market, hands in pockets, looking straight ahead, not talking. You could see the tension, even from a distance. They weren't going down to Powell to ride the cable car with the tourists.

Just before Powell, they descended into Powell Street Muni Station.

Damn.

Nowhere to pull over, even on a Sunday. Boom cut a sharp right on Fifth, parked at the first available meter, which was halfway down the block. Hopped out, locked up his buddy's Trans Am, turned, ran back up to Market for all he was worth. At 220 pounds he wasn't breaking any speed records, probably why he didn't get that football scholarship at City College. That and the fact he'd been drafted and shipped off to Nam.

He tore across Market, dodging a Muni bus, and scooted down the escalator into the Muni station.

Boom saw no sign of the pair in the long subterranean station. Muni was one end, BART the other. Both entrances had turnstiles and steps down to platforms. The pair could have taken either. Sunday, there was no Muni attendant at the window to ask.

A vagrant was sitting on the floor across from the stairs down to Muni, slumped over. Boom approached. The man looked up at the sound of Boom's big feet, a fearful look on his face. A big black dude did that often enough. Boom threw a quarter into the man's hat, put on his quiet, polite voice.

"Excuse me, sir, but did you happen to see a man and woman head this way? He would have been wearing a Giants cap. She, a red beret."

"Sorry, brother."

"You didn't notice anybody going down to Muni in the last few minutes?"

Shook his head no. "Wasn't really paying attention."

Boom jogged down to the BART booth, where there was an attendant. Asked the same question.

"Nobody's come through here in the last ten minutes."

That meant Muni. Boom ran back. On the way he heard a train screeching into the station below. He picked up speed, took the stairs two at a time to see a double L car disappear into the inbound tunnel, heading for Embarcadero Station.

No one else was on the platform except for a few commuters waiting to go outbound, none of them Erich Hahn or the tough-looking woman. He asked a Chinese woman loaded down with shopping about the pair. She nodded at the inbound train that had just left. Boom thanked her, trudged back up the stairs.

This was not his day for following people.

CHAPTER TWELVE

1979

The L Embarcadero clattered through the tunnel, the noise deafening as the train picked up speed. The two of them were standing at the rear of the first car, Erich and Angelica Czarny, or whoever she was.

It had taken Erich a moment to recall her at first, but he remembered her now. She had been a teenager when he met her. Gaunt. Prisoner stripes. Now she was thirty-seven years older. She had aged, but the same bitter, vindictive sneer was still there. The same sharp features.

How could he ever forget?

There were several other people in the Muni car, the driver up front.

Holding onto a pole, she eyed him. He returned a polite smile. She did the same and it was as false as his.

He peered through the window of the door connecting the second Muni car. A businessman in a suit was reading a newspaper. That wouldn't work. He needed an empty car in order to get rid of this woman.

The train screeched into Montgomery Station. The doors squealed open. An electronic announcement full of garbled feedback filled the air. One man in their car got off. Several commuters remained.

There was one stop left before the end of the line. All of these stops were short.

He had to move quickly.

Erich looked into the last car again.

The businessman was now gone. Erich glanced out at the platform, saw him walking toward the stairs, checking his watch. An empty car. *Yes.*

"Follow me," Erich said to Angelica Czarny. He slid the first connecting door open to the second car, requiring a little effort with its heavy spring, hot tunnel air blowing in.

"Why?" she said.

"Privacy," he yelled in the blowing air, nodding back at the driver.

Was she reading his mind?

He pulled open the door to the next car, pushed through, not holding either door for her. Throw her off guard, give him time to get his knife out.

In the next car now, he quickly reached down to his boot, pulled his switchblade.

"You could have held the door!" she said, squeezing through, bracing one door open with an elbow.

He saw the glint of the small gun in her other hand, down by her side.

He had been right.

The door snapped shut behind her.

He pressed the button on his switchblade, the *shick* sound just audible even with the train noise.

She heard it. Her pupils flared. She started to bring the gun up.

Not fast enough.

He drove the blade up under her jacket into her solar plexus, twisting, working against cartilage and bone. She grunted, her eyes staring in disbelief as she slumped back against the door, rocking with the motion of the train. Her beret slid off, fell to the floor.

"Kontrol . . ." she said listlessly.

"No," he said calmly. "Your name is Salak. You killed my grandmother. At Sachsenhausen."

She looked at him in shock, eyes rolling back into her head. She didn't remember what a six-year-old would. To her it had been nothing. She had killed so many.

But then she did. "You . . ." she said in dying recognition. "You . . ."

"That's right," he said. "This week I'm Erich. Next week I'll be someone else. But I will always be Jakob. Jakob Rosenstein. And this," he said, whispering into her ear as he twisted the knife one last time, "this is for my grandmother."

She exhaled weakly as her body slackened.

The gun fell from her hand, banging to the floor of the car.

He yanked the knife from her torso with a scrape of bone. Propped her against the door with one hand for a moment as the train rocked into Embarcadero. Wiped the blade off on the inside of her dark jacket several times. Retracted the blade. Put the knife away. Another kill on it.

It was too bad he hadn't been able to question her, find out who sent her. But there had been no time. One thing was clear, though: Black Cross had been breached.

He jostled her into a bench seat by a window. Leaned her over against the glass. The stinging smell of urine wafted up. Her jeans were wet. She would be bleeding on the seat soon. He looked around. A newspaper on a seat. He grabbed it, pulled two sheets, balled them up, worked them under her sweater. Soak up blood.

He zipped her jacket up to her neck. Retrieved the red beret, put it on her head, pulled it down one side, hiding much of her face.

The rest of the paper he opened, spread it across her lap.

Just another dozing commuter, taking a nap.

The train started to slow down into the final station. Light was filling the tunnel. It came to a jerking stop at Embarcadero.

Through the windows he saw people waiting to board the train, ride back outbound.

He lowered his face, along with the brim of his hat.

Spotted her small pistol on the floor by the connecting doors. He reached into his pocket for a handkerchief, and bending down quickly, picked up the gun. Stuffed it in his pocket. Pushed his way out of the train as commuters crowded to get on.

How did Beckmann know he was here?

Someone had told him. But who?

Up the escalator, out onto Market Street, he dropped the pistol into a cement trash barrel. His prized switchblade would live to see another day. It had been a loyal companion.

CHAPTER THIRTEEN

That afternoon Colleen called her answering machine in her office from a payphone in the Lafayette BART station across the bay where she had been waiting on the outdoor platform to snap a photo of some marital infidelity for a paying client. She couldn't let her real work fall behind. She used the pocket-sized decoder to retrieve messages on her machine.

There was one from Boom, sounding uncharacteristically flustered.

She dug out more change and called him at home in San Francisco. She shifted her camera bag up on her shoulder. The heat of the day in the East Bay felt foreign from San Francisco, as if she'd emerged from a cave.

"Good news and bad news, Chief," Boom said.

Boom explained how he'd seen a woman—not Ingrid Richter—leave the Metro Hotel with Erich Hahn. Something was up; the two were at odds with each other as they set off.

"They definitely weren't friends, Chief."

Boom described how he'd followed them up Market.

"And the bad news?" Colleen asked.

"I lost them when they entered Powell Muni station. I parked and hustled down there but they'd already boarded an inbound L. So I went back and watched the Metro Hotel some more. Half an hour later, Erich comes back—alone. Ten minutes after that, he leaves the hotel in a suit and tie, with his bag, gets into a Yellow Cab."

"Checking out."

"Seems that way."

"Get the number of the cab?"

"And the license plate. Old cabbie driving. Bald. Glasses."

"Good work, Boom," she said. "Remind me to get you a camera."

"Want me to keep watching the Metro?"

"No, I think Erich's a goner," she said. "And I don't want to screw up your studies. I'll follow up. Say 'hi' to grandma."

"10-4."

Colleen hung up, wishing she didn't have to keep staking out cheaters when there were more critical matters to attend to. But it looked like Erich had taken off anyway. Who was this new woman? Had she been sent by Ingrid Richter? And what the hell had happened to Ingrid?

Colleen headed back to the BART platform with her camera bag, craving a cigarette after hours of surveillance. In the interest of her future grandson or granddaughter, she was smoke free—well, since last night at Matt's anyway. She unwrapped a piece of Juicy Fruit, stuffed it into her mouth, savoring the sweet flood of sugar, and resumed her position, with a view of the parking lot below the platform.

*   *   *

Eleven p.m. Colleen was bent down under the desk lamp in her office on Pier 26, darkness spilling around the beam of light as she studied a Polaroid with a magnifying glass that showed a man and woman kissing in a car in the Lafayette BART parking lot. She had waited all day to get that shot. A Polaroid wasn't perfect but proved the point until she got her 35 mm prints back. She'd drop the roll of film off first thing tomorrow.

The phone rang.

She answered, thinking it might be Pam. Colleen had left the house early that morning, hadn't been home all day. She'd been doing a lot of that lately. Too much. She felt guilty but she had an excuse. Work.

"Looks like I've got the right number for your new office," Inspector Owens said. "And it looks like I caught you working late—again." In the background she heard men talking. The sound of work vehicles. Metal on metal.

"Howdy, stranger," she said, kicking back, her tennies up on the desk, cracking out her back. She hadn't heard much from Owens since his divorce from hell.

"Sergeant Dwight said you had some info on a man and a woman possibly linked to ex-Nazis."

That made her sit up. "I did ask Matt to see what SFPD could find out on a couple of curious characters. I'm pretty sure one of them might be up to no good. Quite likely both."

"Then I need you to identify someone for us. I'd like to get a jump on it before she goes to the Coroner's office and gets tied up with processing."

She. That didn't sound good. Owens was Homicide. And the Coroner's office meant a DB.

Ingrid? Ingrid Richter?

"Where are you?" she said.

"Muni Division Yard. Balboa Park."

"On my way."

Colleen stashed her work-in-progress, grabbed her file on Ingrid Richter, thinking it might come in handy, keys and jacket, locked up, and headed out onto the huge covered pier where she fired up the

Torino, and rumbled through the arch out onto Embarcadero. She shot through the East Cut, got on the freeway south, and being late night Sunday, pulled into the Muni maintenance yard by Balboa Park Station less than fifteen minutes later. There was a news truck outside the gate, a woman with big hair in front of a camera and lights.

The sizable maintenance yard was half full of Metro cars for the night, and those due for service, everything pretty much shut down except for one car, an L at a service platform crawling with officers and techs. Two SFPD black-and-whites were parked nearby, along with a black-and-white evidence van, Owens' beige unmarked LTD, and a white city medical examiner's wagon. More cops stood by while techs came in and out of the L car at the platform. Some kind of rolling crime scene. Boom had said he saw Erich Hahn and the mystery woman board an inbound L.

The back doors of the ME van were open. Colleen spotted Owens in a tapered sports coat. He'd lost weight. He was standing while another man sat in the open back of the wagon, feet on the ground, a cigarette between his fingers. Colleen drove up, parked near the ME wagon.

Despite Owens' weight loss, the tautness around his eyes and the slackness of his face didn't look healthy. Cops had high divorce rates, and middle-aged cops with young wives even higher, and Owens was taking it hard. His previously trendy haircut, which he'd sported for his ex, had been shorn back to its former severe crew cut, no longer dyed to hide the gray at the temples. Back to no nonsense. Poor Owens.

"Thanks for coming," he said. The two men had been waiting for her.

The other man was an ME investigator, an older guy with thinning gray hair and glasses that amplified his melancholy bloodhound eyes. He wore a uniform that hadn't changed since the 1930s: black pants, black shoes, narrow black tie over a white short-sleeve shirt. His black jacket with the gold buttons and gold stripes around the cuffs hung from the corner of the open van door. He wore plastic gloves. His city badge was on his black belt.

Owens introduced him as Alistair Laurie.

"Sounds like you've got a DB," she said.

"The driver found her at the end of the L Muni line out by the zoo," he said in a thick Scottish accent. "Thought she'd fallen asleep at first. But then they saw her sitting in a pool of blood."

He stood, stepped his cigarette out, got into the van, and Colleen climbed in behind him and crouched by a black body bag on a stretcher. Owens, the bigger man, stood at the back, looking in, rattling change in his pocket.

"Matt said something about your client," Owens said. "A middle-aged German woman you had questions about. No ID on this one but her clothes aren't American and she's in the right age bracket. And she had this in her pocket which might make her European." Owens held up half an old banknote.

"A 1936 series British five-pound note," Colleen said. "Serial number 57903."

Owens turned the half banknote towards him, read it, shook his head. "Man, do I wish I had your eyes." Apart from the light in the van, it was dark.

"Me too," Colleen said. "The reason I know is that the guy we were following—Erich Hahn—had it stashed in the air duct in his hotel bathroom. Along with a drop gun and a Nazi ID that appeared to be vintage."

"Lordy, Lordy," Alistair muttered.

"Let's forget for a moment how you know what was in the air duct of this guy's hotel room," Owens said, studying the note. "Tell me more about this Erich Hahn." He flipped the note around and looked at the back. "One side is completely blank."

Something on the front of the note caught her eye.

"Can I see that?" she said.

Owens handed her the half note.

Colleen examined the partial banknote, about three by five inches in size.

This was not the same as Erich's half. This half had an ornate engraving of Britannia in a helmet on the left, seated with a shield, holding a trident and olive branch. The design was intricate.

"This is the left half of the note," she said. "Erich had the other half—without the figure and trident. But it did have a serial number—the same one. The right side of the note." Something else about it seemed different from Erich's, too, but she couldn't put her finger on it.

"Two halves of the same note," Owens said. "A pass code. Verification. Between this woman and Erich Hahn. If that's his real name." Owens nodded at the body bag. "Each party shows their half of the note before they proceed with whatever they were about to do."

Colleen nodded, handed the half banknote back. "Which went wrong in this case."

Owens slipped the note into his jacket pocket. "They were in some kind of organization together."

Colleen took a deep breath as the ME inspector unzipped the body bag on the stretcher. "One that hunts down ex-Nazis is my bet. He is, anyway."

And saw that the woman wasn't Ingrid Richter but another woman in her fifties; this one slender, dark-complexioned, sharp cheekbones, prominent nose, her face disfigured by death. Her left cheek looked as if someone had taken an iron to it and flattened it. A red beret was nestled under her head like a thin pillow. Colleen felt the revulsion of seeing a body that no longer lived. You never got used to it.

"That's from having her face pressed against the window all day in the trolley car," Alistair said. "She was found in a seat, leaning up against the glass. Rigor mortis had set in. I had to massage her legs and arms to get her to lie flat on the stretcher."

"She's been riding the train all day?" Colleen said in disbelief. "And no one noticed?"

"You'd be bloody amazed at what people don't notice."

"Well, she's not my client," Colleen said, turning to Owens. "But I kind of know who she is. Boom saw her with Erich Hahn, the guy we were shadowing, around noon today. They got on an inbound L at Powell." She nodded at the car on the platform. "Five bucks says it's that one."

"The timing fits if she was killed and been on the train all day," Owens said, rattling change again. "Looks like this Erich Hahn you were tailing is now a person of interest."

"They walked to Powell Station from his hotel at the Metro—a flop hotel on Sixth Street. Boom said it looked like they were arguing before they set off. How did she die?"

"Stabbed," Alistair said. "Do you need to see?"

Colleen exhaled a sigh. Not her favorite activity but more information was always better than less.

"Get it over with," she said.

He unzipped the bag further and the blood was thick and sticky around her torso, soaked into a thin green sweater with a coarse cable stich. It was ripped below the solar plexus where she had been knifed.

"A professional job," Owens said. "Maybe this Erich Hahn is ex-military."

"Could be," Colleen said, recalling the austere nature of his room, the tidiness of his belongings. "Any jewelry on her?"

Alistair shook his head. "Why do you ask?"

"Erich Hahn—or whoever he is—the guy I was hired to find—is Jewish. I'm thinking a group tracking down ex-Nazis. Maybe she wore a Magen David—a Star of David—pendant, something like that. Just a thought."

"Nothing," Owens said. "No ID, wallet. A few dollars and change. Carfare. And the half banknote."

Then it came to her. She turned to Alistair.

"Have you looked at her arms?"

"Not yet," he said. "Full examination tomorrow back at the shop."

"Do you mind?"

Alistair traded glances with Owens, who gave him a nod of approval.

Alistair carefully unzipped the black body bag further, working one stiff arm free, pushing up the sleeve of her leather jacket, despite the rigidity. Nothing on the right arm.

But on the left forearm, a six-digit number prefixed by an *A*. The number was smudged and hard to discern but it began with A2101.

"Well, look at that," Alistair said. "A Holocaust tatt."

"Not too easy to make out," Colleen said.

"Most of these were done under very harsh circumstances, often by other prisoners during the registration process. They weren't much to begin with. And they fade with time."

"I think you have your connection," Colleen said to Owens.

"It works," Owens said. "But why kill her? If he's looking for ex-Nazis and she's a camp survivor?"

"Something went wrong," Colleen said. It didn't make a lot of sense.

But survivors came in all shades of morality.

"Seen enough?" Alistair asked.

"More than enough," Colleen said, getting out of the van, feeling queasy. "Thank you."

Alistair pulled the bag back over the woman gently, with obvious consideration, before he zipped her back in.

"You said this Erich Hahn is staying at the Metro Hotel?" Owens asked Colleen. "South of Market?"

"He was. But Boom saw him return home shortly after the train ride, come out ten minutes later in a suit with his bag, get into a Yellow Cab."

"So he took off."

"It's what I'd do if I just knifed someone and left her on a Muni train," Colleen said. "Boom's got the cab number and license plate."

"Maybe *she* was the target."

"But the tattoo," Colleen said. "She's no ex-Nazi. They weren't allies. Even if they were both prisoners."

"Maybe she wasn't who she said she was," Owens said.

Colleen nodded. "My client—Ingrid Richter—paid me to find Erich Hahn. I informed her where he was early Sunday."

Owens raised his eyebrows. "She's not looking too innocent right now either."

"Looks like she used me to find Erich with some story about being his aunt, then sent this woman to take care of him. But Erich killed her first."

Owens nodded, then called over one of the uniformed men, a sergeant with a hard build, instructed him to radio in a request to pick up Erich Hahn who was last seen at the Metro Hotel on Sixth and Mission. "If he's still there. Assume armed and dangerous."

The officer confirmed, took off.

Owens turned to Colleen as Alistair shut the back doors of the ME wagon, went up front, got in the passenger side. His partner was behind the wheel, filling out paperwork. The van started up.

"I'm going to need your client's contact information, too," Owens said. "And anything else you've got. And I need you to be forthcoming with me on this one, Colleen." He gave her raised eyebrows. Colleen had been known to play her cards close to her chest. But not this time. This was different.

"Ingrid Richter is—or was—staying at the Fairmont. I've got photos in the car. I thought they might be needed. You might want to have someone stop by the Fairmont too, sooner rather than later."

"Way ahead of you."

"I'm thinking of checking her out myself," she said casually. "Are you heading down there when you're done here, by any chance?"

Owens flashed a sardonic smile. "This is a murder investigation. Back off."

"Correct me if I'm wrong but didn't I just give you a shipload of information? Which gives you a huge jump on this case? I even brought my file for you."

"Great. You're doing your duty as a citizen—as required by law."

"You'd be scratching your head without me."

"And that woman might not be dead if you hadn't gotten involved." Owens nodded at the van as it bounced out of the lot. "Did that cross your mind?"

"Of course. So that makes me invested." Ingrid Richter had played her. And now people were showing up dead. Where did it stop? "The least you can do is let me tag along. I can help you ID Ingrid Richter."

"No," Owens said. "But I will need that file."

She sighed. "You got it."

"Any other thoughts on what this might have to do with your client?"

"Not yet," Colleen said. "Okay if I look in the train car? Where the body was found?"

"Knock yourself out," Owens said, checking his watch. It was going to be a long night. "But there's nothing besides blood and other fluids."

"They got on at Powell. Headed to Embarcadero. If Erich Hahn got back to the Metro Hotel shortly after, he probably stabbed her at Montgomery, Embarcadero at the latest." Embarcadero was the end of the line.

"There might be a weapon in or around either of those Muni stations," Owens said.

"See how much help I am?" she said. "And I don't even draw a city salary."

"Yes, but you're still not working this case, Colleen. I don't need you going off and doing your own thing—again."

Not yet, she thought.

She went to the Torino, got the Richter file out of the trunk, gave it to Owens.

"Always thinking ahead," he said, looking at the photos of Erich Hahn, Ingrid Richter.

"I'd like that back, by the way."

"Of course."

Maybe, she thought. But now he owed her one. She already knew what Ingrid Richter and Erich looked like and she'd been paid. "If nothing else, I'd like to be kept in the loop."

"Will do."

That Owens would do. She didn't know him well personally, but they'd been through a few cases together. They'd butted heads but he was a good cop. One of the few.

"I'm sorry about the divorce," she said quietly.

He cleared his throat, closed the file, patted it against his leg, looked away. "Thanks."

On the way home she pulled over at a gas station across from City College, filled up the thirsty Torino. Many gas stations had recently gone *self-serve* so she had to pump it herself. She left the pump ticking away while she used the payphone, called the Fairmont.

"Ingrid Richter, please." It was almost one a.m. and she didn't really expect to be put through.

"I'm sorry, ma'am, but Ms. Richter has checked out."

Colleen wasn't too surprised to hear that. Disappointed, yes—in herself, for being a sucker. And possibly contributing to the death of a certain Jane Doe.

"Do you have any forwarding information?" Colleen asked.

"I do not, ma'am."

"I don't suppose Nicholas Carr is still there, by any chance?" Nicholas Carr was the Fairmont's night security manager.

"Nick went off duty at midnight, ma'am."

She left a message for him, thanked the desk clerk.

Back at the Torino, the pump had finally clicked off. Over twenty bucks. A first. Eighty-five cents a gallon—up more than twenty cents since last year. And you didn't even get your windows washed or your oil checked.

CHAPTER FOURTEEN

Going home to a pigsty didn't do much to improve Colleen's out-look. The coffee table was strewn with cups, a cereal bowl, an ashtray containing a twisted butt. So much for not smoking. It was a good thing Pam had gone to bed or Colleen might have given her a piece of her mind. She turned off the TV that had been left on a late-night movie, brushed her teeth, went to bed herself.

And didn't sleep.

She couldn't let go of the fact that Ingrid Richter had deceived her into locating Erich Hahn, an ex-Nazi hunter of some sort, and looked to be after Erich herself. The dead woman on Muni, with the Holocaust tattoo, was evidence of that, a hit apparently gone wrong.

That made Colleen partially responsible, for kicking it all off in the first place.

Where would it end? Who else might be killed?

She finally drifted off but woke up early, the skies pitch dark, the silence of early morning humming outside her window. In the distance the whir of 101 North whispered with light traffic. She lay there on the undulating warmth of the waterbed until she couldn't stand it anymore, got up, showered, pulled on her soft denim bell-bottoms and a light blue V-necked sweater because Pier 26 could be an igloo, made coffee quietly so as not to wake Pam, took it in a cup to go, sipped as she drove down to Embarcadero. The streets were near empty, the bay shining with early rays by the time she got to the pier.

She had plans to use the car today so she parked on Embarcadero. proper and walked into the tall covered pier. The rush of water below splashed around the pilings of the old deck. Past the new architect's office, still under construction, Chan Imports with a fresh pallet of sacks of dried beans. The bags were festooned with exotic writing. She headed back to her office, which faced the bridge.

And stopped when she heard a noise. Coming from her office. She stayed to the left, past boarded-up storage rooms, then tiptoed into a dark hallway that split off to her office and several others waiting for gentrification.

Another noise. From inside her office. She was sure of it.

Someone was in there. Her heartbeats quickened.

She turned, padded back to Embarcadero quietly in her tennies, opened the car door, reached under the dash, got the gym sock with Little Bersalina in it, her .22 caliber Argentine semiautomatic that fit just about anywhere.

From the trunk she grabbed her Polaroid OneStep camera, inserted a flash bar on top. There were still a few fresh bulbs left. She hung the camera around her neck, flipped the safety off on the Bersa.

Camera steadied with her left hand, gun tucked in the palm of her right, she stepped quietly back inside Pier 26. The tall ceiling echoed in the early morning darkness.

When she got to the end of the hallway, in the minimal light, she saw a flashlight beam bounce out of the window in her office door. Her nerves tightened.

Something clattered in her office.

She approached slowly, camera and gun ready. She saw that the glass in the upper half of the door that had just been stenciled with her business name had been shattered. Broken glass lay on the floor. A chunk with *Hayes Conf* lay in front of the door. Her nerves ratcheted up.

"I can't fucking find it," she heard a man whisper. He had a young reedy voice.

"Maybe she doesn't have it," another man said.

"Maybe in that safe."

"Good luck with that."

She approached the door, camera up in her left hand, finger on the button. The gun rested in her right.

Stuck her head in.

Two guys squatted by the file cabinet in the corner, flashlights jumping.

She moved into the doorway quietly in her sneaks, camera up.

"Hey guys—what's up?"

The two spun in surprise, and she pressed the button and got a shot, the room flashing briefly with light. In that moment she saw a ball cap on one, a dark watch cap and bushy Fu Manchu mustache on the other, a stocky guy.

"Fuck!" Ball Cap shouted. The two flashlights zeroed in on Colleen. Along with a stubby pistol from Watch Cap's pocket.

Nothing like a gun to elevate the pulse rate.

She jumped back out into the hall as the man's gun went off with a *crack* that reverberated off the high ceilings.

In the hallway she backed away. She wasn't going to shoot anyone for breaking into her office. She was also on parole and the firearm was a violation.

She turned, spun, let her legs do the rest.

At Chan Imports she ducked behind a pallet full of cases of rice crackers. She set her Polaroid on top of a carton, readied the Bersa.

Two pairs of feet came pounding down the hall toward her, into the open area, and she saw the two men running for Embarcadero. One had a crowbar.

At the big arched entranceway to Embarcadero, the two men cut left, disappeared from view.

She pulled the Polaroid photo from the camera, stuck it in her jacket pocket, headed for the entrance herself. She held the camera ready, juggling the gun in her right hand.

At the entranceway, she peered around the corner, hidden in shadow.

The two were getting into a beater car half a block down along the water. The big engine fired up and they tore out and up in an old black primered Camaro with a crunch in the right front fender.

The car screamed by and she got a photo of the rear. No license plate. *Damn.* Probably removed for the job at hand. But a faded Confederate flag decal adorned the dented bumper.

Something told her the break-in had to do with Ingrid, and Erich, and her own involvement.

CHAPTER FIFTEEN

1979

As Colleen's nerves settled, she examined the damage to her office.

The original door, made of Douglas fir, had once had a beautiful old pane of frosted glass with curlicue edging that had survived many decades. No more. To top it off, Colleen had just had the new stencil done to the tune of sixty bucks.

The center drawer to her beat-up green metal desk, appropriated from a condemned warehouse she once guarded, had been crowbarred open with no finesse whatsoever. It looked like the Incredible Hulk had stopped by. Pens, pencils, gum, her emergency pack of Virginia Slims, all lay scattered on the rough hardwood floor. Likewise, the side drawer had been torn open. The gray metal cash box was untouched. Not your garden variety robbery.

Against the far corner by the window with the view of a Bay Bridge pier, the filing cabinet had been jimmied open as well. The floor was littered with scattered file folders and papers. The small floor safe next to the file cabinet was intact.

She gave a sigh, went over to her desk, picked the pack of cigarettes off the floor, shook one out, pulled it the rest of the way with her lips. Found a book of paper matches, lit up her cig. Shaking out the match, she surveyed the mayhem one more time, ran her fingers through her hair.

She sat down in her squeaky roller chair, feet up on the desk, took a deep drag of smoke, let it billow out.

The timing suggested the two thugs were looking for the Ingrid Richter file. That she had given to Inspector Owens. Somebody was trying to get rid of what little evidence there was, perhaps. Or was looking for Erich Hahn. Or wanted to send Colleen a message. Or all of the above.

Colleen called home to warn Pam of any potentially unwelcome visitors but got no answer. Pam rarely got up before noon.

She let the phone ring.

And ring.

No answer.

She called the police, reported the break-in. They said a patrol car would stop by.

She put the files back into their folders, folders back in the file cabinet. She'd need to get the door repaired, sooner rather than later. She pressed the button on her Pulsar watch. Not even six thirty. Too early to call a repair service.

When she did, after the business day started, the guy finally came and she ordered a shatterproof replacement, ugly wire-reinforced glass that set her back another pretty penny. The fire code wouldn't let her put a dead bolt lock on the door. At some point she'd have to get the glass re-stenciled. Or maybe not. Maybe incognito was the way to go. Cheaper, too.

She called Pam again who had finally risen. They had one of their standard curt conversations.

"Please be extra careful answering the door, sweetie," Colleen said, signing off. "Check out front first. Then the back, over the deck. Etcetera. Etcetera."

"Why?"

"There was a break-in here at the office. I just want to make sure you know what to do if anyone stops by." Of course anyone that broke in to Colleen's flat would have to deal with Pam, which might be to their detriment.

"I know what to do," Pam said. "Hall closet."

"Hall closet as last resort," Colleen confirmed. "Better still, call the police."

"Yeah, sure," Pam said, and she could hear her puff on a cigarette. "What time are you picking me up?"

"Picking you up?"

"Obstetrician appointment."

"Oh, right. What time was it again?"

"You forgot, didn't you?"

She had. Colleen took a deep breath. "Just tell me what time."

"Three thirty."

"I'll pick you up at two forty-five. Please be ready this time."

"Two forty-five." Pam hung up.

Colleen worked through lunch, reorganizing the mess. SFPD never stopped by.

CHAPTER SIXTEEN

On the way home to pick Pamela up that afternoon, Colleen swung by the Metro Hotel. She found Nathan, the world-weary resident who had let her into Erich Hahn's room the other day for a handful of twenties. He was outside, hands in the pockets of his warehouseman's jacket. His comb-over blew in the sharp wind that whipped up Sixth Street. He brushed it back into place with his fingers.

"He's gone," he said as Colleen approached, meaning Erich Hahn. But she knew that. Boom had seen him leave and get into a cab with his suitcase.

"No idea where, I suppose."

Nathan shook his head. "The police were here. They questioned everyone."

"And you told them what?"

"I sure didn't tell them I helped you search his room. I don't need that kind of attention."

"That suits me just fine." She went inside the Metro, not expecting to find much. The round middle-aged woman behind the smudged Plexiglas was reading a magazine. Walter of the big girth was not ensconced in his yellow love seat today.

The mail slots for the rooms showed a letter waiting to be collected for number 20, Erich's old room.

"Erich Hahn, please," Colleen said. "Room 20."

"Out," the woman said, flipping a page.

"Out?" Colleen said, "Or gone?"

She gave Colleen a squint. "You were here the other day."

"I was."

She looked at Colleen. "The police were here, too. Last night. Late."

"I bet that happens with more than a few of your clients."

"What is it you want, exactly?"

"I'm actually an investigator," she said, holding up the ersatz Consumer Affairs card allegedly from the Bureau of Security and Investigative Services that she'd had printed up, her approval still pending with Sacramento. It looked quite authentic in its beat-up state. "I'm working for Mr. Hahn's ex. He's late on his child support. Four months. Four kids."

"I see." The woman raised her eyebrows, patiently waiting.

"Oh, right," Colleen said, getting out her thinning money clip, slipping a twenty-dollar bill through the slot. *Here we go again.* Only this time there was no client to bill it to.

The note disappeared.

"Number 20 never handed in his key," the woman said. "His room is paid up until the end of the week, but his stuff is gone."

A low profile exit.

Colleen nodded at the mail slot. "Looks like he missed his mail on the way out."

"A letter from his bank," the woman said. "When the week is up, I'll send it back."

"When did that show up?"

"This morning."

The police had been here last night. So they hadn't seen the letter.

Colleen leaned in, lowered her voice. "That could possibly be very helpful for my client," she said. "Trying to get that back child support and all." She shook her head sadly. "Four little ones to look after."

"I can see where it might," the woman said flatly.

"Just to look at real quick, if you know what I mean. Not to keep."

The woman's dark eyebrows knitted. "Tampering with the U.S. Mail?"

"Wasn't that a song by Elvis Presley—'U.S. Male'? What a loss." Another twenty slid through the slot.

The woman stared at the lone bill.

Colleen sighed as the final twenty slid through. "I'm starting to get a cramp," she said, dropping her empty money clip in her pocket. "And that was my last one." This case was starting to hurt her pocketbook.

The woman collected up the twenties, tapped them together, folded them, pocketed them. Spun in her roller chair, retrieved the letter. Colleen saw a swirling blue Peninsula Bank and Security logo in one corner.

The woman stood up, letter in hand.

"Wait here," she said.

She squeezed out from behind the desk, shuffled down the hall in fuzzy slippers, went into a room. Five minutes later, she was back, holding an unfolded letter. She had opened the envelope somehow. Colleen wondered how well practiced that procedure was.

She handed it to Colleen while she rubbed her leg absentmindedly.

Colleen read the letter. It was addressed to Mr. Erich Hahn, c/o The Metro Hotel.

"This is to confirm that the safe deposit box in your name, no. 1781, has been established with the approved pass code previously set up on file March 14th, 1979."

By Colleen's calculations, Erich had been in Buenos Aires on that date. So the safety box had been set up ahead of time. Interesting. A drop box of some sort for collaborators?

"When did Mr. Hahn rent the room here?" Colleen asked.

"Prepaid, beginning of the month."

So that was set up ahead of time as well. Before Erich's "surprise" visit to San Francisco to "see his aunt." He would need a physical address for a bank account and safe deposit box.

"Can I get a copy of this?" Colleen said.

"No." The women held her hand out.

Colleen folded the letter up, handed it back.

On the way home, she stopped at a payphone, left the engine running while she hopped out and called SFPD's anonymous tip line.

"This is an anonymous tip for Inspector Owens," she said. "Peninsula Bank and Security has a safe deposit box registered to Erich Hahn, number: 1781."

She waited until the phone clerk had written that down, thanked her, hung up, jogged back out to the Torino.

*   *   *

After Pam's doctor visit that afternoon, Colleen drove Pam back up the hill to her flat.

"I might be late home for dinner tonight," she said, the car idling in front of her apartment building on Vermont.

"I thought you had a date with Sergeant Dwight," Pam said.

"I canceled," she said. She had called Matt, let him know she was spending the evening with Pam.

"But you two are getting pretty serious," Pam said, climbing out with a bit of difficulty, her round belly making it an effort. "When's the big day anyway?"

"Don't start," Colleen said.

"Oh?" Pam said, bending down, looking into the car. "I thought Sergeant Dwight was hot to put a ring on my mom's finger."

"It's been discussed."

"And?" Pam brushed her red hair out of her face, eyeing Colleen with serious interest.

"You and Lambert are my number one priority," Colleen said. Lambert was their nickname for Pam's baby, even though they did not know the gender.

Pam blinked. "You sure could have fooled me."

Colleen sighed. "You and I might be going through a rough patch right now, Pam, but that's all it is—a patch. We'll get through it."

"Guess I'll have to take your word for it."

"I thought we could order Chinese tonight. Watch a trashy old movie together."

"You can't afford to stand Sergeant Dwight up too many times, you know. You're no spring chicken."

"Yes, yes, I know—I'm in the twilight of my years. If I'm late and you get hungry, go ahead and order. I'll have the usual."

"Kung Pao," Pam said.

"Don't forget the fortune cookies. They missed them last time."

"Bastards."

"And don't forget to keep an eye out for bad guys paying visits, hmm?" She said it as casually as possible, not wanting to worry Pam too much.

"*Hall closet*," Pam said, meeting her gaze.

"Hall closet," Colleen confirmed.

Pam slammed the car door, waddled off to the apartment building. Colleen's heart went out to her. With all that had happened recently, she couldn't afford to have Pam under threat as well. She had been through so much. Colleen watched Pam unlock the entry door to the apartment building, then go inside. No look back. No wave. *Oh well.*

Colleen headed to the Civic Center where she visited SF Public Library. She hit the index cards, starting with Walter Beckmann, the name on the SS ID that had been in Erich Hahn's air vent, along with half of a 1936 five-pound note and a Hungarian pistol.

CHAPTER SEVENTEEN

1979

A new location. A change of plans.

He took the morning bus from Rome to Lake Bracciano, fifty kilometers north of the capital. The mist hovered over the country-side, ageless. One could look back in time through the swirling white vapor, past centuries, millennia, to when the Romans ruled the world.

But he always came back to this century. To a time thirty-seven years ago. The war. Sachsenhausen.

Last week he was Erich. This week he was Saul. The new passport in the safe deposit box in Rome said as much. And the photograph he held now in his hands that had accompanied the passport showed how his mission had changed. The target in San Francisco had to be abandoned. Here was a new one.

To be effective, one had to be flexible.

Flexible but never forget. Forget what they had done. To his mother. His grandmother.

His people.

Six million souls that hung in limbo, waiting for justice. One by one they would receive it.

Black Cross moved with a life of its own. His life moved with it.

The bus shifted down, descended a winding road onto a cape on the lake to a medieval village, to an ancient square overlooking the shore. Women lugged buckets of water from the fountain. He got off the bus, went to the café. Fishermen standing with cigarettes and coffee chatted about the weather, how today looked to be a good day. Getting ready to go out and fish, drag the nets into shore, each man pulling as his boots dug in, leaving deep grooves in the dirt as they had done ever since the village had been here. The cool morning air. The square. Savoring the early day.

He envied them. Their simple connection with life. Never to be his.

He ordered a coffee, stood at the counter amidst the cigarette smoke and sugar wrappers littering the tile floor, the noise of the day beginning. There was no need to ask where the Church of Saint Mary of the Assumption was. The bells were ringing, echoing through town, down the steps into the square. He downed his espresso, headed for the church, up stone steps. Schoolchildren with satchels ran by, laughing.

He entered the unpretentious church, took a seat in a pew towards the rear. There were a number of people for morning service, still many believers in a small town like this.

The priest appeared at the pulpit, a man close to sixty, in red and white robes and a crown of white hair. Looking almost angelic in the light cast from the stained glass windows.

What an image the priest clung to, hiding amidst his sheep all these years.

Erich-Saul-Jakob examined the old black-and-white photograph in his hand, one that had been in the safe deposit box along with his new passport and money.

A young priest standing with Nazi officers in front of the church in Oranienburg, just outside Sachsenhausen, all of them smiling for the camera. Death with a smile.

The priest was thirty-seven years younger in the photo but it was the same man as in the pulpit. There was no doubt. Doing the Vatican's work then, investing in the factories the Nazis ran with slave labor from the camps.

Jakob's mother one of them.

Hiding all these years, the father of this church thought he was safe.

Erich-Saul-Jakob slipped the photo into his jacket pocket as Mass began, felt the handle of his knife with his thumb.

The beautiful music, the sunlight streaming through stained glass, the smell of incense. He would enjoy it for what it was.

This priest's last Mass.

CHAPTER EIGHTEEN

Early that evening there was a knock at Colleen's office door, which was now locked and sported a new functional, ugly wire-reinforced glass pane. Colleen got up, answered the door. It was Owens, in a smart slate blue suit with wide lapels. Looking trim.

"New suit," she said, showing him in. "Nice."

"None of my old clothes fit anymore."

He'd lost that much weight.

"Well, that's one good thing," she said, although Owens' face was haggard, bags under his eyes. She went around, sat down in front of her notes on Erich Hahn. She closed the file.

Owens stood. "I just got an anonymous tip," he said, squinting.

She frowned in mock confusion. "Really?"

"Yes, *really*: Eric Hahn's safe deposit box number."

"Wow. Some good citizen must really want to help you out."

He gave a droll look as he pulled the knees of his pants up an inch before sitting down. "Correct me if I'm forgetting myself but I thought I told you to stay away from this case, Colleen."

"My office was broken into this morning." She told him what had happened, described the perpetrators.

"Did you call SFPD?"

"Still waiting for them to stop by. But I had to leave for a couple of hours, take Pam to the doctor."

"Everything okay?"

"Oh sure."

Owens nodded. "You think the break-in had something to do with Erich Hahn?"

"Ingrid Richter perhaps. And I don't *think*. I know. No cash taken. Someone wants to find Erich and stop me with what little I know. Which I already gave to you."

"All you need is proof."

"Ingrid Richter knows where my office is. Ingrid is after Erich Hahn. She could be working with some right-wing fringe group."

"How do you make that jump?"

"The two thugs who ruined what little I have here drove an old Camaro with a Confederate flag bumper sticker."

"Might be a stretch but okay."

She shrugged. "What have you guys dug up?"

"Ingrid Richter took the red-eye to Rome last night. But I suspect you might have known that, too."

"I knew she checked out of her hotel. But I didn't know where she'd gone."

Owens gave a mocking smile. "Even though I told you to back off."

Colleen ignored that. "But Rome? Now it makes her even more of a suspect."

"Did you hear what I just said?"

"You know, you may as well just let me help out. I'm not dropping this. You could talk to your superiors about bringing me in as your CI." Confidential Informant. "Make it official." There were distinct advantages. She'd get more support, maybe even a little cash to cover expenses. It would broaden her scope of influence. It would look good for parole.

"We'll see." He grimaced, changed the subject. "We found nothing on Erich Hahn's travels."

"Meaning?"

"He left his hotel, but that's all we know. The itinerary Ingrid Richter gave you shows he flew in from Buenos Aires last Friday."

"I'm not too sure about Ingrid anymore, but the itinerary looked genuine."

"It is." Owens reached into the inside pocket of his jacket, pulled out a folded-up sheet of rough printer paper, unfolded it, set it on her desk blotter.

Colleen leaned over, turned the manifest around, studied it.

The passenger list from the flight from Buenos Aires to SFO last Friday.

"Got in shortly before the cabbie you talked to picked up your Erich Hahn," Owens said.

"No Erich Hahn on that flight," she said, looking up. "Maybe he took an earlier one."

"Or his name isn't Erich Hahn."

She shot him a finger pistol. "Great minds think alike."

"Although the records at the Metro Hotel show Erich Hahn checking in with that name, using a Syrian passport."

"Syrian," she said, "Curious." She studied the manifest, turned the paper around, and pointed to a name.

Owens read the name. "Jakob Klaus," he said.

"He's traveling alone," she said. "Sounds German. And possibly Jewish."

Owens thought about that. "Multiple passports."

"If he's a hit man, that's no big surprise. You should search for Jakob Klaus leaving town."

Owens nodded. "But who is he?"

She sat back. "Whoever he is, he's looking for Werner Beckmann."

Owens put his list away. "Werner Beckmann: the name on the ID in your Ingrid Richter file."

"Which you are going to return at some point. Yep. He was a high-ranking official at Sachsenhausen concentration camp in 1942. He left in 1943, with no further trace. So he could still be at large, as they say."

"That's not in your file."

"Just found out today."

"From who?"

"*Whom*," she said. "SF Public Library is my friend."

"How old would Erich Hahn have been at the time?"

"Young," she said. "Six or so. But he could still have been a prisoner in a camp. Or a family member could have been. Or he could just be following orders—if he's a hit man with a revenge group."

"We're trying to ID the dead woman with the Holocaust tattoo. We're going through the FBI." Owen clicked his teeth. "This is turning into an international thing."

"Maybe she was a prisoner at Sachsenhausen."

"So why would Erich kill her?" Owens asked.

"Good question. But you're assuming prisoners were always allies. They weren't. One of the things the Nazis did was to create classifications that split prisoners into groups who were often in conflict with each other. This was by design. Prisoners were categorized by religion, race, sexual preference, ethnicity, you name it. Jews, of course, were the primary target and murdered in the millions. Prisoners were also used as guards. Not only did that mean the Nazis could leverage their own troops but they didn't have to get as physically close to prisoners themselves. Death and disease was rampant in the camps. None of this was good for prisoner morale, which was exactly what the Nazis wanted."

"Divide and conquer."

"Exactly."

"So the woman with the tattoo might have had some beef with Erich Hahn."

"He obviously had one with her before he stabbed her."

"What would Ingrid Richter have to do with it? And why Rome? Just to get out of the country?"

Colleen gave a frown of uncertainty. "I have my thoughts about her."

"You think she's an ex-Nazi."

"No hard proof. But she did use me to find Erich, and I think she sent the tattooed hit lady after him."

"The conference is still ongoing, we're told," Owens said. "But Ingrid left early. Flight 800 last night, SFO to Vinci–Fiumicino Airport."

Even more damning evidence against Ingrid Richter.

"Rome isn't home for Ingrid," Colleen said. "Berlin is." She drummed her fingers. "Sure would be nice to know what's in Erich Hahn's safe deposit box."

"We don't have enough info for a warrant yet."

"Say what?"

"It's just not good enough to say Erich Hahn might be a murder suspect and that something in that safe deposit box might link him to the murder. The judge needs specific, verifiable information connecting what's in that box to the homicide to Erich."

Colleen took a deep breath, let it out.

"Can't you make something up?" she said quietly.

Owens eyed her. "Other cops might."

Owens was a good cop, which was one of the many reasons Colleen admired him.

He continued, "Besides, if I say I'm looking for a bloody knife and I find Nazi diamonds, the trial judge will rule they're inadmissible."

"This law thing gets complicated."

"Sure does." Owens sighed. "On top of it, if the FBI step in and take over, I'll be dealing with them. And they don't always like to share. That's why I want to beat them to the punch."

Colleen tapped the arms of her chair. "I can't say as I blame you."

"Did Sergeant Dwight have anything for you?" Owens said casually. He knew about her and Matt.

"Why don't you ask him?" she said.

"Because I'm supposed to go through channels. Versus information that he might have just found out unofficially for a—ah—friend. Like you."

"So you *do* want me to help you," she said.

"I just don't want you getting actively involved."

"Someone breaks in my office and shoots at me," she said. "I think I'm actively involved."

"I'll check with SFPD and find out what the status is with your break-in."

She opened the file on her desk, held up one of the Polaroids. Two men staring at her from the office in the dark, lit up by the flash, and the other a black Camaro roaring up Embarcadero.

Owens reached over, took the photo, studied it. "A couple of fine-looking, upstanding young men."

"Particularly the one who fired at me." She nodded at the wall behind Owens. The dark wallboard had a white chip where the bullet had pierced it. "I think it was a snub nose. Loud anyway. A thirty-eight at least."

He turned, looked at the bullet hole, turned back, picked up the photo of the car rushing up Embarcadero. "No license plate."

"Not quite as dumb as they looked."

He slipped the photos in his breast pocket.

"Oh, come on now!" Colleen said.

"You're not actively working this case, remember?"

"Perhaps I want to cherish the memory."

"You've got a bullet hole for that." He stood up. "I'll keep you in the loop though."

"That's the least you can do."

"And you make sure you do the same with me."

"I wouldn't have it any other way."

When Owens left, Colleen realized the time. As dark as the interior of the office was, the reflection of the last rays reflecting off the bay caught the opposite wall. And the new glass of her door.

She wanted to get home and have dinner with Pam, make sure there were no unsolicited visits. And that Pam was okay. She'd been blue lately. Colleen had to remind herself that Pam was eight months pregnant, after all. Not to mention that the father of her child was a nutjob who had headed up a religious cult.

With no lockable file cabinets, she put her important files in her safe, threw on her leather coat, grabbed her keys, headed out. The Torino was parked on the pier next to Chan Imports.

She said goodnight to Harvey Chan, a portly Asian man with surprising strength as he hurled boxes around to ear-screeching Chinese music from a transistor radio.

She was just about to unlock the Torino when she heard a familiar voice.

"Hey, good-lookin', where do you think you're going without me?"

She spun.

It was Matt, with the big pointed collars of a dark blue floral shirt draped out over the lapels of a smart tan corduroy three-piece suit. The men were definitely outdoing the women today, especially with Colleen in her jeans, V-neck T-shirt, and Pony Topstars.

She was surprised to see him and it must have showed. His smile faded.

"The reservation at Alfred's?" he said patiently, perhaps a little edge. Getting into Alfred's was no small feat.

"You didn't get my message," she said.

He came up close. Paco Rabanne. He smelled great.

"No, I didn't," he said with a sigh. "Work again?"

"*Pam*," she said. "I'm really sorry, Matt. I did call. And it's not just Pam for the sake of Pam this time." She could see the disappointment in his face. And God knew the two of them had canceled more dates than not. She couldn't just take off on him now. "Let's go next door for a quick drink and I can bring you up to date."

A few minutes later they were sitting at the bar on Pier 23. Jazz with an African beat pulsated from a trio in the corner. The lights of Oakland shone across the water through the windows.

"Did you report the break-in?" Matt said, stirring his drink with a plastic swizzle stick.

"I did," Colleen said, sipping Chardonnay. "But no follow-up yet. I gave the pics to Owens."

"And now you're worried about Pam," Matt said, taking a measured sip of a Black Russian.

"I think those two who broke in might be locally connected," Colleen said. "The beater car and all. Confederate flag sticker. Their accents. American."

"But you still think they're connected to this Erich Hahn."

"Too much of a coincidence," she said. "And they were clearly looking for something. It has to be the file on Ingrid Richter."

Matt sipped, smacked his lips. "Hard to think otherwise."

Matt was working a case with a local Aryan fringe group and she had her theories.

"Any news yet from the Interpol guy in Lyon?" she asked casually.

Shook his head. "Paquet hasn't got back to me yet." Matt set his drink down on the bar. "But I did see something interesting out of the Buenos Aires Interpol office today on the teleprinter. Since your buddy was just down there, it might be of interest."

"Oh yes?"

"A German ex-pat found murdered in a tourist bar near the water-front. Right around the time Erich Hahn would've been there." Matt continued: "Turns out the dead man wasn't just any ordinary German looking to enjoy the land of sunshine and cheap steaks either. He was a former concentration camp guard by the name of Hermann Kruger." Matt raised his eyebrows.

The news was as much a surprise as it wasn't. "Sachsenhausen?"

"I didn't get the camp name," Matt said, picking up his drink, swirling it. "But he was garroted, killed execution style. Made me think of your buddy Erich the Knife."

"How are you doing with Dr. Lange?" Lange was the mouthpiece for Aryan Alliance, a local neo-Nazi group Matt's department was investigating. Colleen had had a brush with Lange on a recent case at a neo-Nazi/Klan rally. If anyone knew the SF extremists scene, it would be him.

"We are proceeding cautiously. Lange is an eel. Slippery."

"I'm wondering if those two punks who broke in might be linked to Aryan Alliance."

Matt shrugged. "Nothing tangible, though."

"Confederate flag sticker on the bumper? It's enough to go on in my book."

"Right, Colleen, but once again your book and mine are not quite the same. If you're asking me to question Lange's people then I need to remind you that SFPD is proceeding very cautiously with the Lange case. His antennae are already up. He knows he's being watched. We can't afford to scare him off again to chase down a couple of punks on a possible B&E."

"Got it." She didn't like always asking for favors and tonight it was clear Matt didn't like being asked. She pressed the button on her watch. "I better get home. I'm worried about Pam."

Matt took a measured sip of his drink. "Ever think you might be worrying about her a little too much?"

"No." Colleen set her glass of wine down. "Maybe not enough."

"It's none of my business," Matt said gently. "But Pam is a grown woman. One who has put you through the wringer. You rescued her from a cult, you house her, pay her bills, doctor bills, and she watches TV all day while you hustle divorce cases. You've got your own life, too."

"You're absolutely right, Matt," Colleen said brusquely. "It *is* none of your business." She took another sip of wine, set the unfinished glass on the bar. She insisted on paying for drinks, left a tip, gave him a peck on the cheek. "I'm sorry about dinner."

He returned an apologetic smile, swirled his drink. The band was just kicking into a Fela Kuti number so he decided to stick around. Matt was a jazz hound.

*   *   *

When Colleen left, a couple of Qantas stewardesses came into the bar. They had just checked into the Hyatt Embarcadero across the way and had not even changed out of their stylish green uniforms. They were tanned and blond and obviously out to enjoy the City by the Bay during layover. They sidled up to the bar next to Matt and ordered sparkling wine. One started snapping her fingers to the music while the other gave Matt a smile. She had big gold hoop earrings to frame her oval face.

"What a cool place," she said in an Australian accent. "Are you a local?"

"I am," Matt said. "We're a vanishing breed."

"I bet you know all the good spots for dinner."

"As a matter of fact, I know just the place."

The woman looked at him sideways, crinkling her smile.

* * *

Pam was flipping the channel changer, fighting the urge for a cigarette. Monday night, nothing but shit. *Laverne and Shirley*. *WKRP in Cincinnati*. Ugh.

The doctor had admonished her today for smoking. Well, she was right about that.

Maybe she should read a book. But she just didn't seem to have the patience for anything anymore. Having this damn baby was taking it out of her and then some. And still a month to go.

She was getting hungry too, which is all she was anymore as well. She didn't want to end up a whale when this was all over. Mom had said they'd order Chinese when she got home but she wasn't home yet. Maybe she'd just go ahead and order. Yeah, maybe she would just do that.

In her flannel nightgown, Mom's kimono, and her floppy slippers, Pam pushed herself off the low sofa, into the kitchen where she got the menu for Five Happiness off the fridge, took it into the living room, plopped back down. Everything freakin' took it out of her. She dialed Five Happiness from the princess phone on the glass coffee table. The Chinese guy told her to please hold. Hurry up and wait. On *WKRP*, Les Nessman was directing Herb to stay out of his imaginary office, pointing out the masking tape on the floor outlining where the walls of his office would be. Hilarious. The first five times she'd seen it.

The Chinese guy at Five Happiness came back on the line to take her order and they got stuck in the loop where she had to repeat everything several times, even though you'd think "Kung Pao Chicken" would be recognizable by now.

Her thoughts of Kung Pao were broken by a sound outside.

Footsteps creaking up the back stairs, the exterior ones that led to the deck off the kitchen down to the yard. Mom, *finally*. At least she was home sort of on time for once.

Pam reminded the guy at Five Happiness about the fortune cookies.

"You forgot them last time," she said, annunciating clearly.

He apologized, saying he would include extra, said delivery would take forty-five minutes. *Forty-five minutes?* Another late dinner.

She hung up, thinking about that cigarette. Nope. Lambert the little bastard didn't need it.

Mom was scratching at the kitchen door, fooling with the lock, milling around out there.

What the hell?

Must've forgotten her key. She had been pretty scrambled lately.

Pam struggled off the sofa again, propping her arm on the armrest to get to her feet, cricking her back, shuffled out into the kitchen off the deck.

"I'm coming!" She wished she was. She hadn't been laid in months. Maybe that was another thing doomed to the past too. Like fun. The joys of motherhood.

She stopped in the kitchen when she saw a pair of dark figures outside the kitchen door off the deck.

Not her mother.

Her heart shot into alarm mode.

She stepped back, peered around the kitchen door.

Two lowlifes, one in a ball cap, the other in a watch cap, with a stupid Fu Manchu mustache and a crowbar. The fog swirled in the darkness beyond the deck.

She froze as their eyes connected.

All she could think about was what Mom warned her about: the break-in at the office.

She grabbed the wall phone, held it up. Shook it for them to see.

"I'm calling the cops, assholes!" She began to dial.

The crowbar came crashing through the glass. She screeched and jumped.

"Put that fucking phone down!"

Jesus H. She dodged out of the kitchen into the living room with the wall phone on its long cord, flipping the living room light switch off. Semi-darkness. Shut the door.

"How you gonna dial in there, Einstein?"

Fuck, he was right. She dropped the phone on the floor.

Hall closet.

"You need to learn a lesson!" the voice shouted from the kitchen. "And that lesson is for your mother to mind her own fucking business. Got that, bitch?"

She got it. She padded out of the living room into the hall, quietly opened the closet door. Tiny squeak. Not much.

Behind the beige raincoat on the rack, to the right, clipped to the wall, was the sawed-off shotgun Boom had installed. Ghetto Security, he called it.

She unclipped the gun from the wall. Broke it. She knew guns. Had handled them for Moon Ranch, when she ran acid for them. The good old days.

Two shells in the twin barrels. Two more taped to the side of the stock with masking tape. Good old Boom.

"You hear me, bitch?" the voice shouted from the kitchen.

She walked out into the living room with the gun, shuffling in her slippers, stood with the gun leveled at the door to the kitchen.

The man repeated his command. "I said *do you fucking hear me?*"

"Yes," she said to the door. "I hear you."

And pulled trigger number one.

The blast was earsplitting. The living room door to the kitchen erupted, splinters and shreds of wood flying.

The one punk screamed. The other yelled in a more manly fashion.

She heard them make a quick exit from the kitchen to the deck.

They were okay though, apparently. Pam recalled something about rock salt in the cartridges. Safer, Mom said.

Pam went after them, gun up.

They were outside on the deck now, had pulled the door shut.

"Hey!" Pam yelled, shotgun ready. "What about my lesson?"

One guy spun back, the mustache. He had a pistol in his raised hand, made her jump. He swung it toward her.

She raised the sawed-off shotgun.

Another sonic boom and a kick to match as the remaining glass panes of the kitchen door evaporated into granules. Her ears were ringing.

"Go!" she heard him yell to the other guy. "Go! Go! Go!"

Then she heard them both scampering down the twisted stairs, three flights worth.

She broke the gun, dumped the empty shells on the kitchen floor, tore off the other two shells taped to the sawed-off stock. These shells weren't doctored. The real deal.

She shuffled out onto the deck, loading the shotgun as she went. The gun was warm. The air was cool.

The two were halfway down the stairs.

She was good and mad now, went down after them, lumbering with her pregnant belly in front of her.

They were in the dirt yard when she got to the last flight.

"Hey, shitheads!" she yelled. "Come back. Don't you want to tell me how much I need to listen?"

They got to the fence opening to Kansas Street. Turned right.

She went after them, loping across the dirt yard where the residents parked, in her slippers and nightie, kimono flapping. Shotgun ready.

Got to the gate, puffing. Stuck her head out.

They were getting into some piece-of-shit Camaro, primered black. No plate. Starting it up, the starter motor grinding.

She plodded down the block after it. A few car lengths sway, she raised the gun, aimed at the right rear wheel. Fired.

The rear window shattered and collapsed inward. One guy inside screamed: *Christ, get moving!*

Not easy to aim Boom's little security measure. But this was the real thing. Her heart pounded with adrenaline.

The car flew out into the street and she fired the last shot. Smack dab at the rear right wheel this time. It flapped and shredded apart as the car swerved down the street.

They got to the dog leg in Kansas Street where the car died. They jumped out, ran off into the fog.

Pam gave a good heavy sigh. She was shaking. Turned around, headed back.

In the yard she looked up.

All those stairs.

CHAPTER NINETEEN

"What the hell happened, Pam?" Colleen said.

The apartment was a war zone. The door from the dining room to the kitchen had been blown open. In the kitchen the glass panes to the deck door were shattered.

"Long story," Pam said, smoking a cigarette with a slightly shaky hand. She lay back in the recliner, in her nightie, fluffy slippers, Colleen's kimono. The TV was blaring garbage. Colleen went over and turned it off.

She could only think the worst. She turned around, crossing her arms.

"You had visitors," she said.

Pam nodded as she smoked. "Two punks in a Camaro."

"A black one. Primered?"

Pam nodded again as she flicked ash. "It's stuck on Kansas Street. The two punks took off on foot."

"Okay," Colleen said, willing herself to calm down. "Are you okay?"

"Yep." Pam smoked.

Thank God for that. "Did you call the police?"

"No. But Mr. McMurphy downstairs did. I think he was kind of upset."

"I can imagine," she said. "And you're sure you're not hurt?"

"Just my feelings. The one guy kept calling me bad names. In between telling me to remind you to mind your own business."

Just what she had been worried about. "Where's the shotgun?"

"Where no one will find it."

"And where's that?"

"If you don't know, Mom, then you can't get into trouble. You're on parole."

Not bad. Her daughter's thoughtfulness hit a soft spot. Colleen would worry about the shotgun later.

The doorbell rang. Colleen walked to the front of the flat, looked out the window onto Vermont down below. Two SFPD black-and-whites, lights swirling.

"You go ahead and let them in," Colleen said to Pam. "Tell them you locked yourself in the bathroom while they shot the place up. Let them search the place but don't sign a thing until I get back. Be polite."

"Where are you going?"

"To take a quick peek at that Camaro. Then I'm going to call Gus." Gus her lawyer.

"Got it." Pam pushed herself up off the chair, stood, stuck the cigarette in the corner of her mouth.

Colleen went to the hall closet, grabbed a wooly watch cap, tucked her hair up under it, pulled it down over her head for the disguise that was in it, then out onto the deck, stepping over broken glass, down the outside stairwell. Her daughter had come through but something like this couldn't happen again.

On the deck below, Mr. McMurphy appeared in his plaid bathrobe. His hair was askew and his glasses were crooked.

"Really sorry about the disturbance, Mr. McMurphy," Colleen said, flying down the stairs past him. "It won't happen again."

"I had to call the police, Ms. Hayes. It sounded like D-Day up there."

"Yes, I do apologize," Colleen shouted, circling down the wooden stairs.

"Is Pam okay?" he shouted down.

"Yes. And thank you for asking. Sorry again for the commotion."

She hustled down to the street, saw the same Camaro that had sped off that morning from her office, broken down at the end of Kansas Street, doors open, dome light on. A rear tire was flat, reduced to shreds. The rear window was shattered. Shotgun Pam. Colleen jogged for the car.

Once there, puffing air, Colleen rummaged around in the glove compartment. Amidst a pack of rolling papers, a condom in a foil wrapper, some fast-food condiment packs, unpaid parking tickets, she looked for the car registration. No such luck. But she did find a bill for an oil change for the car, in the name of Rodney Walsh, along with an address. *Come to mama.* She pocketed it, headed back.

"Hey!" someone shouted from a window. "What are you doing in that car?"

"*No comprendo,*" Colleen grunted in a low register, head down. She hurried back for her apartment building.

Back upstairs, SFPD were in search mode. Officers and a younger detective with slicked-back blond hair and a shiny face.

"Someone needs to tell us what happened, ma'am."

"More than happy to," Colleen said, grabbing the wall phone. "Just as soon as I talk to my lawyer."

She caught Gus Pedersen at home, some hi-tech electronic music floating in the background. Gus instructed Colleen and Pam not to own up to any shooting or possession of a firearm. Stick to the story of Pam hiding in the bathroom.

Pam gave her statement and waited for Gus, who lived in Stinson Beach and would be over as soon as he could. This time of night, it wouldn't be a problem.

Gus Pedersen arrived in less than an hour, while the police were still there. He was a big guy, surfer-turned-lawyer or vice versa, with a mane of long brown hair in a ponytail, aviator sunglasses, which he probably wore in the shower, and a fringed suede jacket. He loomed over the young detective.

"How can I help you, Detective?" he said in a deep voice.

"There are some holes in our information," the detective said.

Colleen said it might be related to a case she was working on but wasn't sure. "I do make an enemy here and there in my line of work."

"Odd thing," the detective said. "We found their car on Kansas Street. The rear window and one of the tires appears to have been shot out. There was a report of gunshots on Kansas about the time two men were seen running from the vehicle. Yet you maintain *they* fired the shots?"

"Someone did," Pam said tearfully, wiping her eyes with a tissue on the recliner. "I was locked in the bathroom." In her other hand she had a can of Budweiser. Colleen went over, squatted, put her arm around her daughter while she surreptitiously took the beer, set it on the coffee table.

"You poor thing," she said to Pam.

"Thanks, Mom," Pam sniffed, wiping her eyes.

"There's been more gang activity in the neighborhood," Colleen said. The Potrero projects were just on the other side of the freeway. "The police should really do something about it."

"What I suggest," Gus said to the detective, "is that SFPD focus on finding the two assailants who so brazenly attacked my client's daughter, a woman who is not only eight months pregnant, but has just suffered a harrowing experience."

The detective looked at Pam suspiciously.

Then he eyed Colleen. "One neighbor reported a woman rummaging through the vehicle," he said.

"Is that right?" Colleen said with feigned surprise, standing up. "Well, I suppose it's possible. I wonder who it was."

"But you wouldn't know anything about that?"

She shook her head. "I wish I did."

"My client and her daughter won't feel safe until those madmen are brought to justice, Detective," Gus Pedersen said in a haughty tone. "I suggest you get on that sooner rather than later and let my client and her daughter recover from this traumatic event."

"We're running the VIN now," the detective said, regarding Colleen with a look.

*   *   *

It was the wee hours before the police left. Gus sipped jasmine tea at the glass coffee table still scattered with half-finished containers of Chinese food. Pam had gone to bed.

Colleen broke open her fortune cookie, pulled the fortune.

"*You will soon go on a long journey,*" she read out loud to Gus. "Hopefully one that doesn't involve a prison cell."

"You're cool for now," Gus said, sipping tea. "Those two lowlifes can take the heat for the shooting." He set his tea down. "So what *were* you doing in their car?"

She held up the oil change bill. "A little research."

Gus frowned. "Why are they after you?"

She told him about Ingrid Richter.

He grimaced. "Not a great idea to chase these guys down yourself."

"I'm still waiting for SFPD to follow up on my office break-in. I'm not convinced they have the same motivation as I do."

"A lawyer doesn't like to hear things like that."

"They threatened me, Gus. They threatened *Pam*."

"Like I say, the less I know the better. But please, heed my advice. Avoid this like the plague."

"I always appreciate your advice."

"Good. Try following it. Is there somewhere safe you and Pam can stay? Or Pam, at least? You're welcome to my sofa. Stinson Beach is out the front door."

"Thanks, but I think I've got Pam covered."

"Good. Whatever else you've got in mind, stow it."

"And thanks for taping up my kitchen door window." Two more doors to repair.

"I'll let myself out." Gus sighed, stood up. "Talk to you tomorrow. Please take care of yourself. And Pam. And your grand-whatever. "

She got up, showed Gus out, went to Pamela's room, spent a moment gazing at the blue crib, even though they weren't sure if Lambert was a he or she yet. Pam said it felt like a he so they were going with that. The light was still on. As a child Pam couldn't fall asleep with the light off. And for good reason, Colleen thought sorrowfully, knowing what Pam had endured at the hands of her father. Pam lay flat on her back now, mouth open, snoring, the blanket twisted around her waist, her baby belly poking up. Colleen remembered when she was pregnant, too, at sixteen, with Pam. Same thing, exhausted all the time.

She was just relieved that Pam and Lambert had made it this far. But she had to get them out of here for the time being. Until whatever this was, was over.

She pulled the blanket up to Pam's shoulders, tucked her in. Kissed two of her own fingertips, touched Pam's forehead gently with them. She had lost Pam before. She didn't want to lose her again. The feeling was even stronger now with her unborn grandchild. She didn't think she ever wanted something so much, for the two of them to be safe and sound. As if in response, Pam mumbled something in her sleep. Colleen turned off the bedside lamp. The teddy bear night-light glowed from the electrical socket.

On the way out, she noticed the big pile of loot in Lambert's crib, gifts with bows, toys, a box of disposable diapers, things that had been piling up for the big day. The Paddington Bear she had bought was tipped over on its side. She went over to straighten it. Under the packages, under a blanket with ducks on it, was something about two feet long, solid. She moved the boxes, pulled the cover back.

The sawed-off shotgun.

As good a place as any.

She drew the cover back over the gun and rearranged the gifts.

CHAPTER TWENTY

1979

"You ladies stay out of trouble," Colleen said, sitting at the wheel of her Torino in the beige gravel of Alex's expansive horseshoe driveway. She was dropping Pam off at her friend's house—mansion—in Half Moon Bay, down the coast from San Francisco. The morning wind had picked up, coming in from the ocean.

"We'll try," Alex said, flicking ash from a cigarette on the elegant front steps of her mansion. She wore an intense red leisure suit, floppy hat to match, and pink tinted sunglasses. She was as striking as always with her fair skin and curled blond hair, but Colleen couldn't get a good look at her eyes. Alex had been drinking and drugging to excess since her father passed away but had been making efforts of late.

Pam stood next to her on the stairs, wearing her orange hippie dress from Ecuador, which had faded with washings but was one of the few things that fit anymore.

Harold, the butler, stood by, holding Pam's beat-up suitcase.

"You're the one I'm worried about, Mom," Pam said, brushing a strand of red hair out of her face.

"I'm just fine," Colleen said. "But you and Lambert are better off down here until things get straightened out."

"'Straightened out.' There's a euphemism if I ever heard one."

Colleen blew a kiss. "Take care, you two." She gave Alex a wink. "Thanks again."

"What are godmothers for?" she said with a flick of her cigarette.

Colleen spun the car around in the gravel circle, headed down the long private road toward Highway 1. In the rearview mirror the myriad chimneys of Alex's home stuck up over the roiling morning sky. She saw Pam watching from the steps. At the last moment, Pam gave a little wave. Colleen waved back. What it took to bring mother and daughter together.

She cut over to 101 back into the city. According to the oil change receipt she'd found in the abandoned Camaro, which SFPD had since towed away, Rodney Walsh lived off Paul Avenue near Candlestick Park. A rough part of town Colleen recalled, having guarded and surreptitiously lived in an abandoned warehouse not far away.

Pre-lunchtime traffic into San Francisco was starting to thicken. The temperature dropped its customary 10 degrees as she entered the city, and she had to turn on the heater and the windshield wipers to smear away the late-morning fog that was accumulating as she pulled off onto the Third Street exit. On the radio Peaches and Herb were shaking their groove thing.

She found Rodney Walsh's address on a ratty side street. The neighborhood was strictly blue collar, beat-up little houses with tiny front yards paved over to park extra cars, overhead wires crisscrossing everywhere, everything in a state of deferred maintenance. The house where Rodney Walsh apparently lived had handbills hanging from the front doorknob upstairs and a side entrance door next to the garage door downstairs. An in-law apartment. As she drove by, Colleen saw no lights on in the house, heard no sounds. She circled the block and parked down the street in front of a semitruck cab layered in dirt that looked like it wasn't running. She got out, moseyed up to the house, looking around nonchalantly.

Up the dilapidated wooden stairs to the main house she saw a slew of yellowing freebie newspapers lying on the welcome mat. She rang the doorbell, sensing no one was home, and they weren't.

Back downstairs she ambled around to the side door under the stairs. The glass pane had an NRA sticker on the mottled glass. She recalled the Confederate flag on the Camaro's bumper. Quite likely Rodney's pad. The guy lived in the garage. She wondered which one he was, the guy with the ball cap or watch cap. He might even be someone else, who'd loaned out the car.

She knocked, got no answer.

Back to the Torino she got her camera out, eased the seat back, settled in, wishing she had a cigarette to kill the time. She flipped on KGO *Newstalk*. Callers were pontificating about the upcoming trial of ex-cop Dan White, who had shot and killed the mayor and a gay city supervisor, Harvey Milk, last November. Colleen knew all about that case. What bothered her was how many callers were showing sympathy for a cold-blooded killer, insane or not. But in San Francisco, it took all sorts.

In order to stay awake, she switched to KFRC, where the top forty hits kept on coming, when a '57 Chevy with a hood scoop big enough to catch birds came thundering down the street and swerved up into the driveway. The back of the car was perched up on fat mag wheels like a floozie in high heels. Lemon yellow with a black racing stripe. Somebody had spent a lot of money to make the car look like a giant Hot Wheels. Three guys and a girl climbed out, two men clutching 12-packs and bags of booze and chips, the other man dangling a half-gallon of liquor from his hand. Party time. But one was the watch cap guy with the mustache who had broken into her office and fired at Colleen, and later at Pam. He wore pretty much what he had the day before: black jeans, engineer boots, and a beat-up jacket. His buddy was not present, but the other two guys could have filled his spot in terms of dress and style. One guy was leaning toward fat in a baggy 49ers sweatshirt while the other had wild red hair that blew in the fog-wind. The girl wore her denim cutoffs tight on chunky white thighs that probably drove many boys to distraction, along with a black leather jacket and a sneer. She had a big nose and long jet-black hair out of a bottle that matched her eye shadow, and a pair of boobs that would keep men's eyes off her nose. She carried a tall can of Coors, which she drained and tossed over the car into the street. It clattered amid laughter as the four lumbered into the side entrance of the in-law apartment.

The music started blasting, some unintelligible metal with growling lyrics.

They would be ensconced for a while. Colleen fired up the Torino, drove to the nearest phone booth, found a dangling cord where the phone had been ripped out, got back in the car, drove to the next nearest phone, outside a liquor store with a metal grate over the door and windows. She wiped off the slimy receiver with a tissue from a pack she kept in her coat and called Boom.

"You up for harassing some Nazi punks tonight?" she asked.

"How can I turn down an invitation like that, Chief? When and where?"

She told him where. "*When* is pretty much anytime you can get here. Do you have a car?"

"Not tonight, Chief. I got my student Muni Fast Pass, though."

"Take a cab over and I'll pay your way. Pick up something to drink and a pizza and I'll cover that too. We might be here for a while. And don't you dare get pineapple."

"I'm hip."

*   *   *

The sky was dark gray by the time they were ready to make their move.

"I don't think anyone's leaving anytime soon, Chief," Boom said, draining a can of Pepsi. He was sitting in the passenger seat of the Torino, wearing his customary camouflage jacket and thick-framed black glasses.

Motorhead were booming from the garage down the street. "Damage Case."

"Agreed," Colleen said. "But I need to know who's behind the attacks."

"I still think you want to let SFPD take care of it," Boom said, crushing the can.

"When I'm done," she said. The wheels of justice moved too slowly for her liking. And sometimes they didn't move at all.

"Did you bring a piece, Chief?"

"Not today," she said. "Can't risk it."

Boom nodded, reached into the inside pocket of his jacket, came out with a snub nose, put it back, pulled his jacket over it.

"You got a permit for that?" she asked.

"Of course."

"I'm jealous." She nodded at Rodney's garage. "I'll go to the side door. You help me get Rodney into the car. We'll take him somewhere for a quiet chat."

"Ten-four." Boom dumped the crushed empty can into a paper sack by his feet. "I can't take much more Motorhead anyway."

She started up the Torino, the V8 snarling, put the car into gear, pulled out, motored down the street to stop in front of Rodney Walsh's driveway. The music was pounding from the garage. She could hear them hooting and hollering in there.

She donned her black baseball cap, slipped on her shades, got out, the engine running, left her door open. "Hand me that pizza box, will you, please, Boom?"

He reached back to the back seat, got the box full of crusts, handed it to her.

She took the box, held it up in her left hand.

"Ready when you are, Chief," Boom said.

She went around the front of the Torino. She heard Boom open his door partially as she headed up the driveway in between the stairs and the bumble bee hot rod.

She stood at the side door with the pizza box up like a tray.

At the side door, she turned, saw Boom watching her from the passenger seat, his door open a few inches. Ready to move fast.

She gave him a little nod, which he returned.

She knocked on the door.

The music thundered from inside. Voices braying with laughter.

No answer.

She knocked, harder.

The laughter stopped.

A shadow came round the rain glass door, the outline of the girl. Colleen was hoping for Rodney.

The girl opened the door, gave Colleen a confused look. The smell of grass came wafting out. With the door open, the music thundered.

"Pizza delivery," Colleen said.

The girl shouted into the garage. "Who ordered the pizza?"

No one admitted to it.

"Wrong address," the girl said.

"Rodney Walsh?" Colleen said.

"Yeah."

"Large pepperoni."

The girl consulted with the group in the garage again. Colleen gathered they were sitting around.

The girl shook her head. "Nope." She moved to shut the door.

Colleen blocked it with her foot.

"What?" the girl said, her mascaraed eyes flashing anger.

"Someone owes me five seventy-five," Colleen said. "Plus tip. A dollar is customary."

"Fuck you."

"No, I don't think so," Colleen said, obstructing the door. "Now you go get Rodney and tell him I want my five seventy-five plus tip."

"And you go straight to hell, bitch."

The car door creaked open all the way and Boom climbed out, his big frame squeezing up between the Chevy and the stucco wall.

"Fucking incredible," the girl said, leaning into the garage. "Hey, Rodney, this skank says you ordered a pizza and she won't go away."

A moment later another shadow darkened the side door to the garage. The girl moved out of the way and Rodney appeared, still in his watch cap. His mustache was wet with beer and the rest of his fleshy face needed a shave. He reeked of weed.

He looked at Colleen with red eyes. He was half in the bag, didn't seem to recognize her at first in her hat and shades. Boom was lurking to Colleen's left in the driveway, out of sight.

"I didn't order any pizza," Rodney said. "Leave it if you want, but I'm not paying for it."

"Oh?" she said. "You want this pizza?"

He blinked at her, trying to focus. "Wait, don't I know you—"

She smacked the pizza box up in his face, the flap coming loose, crusts tumbling onto the cement driveway.

"Boom!" she yelled.

Boom charged in, grabbed Rodney by the lapels.

"Hey, buddy," he said. "How was the pizza?"

"What the fuck?"

Colleen ducked around the front of the Chevy, giving Boom room to pull Rodney out, kicking and flailing.

Rodney managed to connect a boot to Boom's shin.

"Get off me, you damn spook!"

Boom grunted, heaved Rodney up, slammed him up against the stucco wall.

"One more word out of you," he said, "I break your jaw."

Rodney gasped as Boom dragged him down to the car.

Colleen pulled the side door shut on the garage, then dashed back to the Torino where she slid the passenger seat forward so Boom could shove Rodney into the back of the car, Rodney shouting. Boom climbed into the back seat with him, gave Rodney a slap across the face.

Colleen slammed the passenger door, rushed around to the driver's side, got in, pulled the door shut just as the side door to the garage apartment opened up with a bang and a flash of excited voices.

She threw the Torino into gear as the remaining guests at Rodney's get-together came out the side door of the garage.

Colleen pulled out with a screech. In the rearview mirror around Boom and Rodney's heads, she saw the trio out in the street, watching them leave for a moment before they ran to their car.

Colleen shifted up, stepped on the gas.

CHAPTER TWENTY-ONE

Thirty stories of steel skeleton loomed in the night sky as the Torino bounced along an unpaved access road behind the office building under construction on Mission Street. Colleen dodged parked trucks and construction equipment. Rodney Walsh and Boom sat in the back. Pallets of building materials obstructed much of her path as she pulled up to the shell of a loading dock. She stopped, shut off the engine. Along the Embarcadero the pounding of a pile driver became obvious as the apparatus drove long shafts of concrete deep into the ground, working at night so as not to disturb daytime office workers. More and more buildings were going up south of Market, the new San Francisco skyline.

"Where the fuck are we?" Rodney Walsh said, an edge to his voice. A trickle of blood ran from the corner of his mouth where Boom had hit him. "You guys can cut this shit out any time you like." His anxious breathing filled the car, sour with booze and weed. Boom was keeping a close eye on him.

Colleen made eye contact with Rodney in the rearview mirror.

"You and your buddy broke into my office yesterday," she said, "pulled a gun on me. If that wasn't enough, then you broke into my house last night, threatened my daughter."

Rodney said nothing. Boom examined his nails.

"What were you looking for?" Colleen asked Rodney.

No reply.

"Let me help you try to remember," Colleen said. "You were after a file—on Ingrid Richter. Why?"

Rodney didn't make eye contact.

"Ingrid Richter sent you," Colleen said.

No answer.

Colleen sighed. "Okay, looks like we're doing this the hard way." She opened the car door, got out, went around to the rear, opened the trunk, grabbed her five-cell flashlight. She slammed the trunk, went around to the passenger side, opened that door, pulled the bucket seat forward. "Let's go."

Boom climbed out, dragging Rodney with him.

Rodney tried to pull away. Boom hauled him around, held him up by the lapels. "The lady asked you a question, man."

"I don't know," he said.

"You don't know," Colleen said. "That's not the answer I want."

"I think what he means is he doesn't want to tell you," Boom said.

"You're right," Colleen said. She said to Rodney, "I get it that you're scared to tell me who wanted you to get hold of that file and tell me to back off my investigation. But what you don't understand is that you're going to tell me—because you attacked me and then you attacked my daughter. So you don't have a lot of goodwill built up right now."

Rodney shook his head. "You do *not* know who you're dealing with. Just let me go and we'll call it a wash."

"Not an option," Colleen said.

"So then call the cops," Rodney said. "Turn me the fuck in."

Colleen laughed through her nose. "Yeah, you'd like that. Then whoever sent you can bail you out."

"I got nothin' to say."

"Okay," Colleen said. "Let's check out the view." She walked to the back of the building, no windows or doors yet, took the steps up to the loading dock, Boom pushing Rodney along behind her.

"Nice place, Chief," Boom said, dragging Rodney.

"My company did a security assessment here," Colleen said. "Guess what? Not too secure."

Inside the bowels of the darkened building, she clicked on the flashlight, stepped over equipment and materials, lighting their way. Streetlights on Mission cast scant light through the frame of the building. Pretty much just the floors were in place.

"Where are you guys taking me?" Rodney said, his voice a little shaky.

In the center of the building where a bank of unfinished elevators stood, Colleen got into the only functioning one, lined with press-board and heavy padded moving quilts to protect the interior. She held the gate for Boom and Rodney to enter.

Rodney broke away. Boom jogged after him, grabbed him by the jacket, yanked him back, tearing the jacket. He caught Rodney, threw him into the elevator, slamming him into the quilt on particleboard next to Colleen.

"I can't tell you shit!" he panted.

"Of course you can, Rodney," Colleen said.

Boom entered the elevator.

"What floor, Chief?"

"Top."

Boom was about to press *30*, then turned to Colleen, smiled. "You know, my forebearers used to do this kind of job for a living—operator—and here I am, doing the very same thing for you now."

"Good point," Colleen said. "Allow me." Reaching over, she hit button number 30 herself. Next to her, Rodney was breathing in gusts, anxious eyes darting back and forth between her and Boom.

"If you don't let me go," he said, "you are going to be sorry."

"You already said that," Colleen said. "But I won't be as sorry as you, though. Hmm?"

His eyes flitted away.

The elevator pinged upwards. *Seven-eight-nine.*

"Aryan Alliance," he said.

San Francisco's up-and-coming fascist organization, under investigation by Matt Dwight's team.

"See?" Colleen said. "That wasn't so hard."

Thirteen-fourteen-fifteen.

"So let me go already," Rodney said.

Colleen laughed. "Not even close, Rodney," she said. "I need the person who gave you the order."

Nineteen-twenty-twenty-one.

"Was it Lange?" she said. "Or one of his underlings?" Dr. Lange ran Aryan Alliance, There could be a connection to Ingrid and Lange, tracking down a Nazi hunter like Erich Hahn.

Rodney's eyes flickered.

"What?" Colleen said. "You didn't think I knew about Lange?"

"If you do, then you should know you don't want to mess with him," Rodney said.

"It's not like I have a choice anymore," Colleen said. "You—or he—or whoever—set this thing in motion when you assaulted my daughter."

The elevator dinged *30*. The door opened.

She waved Boom and Rodney out. "Gentlemen? Shall we?"

Boom pushed Rodney out. Colleen followed, the flashlight lighting the way. Wind and fog gusted across an empty shell of floor, devoid of walls and windows. The structure moved back and forth in the wind. Pleasant it was not.

Colleen pointed to the far corner of the open floor facing the Bay Bridge. Ladders and electrical equipment were positioned near the ceiling.

"Come on!" Rodney shrieked. "You can't do this!"

"Do *what*, Rodney?" Colleen said. "Let you enjoy a breathtaking view of our fine city? And I do mean breathtaking."

She walked over to the edge of the floor, feeling ticklish as she stood over thirty stories of open dark space to the ground below. Around them streetlights lined construction sites and parking lots. In the distance the Bay Bridge cut a diagonal to the East Bay.

Boom pushed Rodney closer to the edge. Rodney was stooping, hunching over in fear.

"Hold him," Colleen said to Boom. "We don't want him to slip and fall. It's a long way down."

"Right," Boom said, grabbing Rodney's torn collar. "It might look like a suicide, some Nazi punk loser, high on shit, falls out of a building."

"Wonder if it would even make the front page."

Rodney hyperventilated. Boom held him upright, up to the edge. Colleen was amazed at Boom's nerves. But he had survived two tours of Nam. Everything that came afterwards was gravy, he once told her. He said he was actually lucky in that respect. The wind blew a flurry.

"Okay!" Rodney gulped. "It was Lange's assistant. She wanted that file. I don't know why. I don't even know who this Richter is. I just did what I was told. When you chased us out of the office, she told us to make sure you were scared off. So we came to your place."

"What assistant?" Colleen asked.

"What does it matter?"

"It matters."

"Doris Pender."

Dr. Lange's second in command. Colleen had met her once. "Have you spoken to anyone since last night, Rodney? After you and your pal broke into my apartment?"

Rodney, held up by Boom's big fist, shook his head nervously. "I'm waiting for her to make contact. She said if anything happened, like the police getting involved, to let things cool off a day or two."

"Makes sense," Colleen said. She thought for a moment. "Okay, this is what we do: you're going to call Doris Pender, tell her you got the file despite the fracas. Arrange to meet her."

"Sure," Rodney panted. "Just get me away from this fucking ledge already."

Boom tilted Rodney out for one last thirty-story look down at the darkness below. One or two cars moved on lit streets around the dark site like a child's playset. Rodney's collar ripped another inch. "No funny stuff, little buddy," Boom said. "We can always come back here."

"No problem," Rodney wheezed, looking away from the precipice.

*   *   *

Back in Rodney's garage, his party pals had flown the coop. Rodney hung up the phone, sitting on a ratty sofa that didn't quite cover the faded oil spill on the concrete floor. He pulled off his watch cap, wiped his gleaming brow. He drew a shaky breath, looked up at Colleen and Boom standing, watching him, his arms crossed over his big chest. Colleen had her hands in the back pockets of her jeans, leaning to one side.

"Doris will meet me at eleven o'clock," Rodney said. "The Portals."

The Portals Tavern. A neighborhood dive that had been around since Eve tempted Adam with a shiny apple. Now Dr. Lange's assistant was being tempted with Colleen's file on Ingrid Richter.

"And you're positive Doris Pender will be there?" Colleen asked.

Rodney gave a quivering nod.

Colleen pressed the button on her watch. Red digits told her there were a couple hours before the meet.

"I need to go into the office," she said to Boom. "You okay with him until I get back?"

Boom said yes, showed Colleen the heel of a grip to the 38 special in his jacket pocket.

"I'll be back," she said.

"Semper Fi," Boom said.

*   *   *

Two hours later, the fog drifted up along West Portal through one of the city's quieter residential neighborhoods.

Colleen, Rodney, and Boom waited in the Torino in a small city parking lot across from the pebble-fronted Portals Tavern, a neighborhood pub nestled between the Tip Top vacuum repair store and an alterations shop. The bar's glass-brick window glowed with subdued activity.

It was five minutes to eleven.

There was no sign of anyone else waiting. Parked cars were few. A Tuesday night in sleepy West Portal.

"Okay," Colleen said, gathering up her bag of tricks. "Boom, you go first. Rodney and I will follow. She pulled the Bersa, her not-very-legal 22 caliber, from the pocket of her leather car coat, set it on her knee. "And you know better than to get any creative ideas, right, Rodney?" She looked at him in the rearview mirror.

Rodney bit his lip, acknowledged.

"Give this to Doris." She handed Rodney a manila envelope with an empty file folder in it.

Boom got out, hitched up his pants.

Rodney was still biting his lip.

"If they find out I set this up," he said, "I'm dead meat."

"You might have thought of that before you attacked my daughter," Colleen said. She watched Boom amble across West Portal, go into the bar.

Rodney ran his fingers though his uncombed mousy hair. He had ditched his watch cap. His pale face was stubbled in scratchy five-o'clock shadow. "Christ."

"If it makes you feel any better," Colleen said, "you'll have a witness—me. That will make Aryan Alliance think twice before they consider any serious retribution."

He looked at her, uncertain.

"Let's go." She pocketed the gun and the two of them got out of the car, walked across the empty street. They headed in. Boom was sitting at the bar, turning a glass of draft beer casually on a coaster, pretending to watch a soundless TV. The jukebox was playing the Eagles. *Heartache Tonight.*

The bar was midweek quiet, two small groups of people drinking besides Boom.

Rodney set the manila envelope on the bar, sat on a stool, ordered a draft, jiggled his leg nervously.

No sign of Doris Pender yet, a tall lanky woman with a pixie haircut last time Colleen had seen her. Colleen nodded at Boom, headed back out, bag over her shoulder, back across the street. Her Canon SLR was loaded up with high-speed film, within easy reach. She played at window-shopping in the toy store next to the parking lot, watching the bar in the reflection of the glass. Right at eleven o'clock, a boxy black Mercedes sedan pulled up a few slots down from the Portals.

Doris Pender got out. She was tall, bony, wearing a black pantsuit and high heels. Her short hair was jet black. She wore dark-framed glasses.

From the passenger side a big guy got out, with a bodybuilder torso in a tight suit, crew cut, wraparound sunglasses. Bodyguard was written all over him.

In the doorway of the toy store, Colleen snapped a couple of surreptitious photos of the car and the two going into the bar. Then she headed across the street in a light jog.

She pushed open the door. On the jukebox now Robert Palmer had a *bad case of lovin' you.*

Doris was standing at the bar next to Rodney, still sitting on a stool. The bodyguard was standing back, looking bored but watching everything. Boom was down the bar, hunched over his untouched beer, checking things out from the corner of his eye.

Colleen stood by the door, camera tucked behind her.

"Dr. Lange appreciates all you've done," she heard Doris say to Rodney, taking the envelope. "If this becomes an issue, he wants you to know we're going to take care of things." Meaning if Rodney was busted for breaking into Colleen's office or flat, she assumed.

Colleen snapped a picture of the interaction and of Doris taking the manila envelope.

"Hey!" the bodyguard said, seeing Colleen take photos. "What do you think you're doing?"

"Just a piece on neighborhood bars for the *Chron*." Colleen flashed a polite smile, turned, pushed out of the bar. She waited in the street by the door of the Mercedes.

The door flew open and the bodyguard appeared. Next was Doris, looking pissed.

"Better explain yourself," Doris said. Colleen remembered her sharp nasal voice.

"I need to know why you wanted that file on Ingrid Richter," Colleen said.

Doris' eyes narrowed. She realized then who she was dealing with.

"Yep," Colleen said. "It's me."

"Best thing," Doris said, "is for you to run along. You were paid by your client. You're done."

Colleen shook her head. "Your clowns not only screwed up my modest collection of used office furniture and shot the place up, they destroyed two doors when they tried to break into my house, and threatened my daughter. So forgive me if I'm not quite 'done' yet."

The door to the Portals opened again and Boom appeared on the street. He stood with his arms by his side. Doris and the bodyguard turned for a moment, eyed him.

"Good evening, everyone," he said. "Little chilly tonight." He rubbed his hands together and let them hang by his side, twitching, just waiting for something to happen.

Doris blinked as she put it together, looked at Colleen.

"I believe this is what's commonly called a standoff," Colleen said to Doris. "I didn't want to say 'Mexican standoff' because that's a racially charged phrase."

Doris gave a single nod. "Sorry if the guys got a little out of hand. We're prepared to reimburse you for any damage to your office if no charges are filed."

"And my home."

"And your home."

"Great," Colleen said. "But first I need to know Ingrid Richter's connection to Aryan Alliance."

Doris squinted, then grinned. "Use your brain, chica."

"She's an ex-Nazi."

"You may as well get used to it. We're everywhere. Millions of us. More than you'll ever be able to deal with. So why not do the smart thing and pick a side? You're white. Live up to your race, for God's sake."

"Do you really believe that shit?"

"Do I believe in destiny? The question is: Why don't you? You have a duty to your people. But instead, you're hanging with the trash."

"Don't let Boom hear you say that," Colleen said, nodding at Boom. "He's a sensitive guy."

"Maybe he'd be happier with his own."

Boom snorted. "I'm plenty happy right here with you."

"Ingrid Richter used me to find Erich Hahn," Colleen said. "And then she sent some hit woman. And when things went south, you were brought in to clean up."

Doris shrugged.

"You wanted my file on her," Colleen said, indicating the manila envelope. "That's empty by the way."

Doris's face dropped. She ripped the envelope open, yanked out the manila folder. Swore when she saw it was empty. Tossed everything on the ground.

"Ingrid took off, right after a murder on Muni," Colleen said. "Sunday. And now you're working with her or for her, whatever. How am I doing?"

"I don't have a clue what you're talking about," Doris said.

"That's fine," Colleen said. "SFPD will." She held up her camera. "These pics will help. I even got your license plate. So let's give them a call. There's a payphone in the bar."

Doris stared. "What do you want Ingrid Richter for?"

"That's between her and me."

Doris shook her head. "Not good enough."

"Fine. You know what? I think I'm just gonna let SFPD figure all of this out after all." She turned to go into the bar. "You can let them go, Boom. I've got all I need."

"Wait," Doris said.

Colleen stopped, turned. Raised her eyebrows in question.

"Ingrid for Erich," Doris said.

"Now that's interesting," Colleen said. "You're looking for Erich Hahn. But not Ingrid Richter. Why?"

"You don't need to know," Doris said. "But we couldn't care less about Ingrid Richter anymore. She's small potatoes."

"So much loyalty."

Doris shook her head. "You're on some shaky ground, and it's going to get you killed if you keep it up. None of this is worth it. We're talking about people way beyond my control. I'm pretty much just the office manager."

"Oh, don't be so modest, Doris. You do a lot of Lange's dirty work. You're a bona fide Nazi—well, more the carbon copy type—a *wannabe*."

Boom and the bodyguard were watching each other closely, ready for something to start. Boom had his hand ready to go for his gun.

"Okay." Doris put her hands on her hips. She nodded at Colleen's camera. "Ingrid for that roll of film."

Colleen thought about it. "Deal. You first."

"Hotel Campania."

"Great. And where is that?"

"Rome." Doris smiled. "But you better move fast. I can't say how long she'll be there."

Owens had told Colleen that Ingrid Richter had taken a flight to Rome. So Doris' statement seemed legitimate.

"What is Ingrid doing in Rome?"

Doris shook her head again. "Good question. As I say, we don't care about her anymore. We were brought in to mop up after her after the Erich thing blew up. And then she took off. Flight 800, two nights ago. You wanted to know where Ingrid was. Now you do. We're done here." She reached out a long-nailed hand. "My film?"

Colleen wound the camera, opened it, pulled the 35 mm roll of film, tossed it at Doris.

Doris caught the roll, pulled the film out of the roll with a thumb and forefinger, letting it expose under the streetlight. She dropped a snarl of dead film on the asphalt.

"Don't contact us again," Doris said. "Or you *will* be sorry."

"That's funny," Colleen said. "I was just about to tell you the very same thing—especially if you come near my daughter again."

"We have no reason to," Doris said. "Let's keep it that way."

"One other thing," Colleen said. "That loser Rodney. I better not find he's been punished for setting this meeting up. I didn't give him a choice."

Doris got her car keys out, then stopped, looked at Colleen. "You really need to decide whose side you're on. There's a race war going on and you're backing the mongrels." She turned to the guy in the tight gray suit. "Let's go," she said.

CHAPTER TWENTY-TWO

Just after midnight, Colleen dropped Boom off in front of the twin ten-story cement monoliths he and his grandma lived in along with thousands of other SF residents. The so-called Pink Palace looked as George Orwell might have imagined public housing in one of his darker moments: institutional, run-down, and hostile. The color, possibly an attempt to change the tone, ended up making a mockery of a utilitarian disaster. The usual cast of characters mulled around outside, sitting on car hoods, drinking, listening to music. Cigarettes glowed in the darkness.

"Thanks for your help tonight," Colleen said, stepping on the parking brake. "I couldn't have dealt with Doris Pender without you."

"Absolutely, Chief. What's next on your agenda?"

She rested her hands on the steering wheel. They vibrated with the big engine. "Not sure."

"Sounds to me like you might be thinking of tracking down this Ingrid Richter."

"She's the key to all of this. But Italy is a long way to go on a hunch."

"I'm hip," Boom said. "But if you plan to meet up with those fanatics again—call me. I worry a little bit, the kind of company you're keeping these days."

"It's good for business," she said, turning to give him a smile. "Study hard."

"Always."

"Love to Gram."

"Semper Fi," Boom said, bumping fists. He opened the car door, climbed out, which lifted the car a fraction of an inch. Colleen watched him march across the grounds, a monolith himself. People got out of his way.

Pam was safe at Alex's. Colleen was a free agent. And her mind was full of thoughts that revolved around Aryan Alliance, ex-Nazis, and the like.

Ingrid Richter's hotel was in Rome and Colleen had to move fast if she wanted to catch her. She owed Matt a visit. She owed herself a visit to Matt. They'd missed their date last night.

And Matt might have some info for her. On Ingrid Richter. Or Erich Hahn.

Matt lived less than half a mile away in Nob Hill, although it was another world compared to the Fillmore.

On the way she stopped at Sukkers Likkers and picked up a bottle of champagne. Not the budget-busting stuff that her friend Alex bought, but it didn't have a plastic cork either. She found parking near Matt's, which meant tonight was meant to be, and was soon ringing his buzzer. She had a key. Which she'd never used. But she wasn't ready for that step.

Matt hit the intercom quickly, another good sign. Still up.

"Candygram," she said.

"Just what I ordered," Matt said, buzzing her in.

She walked up the four flights. It felt good to unwind her legs after dealing with Rodney Walsh and Doris Pender.

Matt was waiting at his apartment door in a silk paisley bathrobe. His hair was wet. His eyes twinkled and she suspected hers were as well. He stood back, showed her in, and she gave him a peck on the cheek. Lights were low and the music on the stereo was smooth. Weather Report—one of Matt's latest acquisitions.

She held up the bottle in a bag and shot him an evil grin. "Hope you weren't planning on an early night."

"Just got home from work," Matt said, taking the bottle, going into the small kitchen, and coming out with a couple of glass flutes. "I've been calling you all night. What the hell have you been up to, Colleen? Why didn't you call?"

Matt was obviously referring to the break-in at Colleen's last night, which he no doubt had heard about.

"I've been busy, moving Pam down to Alex's and all." She filled in the gaps of the last twenty-four hours while Matt poured bubbly into glasses and lowered the lights before settling into a leather recliner across from the couch where she was ensconced. She rested back against an overstuffed cushion.

By the time she got to Doris Pender, Matt had lost his sympathetic, attentive look. He eyed her sharply.

"Did you really just say that you met with Doris Pender tonight?"

She took a slug of champagne. She worried about stepping on Matt's toes with work.

"I had my reasons," she said. "None of them had to do with your case."

Matt set his glass down on the coffee table. "After you knew my team has been tracking Lange and his crew for almost a year? Doris Pender is his number two. We're building a case against all of them. I thought you would have respected that."

Colleen set her glass down as well. "I'm aware, Matt. I knew about Lange and his inner circle before you even told me. In fact, that was one of the reasons they got on *your* radar." They were involved in a case Colleen had worked last year. A client of hers had been murdered by several bikers with ties to Aryan Alliance, headed up by Lange.

"That's not the point," Matt said. "The point is that you are now jeopardizing a case that is crucial to this city."

"And I've done nothing that will change that. And," she continued, "if Lange's involved with that woman killed on Muni, then this is more ammunition for your case."

He shook his head. "You don't give a damn about any of that. You're on some kind of personal vendetta—again. To hell with what SFPD wants. To hell with procedure and rule of law."

"Don't hold back, Matt," Colleen said, waving her hands. "Why not just say what's really on your mind?"

"Your client paid you off and you're done, but that's not good enough for Hayes Confidential. No, PI Hayes—*unlicensed,* I might add—is going to burn the house down to stop an arsonist."

She shook her head, keeping her emotions in check. "Lange's goons threatened me, then Pam."

"So let the police deal with it."

"For all I know they are—or aren't. Who knows the mysteries of SFPD? But they'll take their sweet time over it; I'm sure of that. I'm still waiting for them to stop by on my office break-in."

"Did you give them Rodney Walsh's address? That might have helped."

"They towed the car away. They can find who it's registered to easily enough. Or is that too much detective work?"

Matt's face darkened. "This is exactly the problem with you, Colleen. You've got a chip on your shoulder with SFPD so big you can't think straight. I don't mind humoring you when you want information now and then, but when it gets in the way of us trying to do our jobs, it's got to stop."

Humoring her. Matt's words stung as much as they infuriated. Colleen stiffened while Weather Report played on the stereo.

"Is that what you think, Matt? That I just 'get in the way'?"

Matt sat up, reached over, grabbed his pack of Marlboros, shook one out, lit it up. He took a deep drag, let smoke billow across the dimly lit living room.

"Sometimes," he said.

Some romantic evening this was turning out to be.

Colleen sucked in a deep breath, wanting a cigarette herself now. "It's been over six months since Lucky's death," she said, referring to an informant who had been beaten to a pulp and thrown in a dumpster. "No one has been charged, even though I gave SFPD everything. Those bikers did it at Lange's bidding. Just like those two lowlifes who broke into my office and attacked Pam."

"I've told you before, Colleen, Lange is going to get his due. There's just not enough to tie him to that particular murder."

"What you mean is that Lucky's murder isn't worth solving. He was just some nobody who sold newspapers on the street. What the hell does anybody care? You want the big prize."

Matt smoked. "When we take Lange down, it's going to be a strike. All the pins are coming down with him. Don't you dare mess it up for me."

"For *you*." She bit down on her anger. "Now we're getting to the heart of it. Meanwhile Lange's goons attack Pam. Sorry, Charlie. I don't work that way—not when my daughter is involved." Not to mention her future grandchild.

"Well, you're just going to have to learn, Colleen. Notice no one is kicking up much of a fuss about multiple shotgun blasts going off in your apartment last night."

"SFPD searched the place. They didn't find anything."

"Because your hippie lawyer stonewalled them with BS," he said, leaning forward to tap ash into a swirled blue and red glass ashtray. "Believe me, SFPD knows someone on your end fired shots. I did my best to hold them off. You seem to forget, with all of your anti-police crap, you've got friends like Owens and me to smooth feathers for you down at 850."

"I think I know that."

"So show it. You can start by staying out of my case. Don't interfere with Doris Pender—or any of Lange's people. Got it?"

She sat back, less than thrilled at the tone of Matt's voice. "Lange is connected to Ingrid Richter. The killing on the Muni. Why else would Lange have his people break into my office looking for the file? My apartment? Meanwhile Erich Hahn—Jakob Klaus, whoever he is—might well kill someone else. Perhaps an innocent bystander."

Matt squinted. "Jakob *who*?"

Sounded like Matt wasn't up on the case. "You need to talk to Owens."

"So you're working Owens too," Matt said, tapping more ash. "Jesus. It figures."

"If by 'working him' you mean I ID'd the dead woman on Muni, gave Owens a jump start on the case, then yes, I suppose you're right. No one else had a clue who she was. I was happy to help."

"*Help?*" Matt laughed out loud, took a drag, blew smoke. Put his bare feet up on the coffee table. "Is that what they call it now?"

Colleen held her tongue. She was quite partial to Matt, but he was being a supreme ass.

She stood up. "Let's try this 'date' another night."

Matt sat up, cigarette between his fingers, smoldering. "Oh come on, Colleen."

"Come on, *what*? Sit here and listen to you rant? Be a good little girl who stays out of your way? After my pregnant daughter was threatened by two knuckle-draggers who report to some guy you're planning to bust *someday*? When the stars are in alignment?"

Matt stood up too, put his hands on his hips. "Okay, I take it back."

And then she saw it.

Poking out from under the embroidered pillow she'd been resting on, right where she'd been sitting.

A gold hoop earring. Tucked underneath.

"What the hell is that?" she said.

"What the hell is what?"

She pointed at the earring.

He looked over at it, turning slightly red. "Oh, that."

"Yeah, *that*."

"After you left Pier 23 last night, I bumped into a couple of stewardesses. They wanted to see the town."

"And any decent tour of San Francisco includes a stop at Matt's bachelor pad."

"Come on! We went to dinner. I didn't want to waste that reservation at Alfred's after you blew me off. We came back here for a few drinks. It was all innocent fun."

She took a deep breath through her nose. "Did you give them a lecture on minding their own business, too?"

"It's not what you think," he said. "I gave you my key."

"What about Paquet? Your Interpol guy? You were going to ask him about Erich Hahn and Ingrid Richter for me."

"I don't believe it." Matt shook his head. "Now you're going to try and leverage an earring for more info? You don't miss a trick, do you?"

"What did Paquet say?"

Matt took an angry drag on his cigarette, blew it out. "Nothing."

She did her coat up. Took Matt's key out of her pocket. Set it on the coffee table.

"Don't do that," he said.

"I never wanted it in the first place."

"I know you didn't. But just pretend."

She forced a smile. "Let's chalk tonight up to experience. It's late. We've both said too much."

She headed for the door.

"Nothing on Erich Hahn," Matt said. "But now we know that's not even his real name."

Colleen stopped, looked Matt in the eye. Jaco Pastorius' smooth bass playing punctuated the silence.

"And when were you going to tell me that? You just said Paquet hadn't gotten back to you."

"I was going to tell you later."

"*Later?* Or never?"

"I didn't think it was the most romantic subject. I thought we could catch up first. I was going to tell you after," he said, going over to the coffee table, smashing his cigarette out. It smoldered in the ashtray.

Colleen wondered about that. Matt always seemed to push back for one reason or another.

"When can you talk to Paquet again?" she said. "I've got a few questions."

Matt shook his head. "I'm not San Francisco Public Library, Colleen. You don't get to keep pushing for info while you run riot over my cases."

She probably deserved that. But it didn't change things. "You're right, Matt. I apologize. I'm not using you. Except for my physical needs, of course." She smiled. "But this is important."

"Let me tell you something else that's important, to me, Colleen: *you.* You're dealing with some dangerous people. You've got this guy running around town stabbing people on Muni. I don't want you to be next. If Lange is involved, none of this is good for you."

"So you're protecting me now? Don't. I don't like it."

"Call it whatever you want. But until I get a better sense of what's going on, Paquet is going to have to wait."

They'd see about that. "Got it."

"That champagne is going flat," Matt said, raising his eyebrows.

Colleen drew a breath. She had been pushy, even if Matt might have been less than forthcoming. And collecting earrings. She wanted his Interpol connection. If she went home now, all of that would be put on the back burner. Or lost.

So what did that make her? She wasn't going to lose a good lead.

Well, she was a lot of things.

She'd ask herself that question again in the morning.

She broke a smile, peeled off her jacket as she eyed the bottle, collecting dew. "So it is."

CHAPTER TWENTY-THREE

Middle of the night, Colleen heard a phone ringing somewhere. She raised her face from a pillow with a silk pillowcase. This wasn't her pillow. She'd been sleeping like a baby.

She looked around Matt's darkened bedroom. She was warm and exhausted, in the nicest of ways. She reached out to his side of the bed.

Matt wasn't there. She lifted her head. The bedroom door was shut. She heard him in the living room, talking quietly.

"Give me thirty minutes," she heard him say.

She sat up, rubbed her eyes. Blinked at the digital clock. Not quite four a.m.

Matt had been called in to work again. She heard him pad into the bathroom, brush his teeth.

Gently, the bedroom door opened and Matt came in, as naked as she, the subdued light from the living room lamp highlighting all the parts she liked.

"The fun never stops at 850 Bryant," she said.

"Sorry," he said quietly. "I need to go in." He grabbed some clothes from the closet, underwear and socks from the dresser. "I'll get dressed in the other room. Go back to sleep."

"Don't be ridiculous." She climbed out of bed, naked and cold after a deep hibernation next to his warm body. Matt had left his dresser drawer open. She took a faded red T-shirt from the top of the stack, the one with "Simpson, 32" on it, pulled it on. "I'll make coffee."

Since she was getting up, Matt decided to dress in the bedroom. "Go for it, but I've got to run."

She went in the kitchen, put the kettle on the stove, struck a match under it.

Matt could dress quickly. By the time she had the cups out and things ready, he was already in the living room in a smart purple shirt, no tie, slim fitting pants, slipping on his shoulder holster with his 38.

He pulled on a big brown leather jacket.

"Is it serious?" she asked.

"Something like that."

He couldn't share. More so since she'd contacted Doris Pender.

She spooned instant coffee into the two cups. "We need to get you a coffee maker and some decent coffee, dude."

"Leave me a note on which kind of coffee maker and coffee and I'll pick them up," he said, adjusting his jacket, coming over to the kitchen to give her a kiss. "I can't have my women less than satisfied."

She grabbed the collar of his jacket gently, kissed his lips. "You just managed to squeak by this time."

"Thank God for that," he said. "Talk to you later—if I can get away."

Man, did she want to know about Paquet.

"Matt," she said, "I know you're busy but . . ."

He stopped her. "Tell you what: I'll get the coffee maker and coffee and you work on timing your requests. This op is highly confidential. You know the rules about talking out of class. I don't want to say it again: but please back off." He raised his eyebrows. "*Please.*"

She supressed a sigh. "Stay safe out there."

"Same goes for you. *Especially* for you." He gave her another peck, and then he was gone.

She went into the living room with her cup of instant coffee, sipped it, winced at the thin bitter taste, saw Matt's pack of Marlboros.

And that gold hoop earring still by the sofa cushion. Ugh.

She lit up an illicit cig, savoring the buzz after so many days without one, went into the bedroom, pulled on her underwear that had been strewn across the hardwood floor, drinking crummy coffee and smoking while she got dressed. No shower. Four in the morning, she'd go fishwife.

By her calculations it was one p.m. in Lyon, France. She entertained the thought of calling directory enquiries, getting the number for Interpol's Lyon office, calling Paquet "on behalf" of Matt Dwight, probing him for info. But it probably wouldn't get her anywhere and would only make Matt see red if it did. She'd have to find another way.

But how long would Ingrid Richter be in Rome?

She went into the kitchen, took one last drag, ran the ciggie under the faucet with a sizzle. Cleaned up.

This early in the day she could probably catch Owens before he left for work.

CHAPTER TWENTY-FOUR

1979

The sun was rising as Colleen stood on the second-floor exterior corridor of the Breakers Motel and knocked on the blue door, which contrasted with the pink '60s paintwork that had not fared well. Pre-rush hour traffic hummed behind her on Lombard, feeding cars into the city from the North Bay. This was the San Francisco that didn't make it onto the postcards, although plenty of tourists did stay in the area. They were probably expecting the famous crooked street at the other end of Lombard, not a multi-lane, uninspired thoroughfare.

Owens answered the door in shirt and tie, ready for the day.

"Why, hello," he said, standing back, inviting Colleen in.

The bed was made. Everything was in order. No mess. A set of dumbbells sat by the wall. The TV was off and paperwork was neatly lined up on the side table by the window.

He'd been divorced for some time now but was still living in limbo.

"To what do I owe the pleasure?" he asked.

"I'm not sure I'd go that far," she said. "But I have a few updates. I can tell you over breakfast. My treat." He was thin, probably still not eating.

That worked.

"Oh," he said. "Before I forget." On his table lay a manila envelope. He retrieved it, handed it to her. "Your file on Ingrid Richter."

"This *is* a red-letter day," she said, taking it. "I think this is the first time you've actually returned anything."

"Very helpful," he said. "The Feds are already starting to cut me out."

Soon the two of them were sitting around the red U-shaped counter at Zim's down the street. Dishes clanked while waitresses hustled orders.

Owens barely touched a bowl of oatmeal while Colleen devoured bacon, eggs, hash browns, and sourdough toast. There was nothing like a night of passion to work up an appetite. Owens was still pining for his ex. Colleen brought him up to speed with the latest developments.

At first Owens didn't have much to say about her meeting with Doris Pender. It was out of his caseload and she didn't mention dangling Rodney Walsh from the thirtieth floor of Mission Gateway. But he had heard about her apartment break-in. So he seemed to be taking a neutral attitude to her otherwise lawless approach.

She told him what she had learned about Ingrid Richter.

He sipped his black coffee. "Rome, you say?"

"As of last night." She wondered if he was thinking what she was thinking.

"You were right," he said. "There does seem to be a connection between Ingrid Richter and Muni Jane Doe."

"Still no ID on her?"

He shook his head, elbows on the red counter. "The FBI are looking into it. But she's not known to any of the major police departments around the country."

"And nothing on Jakob Klaus yet?"

"No flights since the Jane Doe was found. That doesn't mean he couldn't have used another identity."

"Or he's still in town," Colleen said.

"Possibly." Owens pursed his lips. "Because his work isn't done."

"Exactly," she said. "I'm betting Ingrid Richter sicced Jane Doe on him, possibly through Aryan Alliance, but he beat her to the punch. And he's still after Werner Beckmann. The guy in the Sachsenhausen ID."

"Nothing on him either."

There was no time like the present. Colleen set her cup down. "You know, we've been working together for quite a while."

"That is true," Owens said. "After a rocky start."

"I was thinking of heading to Rome," Colleen said.

Owens set his cup down. "Do you really think you should still be working on this? Because I certainly don't."

"Ingrid Richter's not likely to be there for long, I'm told. Do you want to lose her? More people will likely die. People like Pam."

"No, Colleen, I don't want any of that. But that is what law enforcement is for."

"What would it take to talk to the deputy chief, bring me in as a CI?"

Owens frowned. "No."

"I help you nonstop."

"And I you."

"It would help my parole."

"I'm not saying don't bring you on board at some point, but this is not that point. This case is too hot. The chief is not going to want to sanction you going to another country on the promise of finding someone beyond our jurisdiction. Bad idea. Drop it."

"Got it." She sighed. "If I get anything new, I'll share with you."

"Deal," he said. "How is your daughter?" Owens never asked about her private life.

"Staying with a friend out of town," she said.

"Good," he said. "Safer."

"She's pregnant," Colleen said. "Due next month."

"Oh, you didn't tell me that . . ."

"She's not married."

"Oh, okay." Owens drank coffee. "Well, that's not such a big deal anymore, is it?"

"The father ran the Church of Perfect Death."

"That certainly complicates things."

"Hopefully not," Colleen said. "He's out of the picture. It's just Pam and me at the moment."

"You originally came out to California to find her," Owens said.

"I did." Owens knew the reason for Colleen's prison sentence— killing her ex after she discovered him abusing Pam when she was a girl.

"Well," Owens said. "I wish you and Pam the best." He toasted her with his coffee cup.

It was as close to a personal conversation as they'd ever had.

"When are you going to find an apartment?" she said. "Living in that motel is just plain sad."

He sipped coffee. "My ex got the house."

Owens didn't have children. Colleen was a little surprised that his ex would get the house.

"If you need a good lawyer," she said, "mine works miracles. He even thinks he might be able to get me my PI license."

"Then he must be good," Owens said. "But I don't want to fight with Alice anymore. She can keep the house."

Maybe Owens was hoping for a reunion. But Colleen hated to see him always get the dirty end of the stick.

The waitress plopped the bill in a plastic tray in front of Owens, two soft mints on top of it. He reached inside his jacket pocket. Colleen grabbed the bill. "This is on me. Save up for a deposit on a place. And remember to keep me in the Jane Doe loop."

"Are you sure you should still be part of it?"

"I'm sure," she said. "I'm sure."

CHAPTER TWENTY-FIVE

Back home, Colleen was relieved to see that her contractor had replaced both kitchen doors that Pam had shot up, the one out onto the deck from the kitchen with smudgy new glass in the upper half and a set of bars over it now. This was obviously her week to repair doors. They needed paint but all in good time. She was not as crazy about the invoice that had been left on the kitchen counter. Or the call on her answering machine from the building's owner about gunshots. Apparently tenants were not supposed to have shootouts late at night, or at any other time. Colleen returned the landlord's call, shared his concern, suggested perhaps a secure back gate to the parking area and security lights on the stairs, possibly an alarm system? She mentioned her daughter, eight months pregnant, and men armed with crowbars and guns who'd had very easy access to her flat. That shut the owner up although he made it clear that repairs were her responsibility. But she kind of already knew that.

The next phone call was to a Professor Fisher at SF State where he taught Jewish Studies. On her last visit to SF Public Library, Colleen had seen the professor's name in a number of articles and footnotes. Fisher headed up the fledgling Zeykher Project, a foundation that compiled information on the Holocaust. Colleen saw an opportunity to get some of her increasing number of questions answered. Ingrid

Richter was supposedly at the Hotel Campania in Rome, but for how long?

The SF State Humanities department secretary told Colleen that Professor Fisher had a full day of classes and appointments, with more of the same for the rest of the week. Colleen mentioned she had some information on Sachsenhausen concentration camp she would be willing to share with the Zeykher Foundation. The secretary told her Professor Fisher was in class at the moment but took a message.

An hour later, in between classes, Professor Fisher returned Colleen's call.

"I understand you might have some material on Sachsenhausen?" He had an articulate voice and enunciated every word.

She said that she did, but she also had a few questions, questions that didn't seem appropriate over the phone. Could they meet? She'd bring the file.

Professor Fisher deliberated for a moment. "I might have some time later in the week."

Colleen heard the clock ticking on Ingrid Richter's Rome hotel. "Can you swing a quick lunch in the cafeteria? I'm buying." More expenses she had no client to bill to. But so be it.

"I actually work through lunch most days."

"A quick coffee?"

He thought about that. "If you don't mind stopping by."

She wouldn't mind at all. They picked a time that afternoon.

She called Pam, who was enjoying life with Alex's butler waiting on her and bringing her homemade ice cream. Colleen wondered about the possibility of Alex adopting Pam.

Still full from breakfast, she skipped lunch, caught up on some paid work, then headed over to SF State late afternoon with a file she'd prepared on Ingrid Richter. Fog swept down 19th Avenue between streaks of blue sky.

The sun was trying to come out over the blocky concrete student union building in the center of campus, banks of bleacher seats on top at odd angles like giant fins. But students were making use of them, seated here and there. Colleen entered the Cesar Chavez Student Center and headed downstairs, where the droning dance rhythms of a new wave band reverberated out of the Depot, students spilling out the doors. The singer was a woman who maintained that she might like you better if you slept together.

The Pub next door was doing its best to compete with the noise, loud voices over more music that overlapped the band across the way. Colleen scanned the smoky bar and saw a youngish man sitting alone with a stack of papers and books at a small table. In faded jeans and denim jacket, sandals, frizzy hair resembling early Bob Dylan, he looked more like a grad student than a professor.

She approached.

"Professor Fisher?" she asked.

He looked up. He wore round glasses, with sharp dark eyes amplified by the lenses. The paper he was working on was marked up in red with many small notes in tight handwriting.

"Colleen Hayes." She handed him a card.

He took it. "Call me Aaron," he said, waving her to a spare chair.

She asked if he would like something to drink.

He shook his head. "I only have a few minutes."

She sat down. "I understand you head up the Zeykher Project."

He took his glasses off, wiped them on a loose paper napkin, spoke as if reciting: "I started compiling information on the Holocaust for my thesis, using what is called a database, a computer storage repository to organize and share data with other centers of similar information. Much of that information is spread all over the world, on paper, microfiche, what-have-you. And much of it has been lost either through time, or deliberately. When the Nazis knew they were losing the war, around 1943, many records were destroyed—records that had otherwise been very detailed." He slipped his glasses back on. "Zeykher's role is to rebuild that memory." He consulted a very beat-up watch on a bony wrist, gave a patient frown.

"You founded the program. Secured grant funding. That's impressive."

"We'll see," he said, nodding at the file in her hand. "You said you had information that might be helpful to the program, Ms. Hayes?"

She handed him the file, which contained some, but not all, of the information she had. She knew better than to give everything away at once.

"There are people in there I'm very interested to know more about," she said.

"Is this for a client of yours?"

"No," she said. "Although I'm trying to figure out why a client misled me."

He looked at his watch again and raised his eyebrows. He stood up, started collecting his books and papers. "Let me read your file and get back to you. I have a class that starts in less than ten minutes. Thank you very much for making the trip and assisting the Zeykher Project."

She had been hoping for a little immediate info. "Do you have time for a couple of quick questions now?"

"Let me read your notes first. I need to be getting to class."

She stood up too while he gathered his files, his briefcase. "I'll walk with you."

"Very well," he said reluctantly.

They left The Pub. The band next door were going full bore with a wild sax solo.

"Jakob Klaus," she said as they walked out onto the green. Students were coming and going as the top of the hour approached. "AKA

Erich Hahn. He was in Buenos Aires a week ago, when Interpol reported a German ex-pat had been found murdered."

"Hermann Kruger was the dead man's name," Fisher said, readjusting his loose files as they walked to the buildings on the east side of the campus.

"So you know who he was," Colleen said.

"I just updated the database on him yesterday. He was found garroted in the restroom of a tourist bar in the Boca—the old port."

Interesting. "I think Jakob Klaus killed him. And then he came to San Francisco to target another ex-Nazi by the name of Werner Beckmann. Last week a woman was killed on Muni. I believe Ingrid Richter sent her to stop Jakob Klaus but he got the jump on her. Then Jakob Klaus disappeared. And so did Ingrid Richter."

Professor Fisher nodded as he walked. Noncommittal.

"Do you think Hermann Kruger was assassinated by a clandestine organization that targets ex-Nazis?" Colleen asked.

He gave her a guarded look as they walked. "The Zeykher Foundation needs to be careful who we share information with. Any path to justice must follow strict, recognized—legal—procedures. We are not interested in facilitating revenge. Due process is the way—something the Nazis did *not* observe."

"I just gave you a file that was the result of a lot of hard work," she said. "I want justice—the right kind of justice—as much as you do."

Professor Fisher was stopped by a young woman who needed him to sign a card to add his class. It was clear Colleen was becoming a nuisance. They approached the Humanities building. She held the door for Fisher and he went in with a polite but curt "thank you."

They got to a classroom door. Through the window she saw it bulging with students. The hallways grew silent as class started.

"When do you think you'll have time to answer questions?" she said.

She saw him suppress a frown. "As I said, I'll give you a call. Right now, I'm late for class."

How long would Ingrid Richter stay in her hotel in Rome?

"I don't mind hanging around," she said. "I can meet you after class. Or later this afternoon."

"I have classes all afternoon," he said. "Then I have office hours."

She stifled a sigh.

He noticed that. "I *will* call you this week. Now, I really have to get going."

"Thank you so much," she said, holding open the door to his classroom for him.

*   *   *

The phone was ringing as Colleen walked in the front door of her flat that evening, a sack of groceries under one arm. It was late—after ten p.m.—and she hurried, thinking it might be Pam calling from Alex's. She rushed to the kitchen, set the groceries down on the 1940s tile counter, grabbed the wall phone.

"Ms. Hayes?"

She recognized Professor Fisher's voice. That was quick. She was surprised and encouraged.

"Please," she said, "call me Colleen."

"I've had a chance to go over your paper," he said.

It took her a moment to realize he was using the word *paper* to mean her notes on Ingrid Richter. Shrewd.

"I appreciate that, Professor," she said.

"I'd like to discuss it with you." Then he added, "But not on the phone."

Perhaps he had good reason. "I'm available anytime," she said. "When and where?"

"Can you possibly get away now?"

It was late but she had long since learned that when an opportunity for information came along, you grabbed it.

"Absolutely," she said.

"Where we met earlier today," he said. Again, he was being careful.

The student union. Were they even open at this hour? "I'll be there," she said.

"Thirty minutes," he said before he hung up.

Colleen put the groceries away, threw on a heavier jacket, and headed back out.

*   *   *

Half an hour later, she was walking down the gentle slope of the SFSU campus again, the grass wet with fog, hands in the pockets of her green parka with the faux fur collar up. A typical San Francisco summer night. She kept her eyes peeled, not just for Professor Fisher but for anyone else that might be watching or following. It was becoming her MO, especially on this case, where she was the client. Driving down 19th, it seemed like every car might be a tail. But the student complex was dark and the place desolate. No Professor Fisher, or anyone else.

Then, on top of the student center at the back of the row of cement bleachers facing her, she saw someone light a match, hold it up. There he was. A signal. Then he shook it out.

A minute or two later she was up top herself, climbing the stairs to the final row of cement. Fisher wore a beat-up leather jacket and a scarf wrapped around his neck. His sandals had been switched for canvas wino slip-ons and droopy socks.

"You're careful who you deal with," she said.

"When it comes to something like this." He put both hands in his pockets and hunkered down as Colleen sat next to him. The view across the east side of the campus, towards 19th Avenue, was obscured by fog.

"The Zeykher Project has been known to attract the wrong sort of attention," he said.

"I can believe that," she said, looking around, scanning the shadows across the deserted campus. "Especially with what I've seen in the last week."

"For most people," he said, "the Second World War is long over."

"I'll confess it never seemed to affect me until now," she said. "But it has. I'm not even getting paid for my work. This is all on my own dime."

He nodded in concurrence. "Over eight million Germans were members of the Nazi party. Do you know how many were convicted at the Nuremberg trials? Twenty-four. Yes, subsequent trials took care of more but the bottom line is that plenty of those eight million are still alive and still sympathetic to the party's beliefs."

"Cautious is good."

"I gather you're in a hurry for information," he said.

"I'm told that Ingrid Richter is currently in Rome. I have her location. But I don't know for how long."

"And you think she's one of the eight million?"

"Yes."

Professor Fisher turned, looked at Colleen. "You're not personally thinking of trying to intervene in any way, are you?"

She weighed things up. Say too much, scare him off. But then again, he was going out of his way to assist her. When it doubt, opt for the truth.

"No," she said. "But I need to get to the bottom of things."

"Why? Because Ingrid Richter deceived you?"

"In my line of work being played is almost grounds for immediate disqualification. But that's not what matters. Thugs connected to this thing threatened me, and what's worse, my daughter. On top of it, a woman was killed."

"The woman on Muni?"

"Yes. And part of that was my doing. For tracking down Jakob Klaus for Ingrid Richter. Setting all of this in motion." Colleen took a deep breath. "Jakob Klaus is killing ex-Nazis and Ingrid Richter is trying to stop him. Why? Unless she's one of the eight million."

Fisher was watching her closely. "And what are you going to do if you do manage to unravel this?"

Colleen turned back to the silent, dark campus. A young man and a woman were walking across the green, holding hands and books. Nothing threatening. "Hand over anything I find to the authorities."

Fisher squinted through his glasses. "Are you one hundred percent sure about that?"

"Why wouldn't I be?"

"You've got a police record."

She turned, looked at him again. He'd said it so matter-of-fact. "You've looked into me." The past never let go.

"For anybody we interact with. We're dealing with the deaths of six million. It's a sacred mission. We don't want revenge. We want justice."

There was a pause while the wind rushed across the campus. The young couple had moved on. Colleen heard the woman laugh. To be young and in love.

"It's no secret I killed my husband," Colleen said. "I was sent to prison for it. It gave me time to learn what a hideous mistake I made."

Fisher seemed to take that in.

"How does all of that translate into you being a private detective?" he said.

"I came out to California looking for my daughter, who ran away when I was in prison. This pays the bills in the meantime."

"And your daughter?"

"Pam's never really forgiven me for killing her father. She's twenty now. Well, I found her and we're back together." Colleen held up crossed fingers. "And I'm trying to make amends."

Their eyes met again. He seemed to understand.

"Black Cross," he said.

"Black Cross," she repeated. "That would be the outfit Jakob Klaus works for?"

"*Czarny Krzyż.*" He pronounced it *Charnick Siss*. "Originally a Polish organization of Holocaust survivors that—ah—locates ex-Nazis."

"'*Locates*' is a nice way to put it."

"Another point," he said, "is that the person you're so eager to find is connected to people who aren't benign. You need to be careful."

"I wish I'd been more careful before I let Ingrid Richter set me up to find her so-called nephew."

"Jakob Klaus was a prisoner at Sachsenhausen as a boy. We have no record of the rest of his family. But there must have been some. Children were rarely taken to the camps alone. If they were, they were quickly dispensed with, or used for medical experiments. But somehow, Jakob Klaus survived. Why? How? The man killed in Buenos Aires was a former guard at Sachsenhausen. His original SS ID was found lodged in his throat in a men's bathroom in a bar after he was garroted. It appears that Jakob Klaus has *located* a few other ex-Nazis too."

"And now he's looking for Werner Beckmann."

"Which is odd. Beckmann was a Sturmbannführer—the equivalent to a major—at Sachsenhausen. But he wasn't on any of the camp records—none that we have access to anyway—although he is rumored to have run a secret project. And he supposedly died in a hotel fire in Rome in early 1945 trying to escape the Allies.

Otherwise, he might have possibly been a defendant at one of the post-war trials and subsequently hanged. Call it poetic justice."

Rome again. "Maybe Werner Beckmann rose from the ashes," Colleen said.

"You don't have that SS ID card by any chance, do you?"

She shook her head. "Saw it, though, in the air duct in Jakob's hotel room. I'm no expert but it looked to be the real thing. Sachsenhausen. 1942."

Professor Fisher raised an eyebrow. In his line of work people didn't ransack hotel rooms looking for information. "Maybe Jakob Klaus was barking up the wrong tree."

"If Beckmann died in 1945 in a fire, he certainly would be," she said. "What about Ingrid Richter?"

"That's where it gets really interesting," Fisher said. "Ingrid Richter's father was a well-known university lecturer and activist at the beginning of World War II. A wealthy, prominent Berlin family. His position afforded him privileges to speak his mind until it didn't. He was shot Christmas Day, 1942. It's rumored the execution was filmed for the Führer's pleasure."

Colleen trembled involuntarily. "Talk about the Christmas spirit."

"Ingrid Richter was arrested by the Gestapo. She was seventeen at the time. Taken to the Reich main security office. That's where her trail ends."

"With a father like that she would've been a political prisoner, correct? One of the ones with a red triangle on her coat?"

Fisher nodded. "Someone's been doing their homework."

"Sachsenhausen is just north of Berlin," Colleen said. "Seems she might have been taken there."

"Yes. It is nearby and Sachsenhausen was used primarily for political prisoners. But," he said, "there's no record of her. It stops at the Reich main security office in Berlin."

"Isn't that kind of unusual? Nazis and record-keeping go together like hand in glove from what I've read."

"Unless somebody wanted them erased," Fisher said. "It was always assumed she was taken off somewhere and shot. But, lo and behold, here she is, working for a Swiss bank in 1979—if it's she."

"It has to be," Colleen said.

Fisher shrugged, dug out a pack of gum, offered Colleen a piece, which she declined, selected a stick, unwrapped it, put it in his mouth, chewed. "Ingrid Richter is not an uncommon name."

"But when you match it up with Jakob Klaus, Werner Beckmann, and Sachsenhausen concentration camp, who else could she be?"

He chewed gum. "Agreed."

"What was the special project that Beckmann—who died but maybe didn't—was part of?"

"We don't know. Something very hush-hush."

"No records anywhere?"

"Just a rumor that something went on in Barracks 19 at Sachsenhausen. As you've discovered, Sachsenhausen was a prison for political prisoners, like Ingrid Richter, as well as a center for slave workers for the surrounding manufacturers. Slave labor was a key function of the camps. Unfortunately, most were worked to death. Half the people who went into Sachsenhausen never came out."

Colleen took a deep breath. "So the special project might have been related to something like that."

"We don't know."

"You say it all so matter-of-fact," she said.

Professor Fisher frowned in agreement. "My grandparents perished at Auschwitz. My father too. He wouldn't leave my grandparents behind and they wouldn't leave Germany. But he managed to get my mother and me on a train to Paris in 1941. I was seven years old. I don't remember a thing. I blocked it out. Many did. I'm ashamed to say I'm one. But now I must remember. For all those who lost loved ones. For a world that too easily forgets. I must rebuild my memory, and the memory of a world that doesn't want to remember. Data is truth. I find it, enter it in. What is important is to catalogue that data so it's never again forgotten. That's how I honor the dead—and hopefully provide evidence so that the monsters still out there can be brought to justice."

Colleen pictured a terrified mother and her child leaving the family behind.

She said, "Isn't is unusual, with what's known about Sachsenhausen, that *somebody* wouldn't know about Barracks 19? Those barracks weren't exactly invisible."

"Yet everything about that particular barracks and the one next to it has been scrubbed."

"Except that Beckmann was there. And that he might not be dead. And that Jakob Klaus appears to have a grievance with him."

"Another thing I must warn you about: Allied intelligence were briefed on many things after the war that will never see the light of day. This might well be one of them. Many Nazis were given special treatment in exchange for information."

"So you're saying I've got to watch out for the good guys too?"

He smiled wryly. "Is there really any such thing?"

"Let me have my fantasy," she said. "I wonder if they all knew each other at Sachsenhausen: Werner Beckmann, Ingrid Richter, Jakob Klaus, and Jane Doe found dead on the Muni."

"Perhaps not Jane Doe," Professor Fisher said.

"No?"

"She has—had—a tattoo, your notes said. On her left forearm?"

"Saw it myself."

"You don't have the whole number, do you?"

Colleen shook her head. "All I got was: A2101 and two smudged digits."

"Pity. Tattoos blur over time. But she didn't get that at Sachsenhausen."

"No?"

Fisher shook his head. "The tattoos were used exclusively at Auschwitz from 1941 until 1944. The rest of the camps didn't use them."

"I didn't know that."

"Most people don't. It's a common misconception."

"Could she have been at Auschwitz? And transferred to Sachsenhausen?"

Dr. Fisher nodded as he chewed. "It's possible. That number is from a range used for female prisoners around 1941–42. And prisoners were reallocated to camps as needed—if they were of any value. Jewish prisoners were rarely relocated." His face grew dark.

She knew why. The Nazis had no intention of letting Jews live.

"So she probably wasn't Jewish," she said quietly.

His eyes met hers as he saw her making the connection. "Quite a few Hungarians and Poles were processed at that time in Auschwitz. Those with any usefulness were sent to other camps to backfill. The Russian front was taking every last able German male. The camps were desperate for people with skills. Even those without skills: guards."

"Guards?"

"*Kapos.* Prisoners who worked as guards and block leaders under the SS. They grew in numbers as German troops became scarce. Many of them were more brutal than their Nazi superiors. Some were simply animals who rose to the occasion, others acted out of fear for their own lives."

"Divide and conquer—turn the prisoners on themselves."

Fisher frowned. "It's beautifully architected to destroy the humanity of your enemy. You can thank Heinrich Himmler for that. At the height of the Nazi reign, there were over a thousand camps in operation."

Colleen let a moment of silence pass. "Well, Jane Doe is not as unknown as she was before."

"But remember, there were up to thirty thousand prisoners at any one time at Sachsenhausen. Over two hundred thousand entered its gates. Trying to find one prisoner in any of this is pure needle-in-a-haystack."

She knew that. But she had a start. "Can I contact you for more information?"

He regarded Colleen for a moment. "Here are the conditions: one, you don't mention the foundation, or disclose where the information came from."

"Hayes *Confidential*," she said.

"Two: anything you learn you give to the foundation. To *me*."

"Absolutely."

"Three: I've said it before but now I need to stress: this can't be about revenge."

"Got it," she said. "Now I need to warn you about something, too—someone. Not in the file."

He raised his eyebrows.

"Do you know a Dr. Lange?" she said.

"I'm more than familiar with Dr. Lange's version of history."

"Aryan Alliance are the ones who sent the thugs who broke into my office trying to get that information," she said. "They threatened my daughter."

Fisher blinked behind his glasses. "I see."

"I kind of threatened them back," she said.

"That's not in your file."

"My daughter is my business," she said. "No one else's. But I thought you should know."

"And you just told me this isn't about revenge."

"It's not," she said. "It's about protecting my daughter. But I want you to be able to protect yourself, too."

"My people are used to keeping our eyes peeled for the likes of Dr. Lange—but I appreciate the warning."

"What about the banknote?"

He looked at her questioningly.

"The half of a British five-pound note? It's in that file. 1936. That Jane Doe had? Jakob Klaus had the other half. Matching serial numbers. I saw it in his hotel room too. In the air vent."

Professor Fisher shook his head, possibly at Colleen's investigative methods again. "Some sort of code, I imagine."

"What does it have to do with all of this?"

"Quite possibly nothing at all."

"Right," she said. "But in this case, Jakob killed her. So that doesn't really make them partners, does it?"

"It wouldn't seem so."

"And Ingrid Richter works for a Swiss bank."

He looked at her again, eyebrows knotted.

"Banknotes?" Colleen said. "Swiss bank? See where I'm going with this?"

"Possibly," Professor Fisher said, chewing gum. "But it might be nothing at all."

He stood up. So did Colleen.

"Please be careful," he said.

"And you the same," she said.

They shook hands, parted ways, Professor Fisher heading back to his office where he still had more work to do, Colleen to 19th Avenue where she had parked.

It was coming together. Parts of it were anyway.

She started up the Torino, headed back down 19th.

At Sloat she saw the boxy black sedan a few car lengths behind in her rearview mirror. It normally wouldn't have been too much to be concerned about. Except that it had been behind her on the way over here.

CHAPTER TWENTY-SIX

1942

Ingrid was handed over to the guards posted outside the entrance between Barracks 18 and 19, where the two structures had been almost entirely wrapped with electrified barbed wire and covered overhead by more. The young SS guard at the door to Barracks 19 kept his Luger holstered on his hip and gave Ingrid a nod that almost seemed polite as he waved her into a small room next to a storeroom where the wood paneling had been painted beige and a looming portrait of the Führer hung on the wall. The room was otherwise bare, with only a table and several straight-back chairs. The pounding of machinery from the other side of the barracks was overwhelming, mingled with opera music. She could hear men talking, and the floorboards creaking with footsteps.

The single window was painted over with white paint.

"Wait here," the guard said, shutting the door on Ingrid. The pounding eased with the door shut but was still prominent.

Ingrid couldn't fathom being left on her own in a KZ, although where would she run to? If she did manage to get out, the fence around the barracks would stop her. Beyond that were guards and kapos and more guards and machine gun towers. She would be shot in an instant.

She didn't want to die as her father had. The only way to survive would be to make herself valuable to whatever enterprise this was.

A moment later the door opened and a short stout man in civilian clothes entered, carrying a folio, like an artist might have. He was middle-aged, with a paunch. His shirtsleeves were rolled up. He wore a banker's visor. A tuft of white hair poked up. His dark-complexioned face was shiny and his brow knotted. A man under pressure. He set the file on the table and sat down on the opposite side.

Ingrid remained standing and said *good day*, calling him *sir*, not knowing what else to say.

"Card?" He reached out impatiently. His fingers were smudged with black ink. He wasn't German by his accent. He wore no armband and she saw no prisoner number on his clothing. But he hadn't been accompanied by an officer or soldier. Salak had implied there were privileges in Barracks 19.

Ingrid produced her registration card.

The man took it, sat back, read it, legs crossed at the ankles. He wore socks and shoes, not the rough wooden clogs she had seen on the other prisoners so far. Outside the camp loudspeakers announced a block of workers to assemble for the march to the brickworks.

The man looked up, as if surprised.

"Richter?"

"Yes, sir. Ingrid, sir."

"Do you really speak all of these languages?"

Ingrid confirmed.

He asked her in Russian if she was Professor Richter's daughter.

She replied in Russian that she was.

He gave a somber nod, perhaps acknowledging her father. He set her card to one side. "You know engraving?"

"Yes, sir."

He squinted. "You're not just saying that to try to improve your situation? Because if they find out that's what you're doing, I can tell you right now, they're going to take you out and shoot you for wasting everyone's time. If you admit to it now, I'll do my best to get you put back out there, but you must say so now. Once we talk, there is no going back." He pressed a fingertip into the tabletop for emphasis.

Ingrid shivered. She had studied engraving but she was a novice. She wasn't sure they would give her any kind of a second chance regardless. And "back out there" didn't seem to be much of an option anyway.

"I'm enrolled in the Fine Arts program at Bauhaus Weimar next year."

"You mean you *were*." He sat back. "Dürer is not the real world."

"No, sir." Clearly, she was out of her depth. And not likely to be leaving here.

"No, it's not." He opened the portfolio, which contained many samples of paper, large and small. He selected a small sample, smaller than a business card, cut out of a larger piece, flipped it up, turned it around, placed it in front of her. He shut the folio.

The words "Bank of England" were printed on very high-quality rag paper, from an engraving, the letters with formal curlicue embellishment.

"What is the problem with this sample?" he asked.

She looked at the small piece of heavy bond paper. She could see nothing wrong with the lettering. She studied it over and over, heart thudding.

"Well?" he said, drumming his fingers on the table.

"I'm sorry. I see no problem, sir."

"Take another look."

She did.

"I think it's quite well done, sir."

"Do you?"

"Yes, sir."

He nodded, put the paper back facedown, produced another one. "This one?"

She examined it, blinking while the machines pounded and the loudspeakers outside the barracks droned on about the brickworks. For a moment, she thought she might be going insane. She reminded herself that the war had brought her here and she was fighting the war too. She must survive, as her father would have wished.

"Well?" he said.

"The same as the first, sir. It looks fine—to me, anyway."

"I see." He showed her another one.

Her eyes were good, but she was exhausted from standing all night, and in a state of perpetual fear. She had witnessed young Jakob's grandmother being clubbed to death, the hanging of a prisoner for the theft of 200 grams of bread, and the mistreatment of hundreds of others and she hadn't even been here twelve hours. She needed to use the toilet, her striped uniform was coarse and scratchy and, with no underthings, dug into her to the point of distraction and reeked of disinfectant. She hadn't had a thing to eat since yesterday when she had been shipped from 8 Reichssicherheitshauptamt in Berlin. And that had been a mug of cold tea and a single slice of stale bread smeared with lard.

But she must focus.

"It's fine, sir—again, in my opinion."

"The opinion of a student."

"Yes, sir."

They went over other samples. Was this a perverted test, where nothing was going to be wrong? Where she would eventually see something that didn't exist? The examples were becoming a blur.

Finally, she saw something.

"That." She pointed at the "f" in "Bank of England."

"Something wrong with it?"

"The tail of the 'f' is of poor quality, sir. If you look you can see that it's not smooth, the way the others were."

He narrowed his eyes at her. "Are you sure about that?"

"May I have one of the previous samples in order to show you?"

"No."

Very well. But all she had done were student pieces, two still lifes, and never any text or verbiage. But the "f" wasn't right.

"The 'f' is not as well done as the others. It's very slight but it's there."

He took the paper, put it back in the folio, shut it.

"What if I were to tell you that there is nothing wrong with it?"

She didn't think she could stand the hammering in her chest that accompanied the machinery nearby. "My experience is quite limited, sir, but if I had done that work, I think I would see it as an error."

He gave a single nod. "You are correct."

She let out a massive sigh of relief.

He sat back again, crossed his arms. "What is the reason for the printing problem?"

She drew a shaky breath. "One of three, most likely: poor materials, poor workmanship, or poor setup."

"Now you're an expert? How many print shops have you worked in?"

"My summer internship at Universität der Künste Berlin. And my studies, of course."

"*And your studies*. There are no classes or books here! Describe the cause of the problem, Miss Universität der Künste Berlin."

She took yet another deep breath. "The engraver was possibly working too fast. Or using too little down pressure. Or perhaps had a worn or dull cutter. Tool wear is gradual, after all. Perhaps the plate needed to be cleaned."

Arms still crossed, he nodded. "How would you determine that?"

"I would first clean the plate, check that the materials are all securely fastened."

"Fine. You've cleaned the plate and secured the materials and the problem still exists."

"I would use a 10X eye loupe to inspect the cutter tip."

"You don't have a 10X eye loupe."

She gulped back her nerves, kept going. "If the problem persists, it's not necessarily the cutter tip. I would re-engrave at half speed, sir. It might be the engraver, as I say, working too fast. I would redo it." She hoped he wasn't the engraver in this case.

He scrutinized her. "And what if I said you can't redo it? There's no time. It must be fixed *now*." He pressed his finger into the tabletop again. "Right now!"

"Use a fine brush and ink. Smooth out the ragged bottom of the letter 'f'." She had read where that had been done.

"By hand? Have you ever done that?"

"No, sir. I have always redone my work." That was the point of learning how to engrave.

"Well, we don't have the luxury of redoing our work from scratch here. This paper is extremely hard to come by and we can't afford to waste it."

His explanation gave her relief. She had passed some sort of a hurdle—hadn't she?

"May I ask a question, sir?"

"You just did."

"I beg your pardon?"

"Relax, girl!" He waved his hand impatiently. "Go on—ask your question!"

Relax? "Is what you showed me representative of the work that is required here, sir?"

He finally divulged a grin. "Do you mean: are we making counterfeit Brit currency in Barracks 19? Well, we're not making Christmas cards, girl, I can tell you that."

"I just want to know if I'm capable."

He leaned forward. "You better be capable, Ingrid. You already know too much to go back out there." He pointed outside. "You might know your subject but you're green. Some of us have spent our whole lives doing this. Along with a prison stretch or two."

She would have to be capable. "I have confidence I can do the work, sir."

"Good, because if you don't, it will not only reflect on you, but your workmates as well." He raised his eyebrows. "Do you understand what I'm saying? None of us are here through any act of kindness."

"I understand, sir."

He rubbed his chin. "Well, you're not qualified but, lucky for you, we've lost a couple of people recently. Dysentery."

Who would have thought dysentery would be good news?

He drummed his fingers on the table, obviously weighing her up. Then he stood up, tucked her registration card in his shirt pocket, collected his folio. "Wait here."

Before she could even think, she heard herself say: "Where else would I wait, sir?"

He actually laughed before his face grew serious and he pointed a finger at her. "Don't you dare joke like that in front of the uniforms. Is that understood?"

"Yes, sir." It hadn't been a joke, simply her nerves. She was in a state. She must hang on.

"Good." He left the room, shut the door.

A few minutes later, she heard footsteps approach the door amidst the pounding of which she assumed were now printing presses, blended with Verdi's *Don Carlos*. None of this seemed real.

She heard two men talking outside the door.

"You better not be wasting my time, Alexei," a German man said.

"She doesn't have the experience, Major, but she's very knowledge-able. And she's bright."

"We don't have time to train people. And she's a female, for God's sake. We've nothing but men."

"We're shorthanded."

"Work harder."

"Give her a week. She shows promise." The Russian man's attitude was quite different—subservient—and Ingrid was grateful that he was vouching for her.

The major said, "We'll see."

The door opened and an officer entered, wearing a spotless dark green uniform with black collar, replete with SS patch and the ornamentation of a party paramilitary officer, although his tunic was unbuttoned. Thirties, tall, blond swoop of forelock, all the classic Aryan features one expected. Ingrid stood up. If she had been nervous before, she was shaking now. She checked herself, bowed, head down.

He shut the door, came in, stood on the other side of the desk.

Examined her up and down in her prisoner stripes.

He sat down. He didn't ask her to sit.

He fished a pack of cigarettes out of his shirt pocket. *Chesterfields.* American.

He noticed her looking at the pack. "The party has taken a dim view of smoking. They're actually trying to ban the practice. Something to do with cancer. So I'm forced to smoke my enemy's." He smiled. He was quite taken with himself. "Plus, to be quite truthful, they taste better." He shook one loose, leaned forward, offered it to her. "Cigarette?"

"No thank you, sir. But thank you."

He sat back, pulled the cigarette, put it between his lips. He lit it up with a gold lighter, took a puff. "How old are you?"

"Seventeen."

"Seventeen." He looked around. "God damn it!" He got up, the chair and his jackboots creaking, and marched to the door, yanked it open.

"Where is the ashtray, for God's sake?"

He left the door open, came back, sat down. Took an angry puff. "Infuriating."

"I can imagine, sir," she said.

He smoked more leisurely, smiled. "Can you really?"

"No, sir. Not really, sir."

"You're very polite. Well-bred."

"Thank you, sir."

"Have you ever worked with a group of men? Some not-so-polite?"

Like the Nazis? "I believe I know how to conduct myself with men, sir, and get things done. I handled most of my father's affairs."

"Ah, yes. Your father, the traitor."

She jolted inside.

Another guard came in, a teenager in a baggy uniform, with pasty skin and acne. He was holding a ceramic ashtray that read "Gott Mit Uns" on the side. He placed it on the desk. It actually had a swastika in the bottom. They put swastikas on everything.

"Here you are, Major Beckmann."

"Make sure there is an ashtray in here at all times. I'm holding you responsible. Now get out."

"Yes, Major." The soldier gave a straight-arm salute—which the major didn't return—and left, pulling the door shut behind him.

Major Beckmann blew a smoke ring. "So," he said. "The traitor's daughter."

She didn't reply.

"No response?" he said, smoking.

"My father loved his country, sir."

"Well, he certainly had a peculiar way of showing it."

She couldn't bring herself to denounce her father, even to save her life.

"It's not for me to say."

"No? Then I will. He was misguided at best. His crime accomplished nothing apart from his own demise and his daughter's imprisonment. Had he simply kept his mouth shut and done his job, he would still be with you and you wouldn't be dressed in prison garb with your head shaved, cowering like a frightened puppy."

Despite her situation, she huffed her annoyance. This man wasn't fit to even mention her father.

He smoked. "You have something to say now?"

"Nothing."

"*Nothing?*"

"Nothing, *sir.*"

"Not even that you seek to atone for your father's treasonous crimes?" He waved his hand. "Something like that? Come on, make an effort."

Perhaps she was reaching the end, even though she had been in the camp less than twelve hours. She stood forward, held her head up in defiance.

"You may as well shoot me now."

"*Shoot you?*" He sat up, examined his belt. "Dear me. I seem to have forgotten my pistol." He sat back, smoked. "It will have to wait."

"Perhaps you can get one of your men to bring you one," she said drily. She didn't know where the courage was coming from, only that it was.

He smiled. "Now I'm beginning to see the real you." He puffed. "Sit down."

She stood.

"I said 'sit down.' That's an order."

She sat.

"What has Alexei told you about our little operation?"

"You're printing currency."

"Counterfeit currency. To destroy the British economy—or so Berlin likes to think. But it's too late. The war is already lost."

She couldn't quite believe he said those words.

He took another puff, blew a smoke ring. "It's true, Ingrid. And, in these times, the truth is a precious commodity, more valuable than any currency, especially fake currency. I have no illusions about Germany winning this war. You should likewise have none that once you cease to provide value to this operation, you will have any more value to Germany, either."

His coldness chilled her. But if the war was lost, surely she could survive until then, a day at a time. And perhaps save one or two others. She thought of young Jakob. A foolish dream?

"I understand," she said.

"So, the truth: Operation Bernhard allows a brief respite for you and a few chosen fellow prisoners. Three-hundred-gram rations of bread instead of two. A bed—a real bed, with bed linen. Proper clothes—well, castoffs." Ingrid shivered at the thought of the origin of the civilian clothes. "Interesting work that won't break your back. Recreation. Safety—well, relative safety. As long as you all perform to the highest standards, and Berlin is happy, you all get to live. Until we're done with you."

And you, too, perhaps? she thought.

"The program was already started once at another location," he said, "then shut down at the displeasure of Berlin. I have no intention of upsetting Reichsführer Himmler. Neither will you."

"Of course not, sir."

"Tell me, Ingrid, do you have a problem taking direction from a Jew?"

Her father had given his life to champion the rights of others and instilled that in her as well. But she couldn't be certain what an SS officer might think. She mustn't be too forceful in her opinions. This might be a trick. "Some of the world's most capable men are Jews, sir."

"Well said. All of my Jews are quite capable. They should be. I spent a good deal of time hunting them down, bringing them here from camps all over the Reich. And in here, they will be treated respectfully. We are still building our operation and everyone will work as one." He took a puff on his cigarette. "Until we're done, of course."

He was making no bones about their usefulness once the operation was finished.

"Any questions?" he asked.

"No, Major."

He got up, and she stood up as well, and he went to the door, opened it, the sound of the presses and music filling the air. "Someone get Alexei!" he shouted.

Ingrid heard footsteps rushing down the hallway. The Russian man who had interviewed her appeared.

"Ingrid is on a day's trial," Major Beckmann said. "I want a full report on her progress by end of shift."

"With all due respect, Major, today's shift is already well underway. Tomorrow would be a more accurate measure."

"Oh, would it now? I do apologize, Alexei. I didn't realize that you had been put in charge. Thank you so much for bringing that to my attention."

Alexei bowed his head. "I meant no disrespect, Major. I merely—"

"*End of shift*," Beckmann snapped.

"Yes, Major Beckmann."

"Good." Beckmann turned to Ingrid. "Well, Ingrid, what are you waiting for?"

*   *   *

They immediately put Ingrid with an elderly man with a straggly white beard whose name was Mr. Kessler. She handed him large sheets of rag bond that he slipped into the press with surprising deftness and then removed, handing them back to her to dry and stack. Each sheet contained four British five-pound notes, dated 1936, black and white, printed on one side. She learned that such currency was printed on one side only, which made it easier to forge. One other press was in operation with two men working it.

Several other men, at the direction of Alexei, were setting up a third press, taking it out of the crate. All wore civilian clothes. They worked quickly and efficiently, although Alexei took time to praise the quality of workmanship of the new press. Ingrid saw there were going to be six such presses packed into the small print room. A tall SS guard with an expressionless face watched, often looking Ingrid's way. Her ears thrummed with the noise. The sound of opera, coming from a gramophone, helped mask the machinery.

She had until end of shift to prove herself. She mustn't make a mistake.

As soon as the new press was in place, the SS guard left.

"Take over," Mr. Kessler said to Ingrid, who had been watching the guard.

Ingrid flinched. She had been handing sheets of paper back and forth for an hour, with no real introduction to the press or process.

"Are you sure, Mr. Kessler?" she asked.

"I need to use the toilet!" And he was gone. And there she was, feeding what she knew was very expensive paper into the press.

One sheet came out crooked. Her heart leapt with panic.

Then another. She felt the eyes of Alexei and the two men on her.

Mr. Kessler returned, his face pale. He admonished her when he saw the crooked sheets drying. "Pay attention, girl!" He wiped his brow with a rumpled handkerchief. "Do you know how valuable this paper is?"

"Yes, Mr. Kessler," she said, returning to her support role. "Are you not well?"

"Don't ask stupid questions!" he said. "And you will *not* share my little breaks with Major Beckmann or the guards."

"Of course not, Mr. Kessler."

The guard returned, watching everything.

Mr. Kessler required another break less than fifteen minutes later. He was obviously feeling poorly and didn't want to say so.

The guard, who had been watching, left again.

He returned with another guard.

They approached Mr. Kessler.

"Let's go outside for a smoke," one said.

"Very well," Mr. Kessler said, head bowed, defeated. He switched off the press, turned to Ingrid. "Good luck to you, young lady."

She felt awful, sensing what was coming.

Mr. Kessler was taken outside in between the fenced-off barracks. Another guard appeared inside and turned the gramophone up.

There was a single pistol shot.

Then a moment of relative silence.

Alexei came over to her, turned the press back on. "Get back to work, Ingrid. You're in charge of this press now. I'll give you a hand until we get someone to help you."

She felt a chill run through her, exacerbated by the hunger, exhaustion. and disorientation of this new world.

"Did they have to shoot poor Mr. Kessler, Alexei?" she said quietly as he handed her sheets.

"Dysentery," he said.

She took a deep breath as she fed paper into the press, recalling how many sheets she had taken from Mr. Kessler. Dysentery was contagious.

"Don't they have any medical facilities?" She knew this was a KZ and Mr. Kessler was a Jew but this currency operation seemed important.

"Operation Bernhard is top secret," was all Alexei said. He nodded at the press. "Keep your mind on your work."

She did. She was getting the hang of it.

By the time the shift ended, the silence of the machines being turned off was welcome.

The prisoners were led next door to Barracks 18, where Ingrid waited her turn, used the toilet, washed her hands raw with cold water and coarse lye soap.

In a large common room with half a dozen dining tables, she sat at one end of a table on her own and devoured a bowl of thin turnip soup and a quarter loaf of grainy rye bread, forcing herself to slow down. There were about thirty others, all men, all dressed in civilian clothes. She was the only female, and the only one in prisoner attire. No one spoke to her. Alexei was not there. She wondered if he was giving his report to the major. She told herself she had done all she could and if it wasn't enough, it was fate. She told herself to be happy for a simple meal and another day of life. It was late, dark. The camp was silent.

Alexei entered the common room, came over, sat next to her. What news did he have? Her nerves were raw.

"Major Beckmann is not unhappy with your progress," he said.

"Thank you," she said, breathing a massive sigh of relief. She knew Alexei had given her a good report, despite the mistakes. "*Thank you.*"

Alexei stood up, spoke to the rest of the room.

"This is Ingrid," he said. "She will be joining us."

Heads nodded around the tables. One or two "welcomes" reverberated before the men stood and clapped.

She had never felt quite so relieved. Or welcomed. What a place for it to happen.

"You will treat her as you would your sister," Alexei added with a firm tone that was unmistakable in its meaning. He turned back to Ingrid.

"There are no separate sleeping facilities," he said. "Take a bunk by the far wall. Linen and blankets are in the storeroom. Thanks to the major we do much better than the rest of the camp. We will be up to 140 in short order but for now, enjoy the relative privacy."

She thanked him for his thoughtfulness. The thought of climbing under clean sheets and a blanket and sleeping, even for a few hours, sounded like heaven. Alexei produced a notebook and pencil. "What size clothes do you wear, Ingrid?"

She thought of her fine velvet coat and her dress, now lost somewhere in a pile of prisoner clothing. She told him her size. He wrote it down. It meant she was somewhat permanent.

Alexei cleared his throat and dropped his voice. "Ingrid—if anyone—ah—*bothers* you, you will report it to me immediately." He raised his eyebrows to make sure she got the message.

She truly appreciated that. "Even the guards?" she whispered. The tall one had been watching her closely much of the day.

"Even the guards."

No mention of the officers. One in particular concerned her. A certain major.

*   *   *

By the end of the third week Ingrid was bent over one of a stack of British five-pound notes in the sorting room, touching up the eyes of Britannia with a fine-haired brush. She was getting good at it, if she did say so herself. She took a moment to admire the female warrior personifying Great Britain, holding a trident in one hand, an olive branch in the other, seated in front of a shield.

"Excellent work."

Startled, she turned in her chair, looked up. She had learned to phase out the constant noise of the presses and music and live in her own place.

It was Major Beckmann, smiling down. "The hardest part in forging British currency," he said, nodding at the fiver. "Britannia's eyes. It's almost as if Tommy knew what he was doing."

"Almost," she said. Secretly she wished Tommy every success. She took the fiver, put it on the "fixed" stack, picked another off the to-do pile.

"I see you've been well taken care of," Beckmann said, noting her new burgundy dress with long sleeves and frilly cuffs and collar. It went well with the black hose and lace-up Oxfords on her feet. She tried not to think of the poor woman who had given up the dress. She could smell a hint of her perfume on it. She just hoped she was still alive.

"Your hair is growing out," he said. She knew it looked quite dramatic short but she couldn't wait for her tresses to return, if she lived that long. It had become a goal.

"Will you finally be joining us onstage for music night this Saturday, Ingrid?" he said.

Music night was a competitive affair between the prisoners and uniforms on a "stage" of ammunition cases full of forged British currency in the recreation room. The world's most expensive stage, Alexei called it. Songs, jokes, impressions, snippets of acting; everyone tried to forget where they were for a few hours. "I'm told you might have something new for us, Major," she said, punching a tiny hole in Britannia's left eye with a pin to fill it out.

"I'm singing tenor in an American-style barbershop quartet," he said. "We're not too terrible, I might add. And what talents have you been hiding from us, Fräulein?"

If Major Beckmann was going to be taken with her, it would be to her advantage.

"You don't want to hear me sing, Major—not unless you want a repeat of Kristallnacht. My father said my singing could break glass."

"Ha!" He smiled as he lit up a cigarette. "But don't think you're getting out of it, Ingrid. You can't hide forever."

Couldn't she? "I can play piano."

He rubbed his chin. "One of the officers does have a Galanti."

"An accordion?" she said. "I know a few *chansonnettes* that might fit the bill."

"*Mais oui!* You shall bring a certain *je-ne-sais-quoi* to our little *soiree*."

She had let the flirtations drip carefully, slowly, like water on a dry plant. It was a dangerous game. She also had her fellow prisoners to watch out for. Right now she was little sister but that could change if she was seen as the major's pet.

But this wasn't some idle game. It was life and death. They were all assisting the Nazis in one way or another to save their own skins—even the poor souls in the brickworks starving to death.

She would just have to make hers worth saving. By saving someone else.

"With all due respect, Major, your French could really use a little polishing."

Beckmann nodded, took a drag of his cigarette, blew a smoke ring. "It's awful, I know it."

"You just need practice. We could chat, if you like. *On peut discuter en français, de temps en temps.*"

"*Mais bien sûr,*" he said.

She turned back, touched Britannia's left eye with the tip of the brush, filling in the tiny pinprick. She hummed a little tune. "But you are always so busy."

"Yes," Beckmann said. "Yes."

She stopped, looked up as if she had just thought of it. "I know—I could help you in the office now and then. We could practice while we work." The office was strictly SS and approved staff only. But there were always exceptions to any rule. And getting her foot in that door wouldn't hurt a bit.

"Can you type, Ingrid?"

"Type, shorthand—and the rest of it. I was essentially my father's secretary and editor."

"Standartenführer Kaindl is stealing Hilda from me," he said. But she already knew that from the gossip that circulated. Anton Kaindl was camp commandant. "My correspondence to Berlin must be kept up at the very highest level. Every communication must be flawless. Any grammatical slip, typographical error, late report, only shortens the distance between me and the Russian front. And that affects all of you too."

Ingrid worked on Britannia's right eye. "I never thought of it that way, Major."

"You have a keen eye for detail, Ingrid. Much better than Hilda, actually. You'd be very good in the office. Yes, very good."

Yes, she would be. She worked Britannia's eye.

"Whatever serves the Reich, Major," she said.

"Good answer." He raised a finger to accentuate his point. "You're glibness is well noted. You're learning. We'll make a Nazi out of you yet."

We'll see about that. But she beamed anyway.

"Can I possibly ask a small favor in return?" she asked.

He took a step closer. "I draw the line at a fur coat, Ingrid. My Jews would never stand for the favoritism."

She laughed brightly. "No such thing, Major."

He puffed. "Come on. Out with it."

"I'm curious about two prisoners I was brought in with."

"I see. And what are their names?"

"Jakob Klaus," she said. "A boy, six or so. And his mother—Sheila. I'm told she's on the shoe testing track." Eleven hours a day, with a twenty-kilo pack on your back, walking over stones and rough terrain in oversize boots, testing footwear for the troops. Shoe testers didn't last long.

"Jews, Ingrid." He shook his head sadly. "Are you sure you wouldn't rather have that fur coat instead? It'll be a damn sight easier." But Major Beckmann, for all his faults, was known to make an effort for those he took an interest in, unlike the rest of the goose steppers. He had two barracks full of Jews to prove it.

"I think Jakob's father actually has a baptismal certificate," she said, knowing he would never be able to verify as much. "Yet somehow— his family wound up here. It must have been a mistake." She turned, made eye contact. "Jakob was very sweet to me on the truck coming here. My father had just been shot. I was beside myself. He held my hand the whole way. A very brave little boy, thinking of others." Was she overdoing it? "Well, if there's anything you can do, Major . . ."

"Noted." Beckmann took a puff. "Let me look into it. Now, you get back to your Britannias, Ingrid. You're falling behind."

CHAPTER TWENTY-SEVEN

1979

Colleen watched the headlights in the rearview mirror. The black sedan had been following her down 19th Avenue since her meeting with Professor Fisher on top of the SF State Student Union. A couple of miles now.

She approached the crossover that cut through Golden Gate Park, up to the traffic light that had just turned from green to yellow. The sedan stayed half a dozen car lengths behind, a station wagon in between them. A professional tail. The car had tinted windows, obscuring the occupants. Law enforcement? Aryan Alliance?

The stoplight turned red and Colleen slowed with the rest of the traffic. Then she took a deep breath, shifted down, and gunned the Torino through the red light, cutting off a Pinto with a tinny horn, the little car squealing sideways into the intersection as she snaked around it and shot through. Past the intersection she turned off into the park, pulled over, flipped off her headlights. Her eyes were on the rearview mirror.

A minute later she saw the black sedan fly past on the crossover. It would take them some time to realize she was no longer on that route.

She wound her way back to 19th and Lincoln, parked in the back of the Peppermill, went inside the busy two-story bar restaurant, with its orange and yellow and earth colors represented both in the décor and the outfits of the waitresses. She used the payphone to call Professor Fisher.

"A car followed me," she said. "After our meeting. Black sedan. I think they're more interested in me than you but I wanted to let you know so you can keep your eyes peeled. I'll let someone at SFPD know too."

Professor Fisher took a breath. "I appreciate the warning. You be careful, too."

She cashed in some dollars for change and dialed the long distance operator and placed a call to the Hotel Campania in Rome. The desk clerk told her Signora Richter was at breakfast. Did she want to leave a message? Colleen said she would call back at a better time.

Ingrid was still in Rome. But for how long?

Even though it was close to midnight, she dropped a dime in the slot and called Owens at his motel on Lombard. She needed to know who might have been following her. She needed to find a way to Rome.

"What's up?" he said.

"We need to talk."

"I'm listening."

"I could use a drink," she said. As in, *not on the phone*. She was getting paranoid about the tail. Plus she had a request that would fare better face-to-face. It was time to push things.

"Okay," he said. "Got it."

Half an hour later they were sitting on the open side of the minibar in the Pierce Street Annex, one of the trio of the Bermuda Triangle bars that attracted the city's young and upwardly mobile. Around the top of the bar hung pencil sketches of various San Francisco celebrities. It was rumored that Joe Montana, a new hire with the 49ers, drank here. Despite the cool weather, the floor length windows were open to the street. The fresh air created an almost European atmosphere. Business was slow tonight.

"I saw Linda Ronstadt and the Stone Poneys here," Owens said, sipping a bourbon and water. He wore a faded black USF Dons sweatshirt, loose jeans, and beat-up white leather sneaks. Since his divorce he'd given up on the disco look. To Colleen, it was a definite improvement.

"That must have been a few years ago," Colleen said, drinking a glass of Chardonnay and smoking a Virginia Slim. With Pam temporarily at Alex's, she could indulge. "Linda Ronstadt is Governor Brown's main squeeze now. And a pretty big star in her own right."

"1968," Owens said. "I was still in uniform."

Colleen was in Denver Women's Correctional Facility at the time. A year into her sentence.

She told him about her meeting with Professor Fisher, and the black sedan.

"It wasn't us," Owens said, meaning Homicide. "I've yet to see a black SFPD unmarked. Did you get a plate?"

"No. I did have a run-in with Doris Pender last night, but she drove a black Mercedes. This car was American. So it wasn't her."

"That leaves the Feds." Owens took a drink, smacked his lips slightly.

"Not good."

"No," he said. "Not at all."

"Any news of Muni Jane Doe?"

Owens shook his head. "The coroner's office lifted some prints. Nothing. They've been handed off to the FBI. But it's always a crap shoot whether they'll share."

She swirled her wine as she smoked. "Isn't that par for the course?"

"Seems more so with this case. Matt is being especially tight-lipped."

As was she. She told Owens what she'd learned from Professor Fisher, about Ingrid's time in a concentration camp. She filled him in on Black Cross—*Czarny Krzyż*. "There's got to be a tie-in with that 1936 British five-pound banknote."

"It's tempting to try and make a connection. But sometimes it simply isn't there."

"It seems more than simple authentication between the two parties."

Owens frowned.

"What kind of resources does SFPD have as far as sending an investigator to Rome?" she asked casually.

"That's the FBI's wheelhouse."

"Doesn't have to be, though," she said. "Does it?"

"We may not know each other that well, but there are times I can read your mind," he said.

"That's because it's an open book."

He gave her a wry look. "You want the department to fund you going to Rome to look for Ingrid Richter."

"Why not? Ingrid Richter sicced Jane Doe on Jakob Klaus and after he killed her, he took off. Aryan Alliance has washed its hands of Ingrid so she's going to make sure he's taken care of. She went to Rome after him."

Owens nodded. "I buy it."

"You could bring me on as a CI."

"And then ask to send you to Rome?" He swirled his drink. "That would have to go up to the chief. And I don't have that kind of clout."

"You could, though. You've got a hell of a record."

"Matt is working the Lange case. The chief won't like stepping on that."

"But you're all getting cut out of the loop. The FBI is going to grab all the glory. I'm sure the chief won't like that either."

Owens set his drink down. "I'd have to do some fancy talking, with your history with the department." Owens picked up his drink again, swirled it. She could tell she had his interest. Finally. "Let me think on it."

"Well, don't take too long. Who knows how long Ingrid Richter is going to be at her hotel in Rome?"

He looked at his wristwatch. "I need to be getting back. Some of us have work in the morning."

"Do you still have that banknote?"

"I've actually got the murder book in my motel room." The murder book was the origin document for any homicide, containing much of the paper evidence and subsequent reports.

"Is that kosher?'

"You're going to lecture *me* on protocol?"

"Does it have both halves of that note?" she asked.

He nodded. "The half we found on Jane Doe and the other half when we cleaned out Jakob Klaus' hotel room."

"Well, are you going to invite me back to your motel room to check out your banknotes, sailor?"

Owens divulged a rare smile, finished his drink, left a tip.

*   *   *

"Look at this," Colleen said, holding up the two halves of the 1936 five-pound note as she sat at Owens' table in his motel room. She had removed them from the plastic inserts in the murder book. Together the whole banknote was much larger than any currency she had ever seen, about the size of a paperback. The white fiver was printed on one side only, customary in Britain at the time, with black ink on white linen rag paper. The print work was particularly intricate in one area, the upper left, with a graceful rendering of Britannia seated in front of her shield with a spear and olive branch, next to a serial number.

Owens held a long-neck Budweiser as he stood behind Colleen, looking over her shoulder.

"Five pounds was a chunk of money at that time," he said.

"About what the average Brit made in a week in 1940," she said. "Most of those guys never even saw one of these." Colleen held up the two halves. "Same serial number on both halves. But look." The left half was still in decent shape, the right tattered and beat up.

"One half was taken better care of."

Then she held up the right half, the one she had initially seen in Jakob Klaus' air vent. "The ink is slightly darker. Even though it's more weathered."

"We're talking a banknote over four decades old," Owens said. "Time and conditions have treated the two halves differently. And the note could have been torn in half forty years ago."

Colleen flicked the edge of the right half with her finger. It had a substantial feel and responded with a satisfying riffle. She did the left. Not quite the same. "It's as if the paper is different too."

Owens put his beer down, reached over, tested her theory. "You're right."

She held the two halves together. There was a very slight offset. "The tear doesn't quite line up."

"I agree," Owens said. "But the two halves were meant to be used as a coded interchange between two parties. Their only function perhaps."

"Two parties who ultimately had a disagreement that ended in one's death."

Beer in hand, Owens nodded.

"I'm no expert," Colleen said, holding up the left half again, Jane Doe's. "But is this one a fake?" She set them both down, turned in her chair to look up at Owens. "Jane Doe faked her greeting card? And Jakob Klaus noticed it? Knew she was a fake too?

Owens sipped his beer. "And then he stabbed her."

Colleen bent over the left-hand part of the banknote. "Look at this: a tiny hole in one of Britannia's eyes." She held the banknote up again for Owens to examine. "Like a small pinprick."

He squinted. "I see that."

"Can I borrow these?"

"I'm not really interested in losing my job just at the moment. I've got alimony payments."

Colleen pushed her chair back and stood up. "I'm going to run to the car, grab my Polaroid. Meanwhile, you think how you can talk the chief into getting me to Rome."

"Confidential informants aren't much better than stool pigeons. You sure you want that?"

She shrugged. "If it gets the job done. I can get away with stuff SFPD can't. I work cheap. As in *free*. I'm running out of money. Plus mostly I don't want to be wandering around Italy without a lifeline. I hear they don't even have the common courtesy to speak English over there."

"You know who's not going to like it in particular, don't you?" Owens said, raising his eyebrows. Owens knew about her relationship with Matt. And Matt keeping Owens—and her—at bay.

"Let me worry about him," she said.

CHAPTER TWENTY-EIGHT

The message light was blinking on Colleen's answering machine the next morning when she checked into her office on Pier 26. It was Owens.

"I'm at 850 when you get a moment," he said. "Stop by."

With any luck it was related to her travel request. She grabbed her coat and car keys. 850 Bryant, the Hall of Justice, was just over a mile away and she was there in minutes. The hardest part was finding a parking spot.

She met Owens in the marble lobby before the metal detectors. He was looking natty in his blue suit, carrying a file folder.

They stood to one side.

"I spoke to the chief."

"Sounds promising," she said, already working out how she was going to find Ingrid Richter once she got to Rome.

Owens continued: "Fortunately for you, the airlines deregulated last year. They're falling all over themselves to keep business. They've got this new gimmick: frequent flyer programs."

"Frequent flyer *what*?"

"Basically, you rack up free miles for being loyal. The department has a few hundred thousand miles socked away. The chief let me use a few. What I mean is, he's going to let *you* use a few."

"So do I fly with the baggage? Steerage? Are there goats involved?"

"A little better than that—hopefully," Owens said. "The chief doesn't want to lose this case to the Feds any more than I do. And with you as a CI, we have it both ways."

"I like it," she said. Never mind that it had been her idea to begin with.

Owens flipped open the folder, showing her a form while he produced a pen.

SFPD Confidential Informant Program.

"Sign this."

She did.

A receipt for an airline ticket, attached.

"And this."

She did.

She read the ticket.

"I'm flying to Rome *tonight*?" she said.

"You said there's a risk of Ingrid Richter moving on."

"I did," she said, examining the ticket. "I just called the Hotel Campania. But this ticket is a return. This Friday."

"The chief wants you on a short leash."

She'd have to find Ingrid in a few days. But this wasn't the time to look a gift horse in the mouth.

"I really appreciate this," she said.

Owens shut the folder, put his pen away. "Hopefully you find Ingrid Richter. Conditions: daily updates. Call me collect. Two: anything you find out in the course of your trip is to be communicated to myself or the chief. No one else," he said. "No one else."

"Understood," she said.

"Three: this is fact finding. No—I repeat—*no* physical intervention whatsoever. If you do run into something, we'll do what we can, but it will have to be through diplomatic channels. As I'm sure you're aware, SFPD doesn't have any jurisdiction in Italy. The department is responsible for nothing. So, to repeat, *limited contact*. Observe and report. Then come home."

She looked at her watch. "Guess I better go home and pack my toothbrush."

"There's just one more thing," Owens said. "Some people won't like this."

She looked at him. "Matt Dwight," she said. "I know."

"You can't tell him where you're going."

"He's going to find out eventually."

"*Eventually* is fine. But not until after this case is cracked."

Owens and Matt were competing. Okay. Matt might even throw a stick in Homicide's spokes if he thought he was going to be overtaken.

"Got it," she said.

"So what are you going to tell him, Colleen?"

"Are you prying into my personal life, Inspector?"

"Yes."

"I'll make something up," she said. "I'm female. We have a gift for that kind of thing."

"But there are other people most likely watching you, too." His eyes narrowed. "You know that, right?"

"Aryan Alliance."

He nodded. "So, again, all this is between you and me and the chief. Don't even tell your daughter." He cleared his throat, reached into his pocket, came out with an envelope. Handed it to her.

She opened it.

Two hundred dollars in crinkled tens and twenties.

She looked up. "Where did this come from?"

"Department money—off the books. It's not much, but it will help. Do you have any idea how much taxpayer money goes to snitches?"

"So now I'm really a snitch." She put the envelope away. "Thanks—I think. I'm sure you had to fight for that too."

Owens's face grew solemn. "Just don't let me down."

*　*　*

The sun was going down, the San Francisco sky that had been gray all day turning darker. Colleen checked the modest contents of her red vinyl flight bag, enough for a few days away, before zipping it up. She wore a navy track suit, ideal for sleeping on planes. Her third international trip. Her third for work. One of these days she'd take some time off to actually see the world. She stepped into her Pony Topstars and slipped on her black leather car coat, tucked her passport and airline ticket in her pocket for her red-eye to Rome in a few hours.

The doorbell rang. She hit the intercom.

"I wondered where the hell you'd gotten to," Matt said.

Matt. She didn't have time.

"Just on my way out, Matt," she said. "I'll catch you downstairs."

She grabbed her bag, headed out, double-locked the door, took the few flights down in a sprint. On the ground floor, on the other side of the old beveled glass door, Matt stood in his stylish plaid sport coat and big tie. His beige city Ford LTD was double-parked.

Outside he saw her flight bag.

"Looks like my impromptu idea to take you out to dinner is a bust," he said.

"On my way to spend a few days with Pam," Colleen said. "She's staying at Alex's. Half Moon Bay. It's safer there. Alex doesn't allow gunfights. Too much expensive art."

"I can relate. I hate bullet holes in my Rembrandts."

"Pam needs a break," Colleen said. "She's still shaky after the shoot-out."

"For someone who fended off a couple of punks with a shotgun, she does *shaky* pretty well," he said.

"Like mother, like daughter."

She didn't need Matt trying to find her.

"We're going to head up the coast for a couple of days," she said. "Mendocino."

"Crystal shops. Incense."

"Something like that."

"Got time for a quick drink?"

"Not really," she said. "I'm already late."

"What, you guys are leaving *tonight*?"

"Dinner with Alex and Pam tonight."

He sighed. "I'll have to meet this Alex sometime," he said. "Where does she live again?"

"I know when I'm being questioned by the police, dude. And I'm being questioned by the police."

"Sorry. Second nature. I just miss you."

"Yeah," she said. "Me too."

"I didn't like the way we left things last time."

"Me neither."

"I can be a horse's ass sometimes."

"I'm not going to argue with a realization you obviously worked very hard to come to grips with."

He smiled. "So, everything okay?"

"Sure," she said, checking her watch. "Why wouldn't it be?"

"I thought you might still be upset."

"With you?" she said. "No, you might be a dipshit at times, but I'm used to it."

"It's just that I know Owens had a pow-wow with the chief today."

Uh-oh. "I'm sure he does that all the time."

"A little bird told me you've been brought in as a CI."

"What little bird was that?" she said, starting to get annoyed.

"I can't say."

"Then don't even bring it up, Matt. You don't get to play it both ways."

"Okay." He put his hands up in submissiveness. "But you're still working with Owens?"

"All the time, on all sorts of things. And vice versa. And the CI thing—we figured we might as well make it official. It sure won't hurt my parole. And my request for a PI license. Gus likes it." Gus Pedersen, her lawyer.

"Yeah." Matt nodded. "I can see that."

She reached over, gave him a soft kiss on the lips. "Got to run. Be careful."

"You too," he said. "I mean it."

"Well, I hope so."

"That earring, Coll," he said. "I have no idea how it got there. Those two girls came in for a quick drink after a night on the town, and I called them a cab. End of story. We were all a little toasted but nothing more than that."

"It's 1979. Times have changed."

"Not with me, they haven't. I wouldn't do that to you."

He was being sweet. Was there any way to frame a moment? She gave him another kiss, which turned into a longer one. Which turned into steam.

She pulled back, heart beating, face flushed. They eyed each other hungrily. "You know, it occurs to me that we've never actually christened my place," she said. "Pam has always been around, cramping our style."

"That would be true."

She brushed his hair off his collar. "How fast can you come upstairs, remove your fashionable outfit, throw me on the waterbed, and ride the waves? Like you mean it? And then be on your way? I don't want any boring chitchat. I'm in a hurry."

"I think I can honor that request."

"No half measures, though. I have my needs."

"Wouldn't dream of it."

Fourteen minutes later, they were back out front, blushed and ruffled and breathing deeply. But feeling real well.

"We good now?" she said.

"Better than. Hurry back." Matt jiggled his keys, smiled, went to his car, got in, gave her a wave, drove off.

He still didn't quite seem to believe her. Well, why should he? She wasn't quite telling the truth. But she wasn't going to dwell on the thought that he might be tracking her. She would just have to stay one step ahead.

She jogged over to her Torino parked across the street, threw her flight bag onto the passenger seat, started up the car.

SFO, running late.

CHAPTER TWENTY-NINE

1979

The tires of the 747 skidded on the asphalt at Fiumicino Airport, waking Colleen with a jolt. She blinked herself into consciousness as misty runway lights rushed by in darkness, the jumbo jet bouncing toward the jetway. Three stops and one delay meant she had spent a day traveling and her internal clock was going backwards.

A slow trip through customs and passport control bombarded her with the sights and sounds of a new country, everything foreign and animated, which was followed by a tiny cab that whined like a hairdryer as it shot in and out of traffic that was likewise going at breakneck speed. If she hadn't been awake before, she was now.

Hotel Campania was located on Piazza Mattei, a small and intimate square in the heart of Rome, flanked by ancient buildings around a whimsical fountain with sculptures of boys tossing turtles into the water. You could walk through the piazza and almost miss it. Low key. What Ingrid Richter most likely wanted.

Colleen paid the driver and got out with her flight bag. Her navy tracksuit had taken her shape after hours in an airline seat.

She found a modest pension just off the piazza on a narrow side street, where she asked for a room facing the square. No such luck. But the Campania's entrance was visible from an angle if she leaned out the window and looked down the street to her right. Sylvia, the petite matronly woman who showed Colleen to her small room with its high ceiling, making it seem even smaller somehow, took Colleen's passport, told her they were still serving dinner. Colleen's Spanish was good enough to follow most of what was said.

She declined dinner, although the smells were tantalizing and the dining family style, everyone gathered around a big table in a rustic dining room. She needed to check whether Ingrid was still at Hotel Campania. It was getting late.

Even so, she grabbed a five-minute shower in the shared bathroom to wash away the flight grime and wake herself up, quickly changed into jeans, a light V-neck sweater, and ankle boots. She tucked her hair up under her black floppy hat and headed down to the piazza wearing her leather coat and a pair of very light tinted sunglasses. Change the eyes, change the look. Almost no traffic passed through the baseball-diamond-sized square. The whir of a Vespa echoed off stone buildings and cobblestones. It felt good to stretch after hours confined to an airplane seat. The ground was still warm under her feet, but evening was cooling things off.

She strolled over to the Campania where a small, warmly lit lobby dating back centuries sat empty. An embroidered love seat and two armchairs were placed around a fireplace. Cozy, not a place where one could lurk without being noticed. To avoid raising suspicion, Colleen held off asking for Ingrid Richter at the front desk. The desk clerk, in black vest and white shirt, asked her a question in Italian and she merely said "caffè." He told her the restaurant was closed and pointed to an outdoor café across the square. She thanked him and made her way over. The late evening air was pleasant.

She noticed a car idling on the other side of the square. Two figures. Colleen's antennae rose.

As she passed by the fountain, the car started up, a boxy black Alfa Romeo Giulia. It drifted by. A woman was hunched over the steering wheel, a man next to her in the passenger seat. Colleen's nerves prickled as she felt them eyeing her. The woman had long dark curly hair. The man was slender and wore a light-colored jacket. They passed, slowing down in front of the Campania, which had dimmed its lobby lights. The Alfa hovered a moment, then came shooting back, and pulled over in front of the café, engine whining. Watching her.

Then the car exited the square.

What was all that about?

A few minutes later, Colleen was sipping an espresso and leafing through an unintelligible Italian newspaper at La Tazza café on the opposite end of the piazza where she had a clear view of the Campania beyond the fountain. The waiter was a good-looking guy named Marco, with sleepy eyes and tousled hair, who helped her with a word or two of Italian.

By the time Marco was turning off lights and dragging chairs and tables under the awning, two persons had returned to Hotel Campania, neither of them Ingrid Richter. Colleen was the last customer. She hoped Ingrid Richter was still around. She left a nice tip, said *buonanòtte*, headed back to her pension.

As she passed by the fountain again, she heard a car reverberating into the square from the other side. It sounded like the Alfa. She turned to take the side street back up to her pension and saw it was indeed the Alfa returning. Colleen's nerves jangled. Doris Pender said Aryan Alliance was done with Ingrid Richter. But the police were always a possibility.

The car circled the square and slowly took off again.

In her centuries-old pension building, Colleen tiptoed to her room.

She had two days to make contact with Ingrid Richter.

* * *

Early the next morning, the piazza was busy as Colleen sipped a morning cappuccino. She wore her jeans, and had opted for a light blouse as it promised to be a warm day. Her floppy hat was low over her brow, along with her light shades. She was feeling more settled in the time zone as the sun reached over the rooftops and slanted down into the square. The fountain splashed. She had her camera on a strap.

An hour passed. She was halfway through a paperback, watching everyone that came and went. Nothing. But there had been that Alfa last night.

"Qualcos'altro?" the waiter asked.

She ordered orange juice in Spanish with an apologetic smile at her limited Italian and he told her: *succo d'arancia*. Then he went off singing, metal tray slapping against the side of his leg just as she noticed a familiar figure exit Hotel Campania.

Ingrid Richter in a mid-length gray traveling skirt, pale blue windbreaker, sensible walking shoes. A brown bag over her shoulder. Sunglasses on top of her head. She *was* here. A bolt of reassurance made Colleen sit up. She left money anchored down by her coffee cup and got up and followed.

She trailed Ingrid Richter at a distance to the center of Rome, getting glimpses of places she'd seen pictures of. It felt surreal to be walking through the Piazza Navona, past its elegant fountain, and sidewalk cafés populated with the well-heeled lingering over coffee. It was the closest thing she had had to a vacation since she'd been a girl. She stopped to take a photo, play the tourist strolling through Rome in case she was being watched.

Ingrid Richter crossed the river on the Ponte Sant'Angelo and headed towards the Vatican. Colleen stayed well behind, tailing Ingrid Richter into St. Peter's Square, bowled over by the sheer size of the plaza, the grand colonnades on either side, the basilica, everything more majestic than any picture could do justice. But Ingrid wasn't taking photos, consulting a guidebook, or a map. She seemed to be heading somewhere with determination.

Behind the basilica, Ingrid entered another picturesque square, of which there seemed to be no shortage. This one had an administrative feel to it with its stately official buildings on three sides. Office workers came and went. Vatican gendarmes in blue caps and shirtsleeves were posted here and there.

Ingrid entered an 18th-century office building as Colleen snapped a photo of St. Martha's Square. If nothing else, she could at least show Owens her vacation shots.

She followed Ingrid into the building. Marble floors reflected ambient sunlight. She was in some sort of legislative or judiciary building judging by the directory near the front doors.

She didn't see Ingrid Richter downstairs.

Colleen ventured up a marble stairwell to the second floor.

On the second floor there were echoes of doors being opened and closed, low conversations, but mostly silence in the long hallway of offices. She cursed under her breath. To have followed Ingrid all this way and then lose her.

Colleen wandered down the tall hallway, pretending to admire the paintings of various dignitaries and the baroque ceiling murals. Italian architects and artisans certainly earned their money.

She heard voices at an open door as she strolled past. A secretary in a black-and-white diagonal striped summer dress sat at a typewriter, giving it a workout. In between rapid key punches, Colleen overheard two people speaking Italian in a side room.

One of the voices was female, speaking with a German accent. Ingrid Richter.

Colleen stopped, out of view, examined the plaque to the side of the door. Loosely translated, the office belonged to a Judge P. Pibiri, Vatican City Legal Counsel.

She tried to eavesdrop on the conversation between Ingrid Richter and who she assumed was Judge Pibiri, wishing the secretary would hold up on the machine-gun typing.

But she did catch a phrase in the midst of it: *lui è qui. He's here.*

There was a pause afterwards and the man whom she assumed was Judge Pibiri asked Ingrid a question with a gravity to his voice.

Sei sicuro? Similar to the Spanish for "Are you sure?"

Yes, Ingrid was sure.

Dove? he asked. Spanish for "where" was "donde."

Ingrid replied, a phrase that sounded Germanic but the rat-a-tat typing and high ceilings obliterated it, along with the remainder of the conversation. But whatever was going on in there had a portent tone. They appeared to be making arrangements.

Then with a start, Colleen heard chairs shift. The two wished each other a good day.

Colleen spun, headed down the hall where she'd spotted a woman's room sign earlier. She ducked in, waited, ready to hide in a stall if Ingrid Richter's footsteps ventured this way.

They didn't. Ingrid's heels marched in the opposite direction, then clipped down the marble stairs.

Follow or stay? Colleen could always pick up Ingrid Richter later at her hotel. She opted for staying.

When the coast was clear she left the restroom, scanned nearby doors. Toward the far end, by the opposite stairwell, she found "*Custode.*" Janitor.

It was. In a dark janitorial closet, Colleen stashed her camera, sunglasses, and hat on a shelf behind some cleaning supplies, rolled up the sleeves of her blouse, and donned a blue apron. She pulled her hair back into a ponytail with a rubber band she found on the cart. There was a cleaning cart with supplies and plastic trash bag in a wire rim, partially full. She pushed the cart out into the hallway. Footsteps approached.

A shortish round man with a face to match walked toward her in a black robe with fancy gold-braided epaulettes. He had a light gray beard, neatly trimmed, and files under one arm and appeared to be in a hurry. Despite Colleen's janitorial getup, he gave her a polite nod and wished her a pleasant day.

She muttered *buongiorno*, keeping her head down. Behind her, his quick steps descended the staircase.

Colleen stuck her head into Judge Pibiri's office. Ms. Efficiency's fingers were a blur. She shot Colleen a quick smile without stopping.

Colleen wheeled in the cart. The secretary stopped typing, shifted back in the roller chair, waited with a patient smile while Colleen emptied her wastepaper basket into the plastic trash bag in the cart's holder. For added panache, Colleen got out a feather duster. The secretary motioned that that wasn't necessary and went back to her typing. Colleen pushed her cart over to the office.

In Judge Pibiri's office she emptied the ashtray and the wastepaper basket, which was full. She wiped the ashtray clean while she scanned the desk, blotter, calendar, notepad, and learned that Judge Pibiri was either extremely neat or didn't get much done. He didn't seem to write anything down.

The typing stopped. The secretary was calling her. Colleen's heart jumped.

Head down again, she guided the cart out into the outer office.

The secretary asked her a question she didn't understand. She responded with a polite *si* and pushed the cart out into the hallway. And picked up speed towards the janitorial closet.

Colleen wheeled the cart into the closet, ripped off the apron, grabbed her stuff, donned her shades, grabbed the plastic bag of recently acquired trash, left.

The secretary was standing by the door of Judge Pibiri's office, looking at her curiously.

"Cosa è successo al custode regolare?"

Something along the lines of: *Where is the regular janitor?* Damn. Colleen ignored her, walked calmly down the far stairs by the janitorial closet, bag of trash in hand, keeping it upright to hopefully preserve the order.

Back at her pension, Colleen grabbed a towel, laid it out on the floor, sat down cross-legged, and went through the trash piece by piece. Everything was dusted with cigarette ash, but she had emptied the judge's ashtray first so the recent contents of the wastepaper basket were on top and less so. That was a good separation point.

An empty cigarette box. A copy of a legal magazine.

Where the cigarette butts began she found a crumpled scrap of paper with the word "Lindenhof," followed by a date, which was today, and a phone number. Was Lindenhof the German-sounding word she'd overhead before Ingrid's conversation had been cut off by speedy fingers? Colleen bet it was. The note would have been on top of Judge Pibiri's trash, the last thing he'd tossed away before he left his office.

Sylvia, the signora who ran the pension, let Colleen use the phone for a charge, telling Colleen the number was in northern Italy and hence long distance.

A clerk answered at the Hotel Castello di Lindenhof.

Colleen asked if he spoke English. He did. She enquired about vacancies. He said they were closed for the season. But that was the address Ingrid Richter had given. She could well be headed there.

Colleen called the long-distance operator and placed a call to her answering machine in her office on Pier 26 in San Francisco, punched in the two-digit code to interrupt her canned greeting and go to any messages. Modern technology.

There was a message from Professor Fisher at SF State. The Zeykher Project.

"Just to let you know, I've found something on that woman you brought to my attention—the one with the tattoo on her left forearm? Jasia Salak. She was a Polish kapo—a prisoner guard recruited by the SS—moved to Sachsenhausen from Auschwitz. She is—*was*— wanted for war crimes. Quite a few kapos were hung after the war by the Russians when the camps were liberated. She, however, escaped somehow. She has—*had*—a brutal reputation."

Colleen pondered that. An ex-kapo, a minor war criminal, aligned with the Nazis. Recruited to kill Jakob Klaus? By Ingrid Richter. But Jakob got the jump on Jasia Salak, killed her first.

Colleen hung up. Three in the morning in San Francisco, too early to call Owens and give him an update. She wanted to call Alex, too, check in on Pam, but again, too early.

She went back down the hall to her room, tucked Judge Pibiri's note in the pages of her paperback on the nightstand, gathered the rest of the trash she had fished through, put it back in the bag, knotted it, set it next to her wastepaper basket. She changed into the one good outfit she'd brought along, a blue polyester pantsuit.

On the way out she told Sylvia she'd like to stay until the end of the week if that was possible. It was. She noticed that the newspapers had arrived and were splayed out on the miniscule reception table.

Today's copy of *La Repubblica* caught her eye. A grisly picture of a priest, dead, robes splayed, his head in the bushes behind a church.

Prete Trovato Assassinato. "Priest Found Murdered." She picked up the paper, stumbled through the article. A village north of Rome. A beloved local priest, his throat cut after morning Mass. There was a photo the police had found stuffed down his throat, half-chewed, of him posing with Nazi officers in 1940s Germany as a young man. A shadowy Vatican connection was implied.

"*Terribile!*" Signora Sylvia said when she saw Colleen reading. She was dusting and straightening up cushions.

All Colleen could think was that the murder bore a very familiar pattern—one Jakob Klaus and Black Cross seemed to favor. And Ingrid was in Rome. On Jakob's trail again, hunting him down as he plied his dark trade. Colleen had no clue who the priest was, but surely he didn't deserve to die in such a brutal, lawless manner. No one did.

Out in the Piazza Mattei the day was warm, reflecting off the cobblestones. She headed over to Hotel Campania. A lean, good-looking man in his forties in a light suit with a sweep of dark hair and a pencil mustache stopped her. Her nerves buzzed as she recognized him. He'd been the passenger in the black Alfa Romeo trolling the square last night.

He spoke in accented English. "May I have a word with you, please, Signora?" He flashed a badge in a brown leather holder and put it away. She caught *Guardia di Finanza*.

The police. She took a deep breath. "Do I have a choice?"

"This will only take a moment." He gestured politely across the square. "Please."

The Alfa sedan was parked in front of the café. At his signal it fired up and came darting around the fountain. At the wheel was the same dark woman with her long frizzy hair tied back. She wore wrap-around sunglasses and a blousy floral top unbuttoned for the heat of the day. Her beat-up leather jacket hung over the back of her seat.

She hopped out, promptly flipped Colleen around against the car, and slapped a pair of handcuffs on her.

"I demand to call the U.S. embassy," Colleen said, staying cool. This could escalate into the wrong thing very quickly.

The woman didn't appear to speak English.

Colleen repeated the same in Spanish. The woman turned Colleen around and gave her an *I'm sorry* shrug.

"Please," the male cop said, opening the rear door of the car for Colleen. "Just a few questions." She had to scoot over an empty child's sippy cup and a stuffed pink dolphin to sit in the back seat. She sat back uncomfortably against the cuffs, and the man shut the door, got in front, and they took off like a shot, barreling down the narrow cobblestone street past her pension.

"Where are you staying, Miss?" he asked. The woman was watching her in the rearview mirror with a smirk.

"Pension Sylvia," she said. "You just passed it."

The man instructed the woman to back up. She hit the brakes with a squeal, threw the small sedan into reverse, juddered back up to the pension, dispersing an old woman with a string bag of vegetables up against a wall. The old woman gave them an earful, and the female cop snapped an apology out the window that didn't sound very apologetic.

At the door to her pension, the policeman asked Colleen: "Your name, Miss?"

Colleen told him.

He gave another instruction to the woman at the wheel, calling her *Pimpi*.

Pimpi huffed, got out, slammed the car door, and marched up to the tall old double doors of Colleen's pension, a pistol bouncing on her round hip. Her snug faded black jeans accentuated a butt she was obviously not ashamed of.

"Am I under arrest?" Colleen asked the policeman in the front seat.

"A few questions, Signora," he said again in a soft tone. It was as if he were a maître d' in a busy restaurant and there might be a short wait for her table.

"What is this about?"

"All in good time, Signora."

Time she didn't have.

She asked for his name. He had displayed his ID so quickly she hadn't caught it. He retrieved it from his breast pocket now, turned in his seat, showed her.

Ispettore Superiore Ugo Toscano. Repubblica Italiana. It all looked legit.

"And who is she?" Colleen asked.

"My associate is Agent Albini," he said.

Agent Albini returned, got in the car, tossed Colleen's U.S. passport at Inspector Toscano, slammed the car into gear, took off with a jolt.

Colleen was going in for questioning. And now they had her passport. Not in the plan.

*   *   *

After the nice American woman who left big tips got picked up by the police in the piazza and handcuffed, then put into the back of the Alfa, Marco, the waiter at La Tazza, went into the café, dialed the number he was told to call.

"That woman you wanted to know about," he said, "just got taken away by the two *sbirri* watching Hotel Campania."

"Where did they take her?" the man said. He had a gruff voice, working class.

"How do I know? You wanted to know if anything unusual happened. I'm telling you something unusual happened."

"Don't get smart, Marco. Or that cushy little job of yours can go to someone more agreeable. While you're walking on crutches."

Marco fought a shiver. *Terza Posizione* were crazy people, not to be messed with. "Understood," he said. "I have to get back to work now."

"Not just yet," the man said. "The Americana who got picked up—she's staying at Pension Sylvia?"

Marco hated ratting out his customers. But what choice did he have? "Yes."

"You just make sure you keep me up to date if you see her again. Or those pigs. You got that?"

He got it, unfortunately.

*　　*　　*

A breakneck ride involving knife-sharp turns through central Rome, shooting by the Trevi fountain at one point, ended at an imposing four-story stone-fronted building that resembled a museum with bars on the windows. Carabinieri stood guard at the drive-through entrance. The building took up a block and looked like a suitable place to be sentenced prior to being burnt at the stake. 850 Bryant paled in comparison.

Pimpi squeezed the Alfa into a large central courtyard packed with Polizia vehicles and motorcycles. Colleen was instructed to get out, awkward with her hands cuffed behind her back.

"Please, Signora," Toscano said again, waving Colleen into the building as if she were a guest. Cops were coming and going along with the usual crew of hard-faced individuals connected to law enforcement and those unfortunate enough to be there otherwise.

She was taken to an interrogation room that might have last been painted sometime between the world wars. The green and beige colors had an appropriate Tuscan flaking, covered by decades of graffiti. The smell of damp lingered.

Pimpi removed Colleen's cuffs, and left the room. Toscano pulled out a seat for Colleen and sat down across from her. He crossed his legs, flipping through her passport. Midday, his five o'clock shadow was already darkening his lean cheekbones.

"Why are you interested in Signora Richter?" He pronounced Ingrid's last name *Reek*ter. "Last night you were watching her hotel. Today you followed her."

They were looking for Ingrid Richter as well. "It's a long story."

"We have plenty of time," he said, breaking out a pack of cigarettes. He offered her one. She declined. He lit one up and took a luxurious drag, blew smoke. "Please."

She told him her visit was related to a murder investigation in San Francisco. Ex-Nazis, as much as she could withhold revealing Ingrid Richter's supposed destination—Lindenhof. She mentioned the murdered priest in Anguillara, the village north of Rome, and how she believed the killer might be Jakob Klaus, and how Ingrid Richter was on his tail.

When she was done, Toscano looked at her in apparent surprise.

"That *is* quite a story," he said.

"I'm a confidential informant." She gave him Owens's contact information. "I'm here on behalf of the San Francisco Police—unofficially."

"And why is San Francisco Police sending an unauthorized informant to Rome for this business? Surely that is the function of your federal police? Once they have been cleared to do so, that is."

"Another long story," she said. "But I notice you're also looking for Ingrid Richter."

Toscano blew a plume of smoke, didn't answer.

Colleen said, "I'm assuming 'Guardia di Finanza' is responsible for dealing with financial crime? And that's why you're interested in her?"

More smoke. "You will understand if I don't answer your question?"

She said she did.

"Senora Richter has checked out of her hotel," he said.

"I'm not surprised."

"Really? Do you know where she is going?"

"I do. And why."

"And where is that?"

"Give me back my passport, let me out of here, and I'll be happy to tell you," she said with a smile.

"Withholding information from the police is a serious offense in Italy, Signora Hayes—as is interfering with an investigation—unofficially or not."

"You need to talk to Inspector Owens, SFPD Homicide."

"So, this Inspector Owens has the authority to disperse confidential agents all over the globe without any notification? So much power the American police have! Unfortunately that power does not translate into the same power here."

She gave him Owens' number at his motel, explaining that he would be waking him up.

"We can wait," he said. "You in a cell. Until you tell us what you know. Pending deportation."

Colleen took a deep breath. "You're after Ingrid Richter for some financial matter," she said. "But if you could get her for a connection to a murder in San Francisco, and possibly another one here, surely that would strengthen your case, wouldn't it? It would be a feather in your cap."

He squinted in confusion. "A *what*?"

"A good thing—for both you and SFPD."

Toscano stood up, slipping her passport back into his breast pocket. "I will verify your—ah—assignment with this San Francisco Police Inspector Owens."

"He'll vouch for me." He'll be pissed, too, Colleen thought.

He left her in the interrogation room but locked the door.

Not long after, Pimpi returned, got Colleen.

"Come!"

Colleen was led by the arm down a hallway echoing with multiple conversations as they entered a bullpen office full of detectives, many on the phone speaking rapidly. Colleen was shown into a cluttered office where Toscano was on the phone. His jacket off, he sat amidst a pile of documents, a green-and-white bar computer printout open on his desk, of what appeared to be financial data. He stood up, handed Colleen the receiver. Pimpi stood by, one hand on her hip, studying the long red fingernails of the other.

Colleen put the receiver to her ear.

"What the hell is going on?" Owens said.

"I'm somewhere between being arrested and deported," she said. "The good news is that I'm not in handcuffs anymore."

"You were supposed to keep this low key, Colleen. This Toscano says you're withholding information."

"I found Ingrid," she said. "It's a strong lead, one we can't miss." She told him about Ingrid Richter meeting Judge Pibiri, not mentioning the Hotel Castello di Lindenhof by name in front of Toscano. She told Owens about the murder of the priest north of Rome. "It's got to be Jakob Klaus. And Ingrid is after him again."

There was a pause while the click of long distance broke the silence intermittently. "You absolutely sure about this?"

"Ingrid's a Person of Interest with the treasury cops here, too, which makes her even more suspicious. Ask him if I can tag along," Colleen said quietly into the phone. "We need to be part of this." Then she raised her voice, smiling at Toscano—"Inspector Toscano has been very professional *and* courteous. I think you'd be impressed with the way they do things over here."

Toscano gave her a polite nod.

"I'll give it a shot," Owens said. "But if they don't go for it, just give them what you've got or they'll charge you. And I won't be able to do anything about that. Now put Inspector Toscano back on the phone."

She handed the phone back to Toscano.

Toscano spoke with Owens. Hung up.

"Well?" he asked Colleen. "Where is Signora Richter?"

"Hotel Castello di Lindenhof," she said. She told him about the meeting with Judge Pibiri, and the note she had found.

"Northern Italy," Toscano said, nodding. "Near the Austrian border. It makes some sense. That place has a history."

"It does?"

He spoke with Agent Albini in Italian. Colleen detected the words *ex-nazista* and *contraffazione*. They had a discussion that appeared to revolve around how long it would take to get to northern Italy. Toscano stared through the glass wall of his office for a moment in thought. Then he stood up, put on his suit jacket, buttoned it, left the office. Agent Albini kept an eye on Colleen, used Toscano's phone to call home and ask about her *bambino*.

Toscano returned about ten minutes later, undid his jacket. Colleen assumed he had been to speak with a superior.

"What is the status of my passport, please?" Colleen asked. She had a leery feeling they were going to hold her until they detained Ingrid Richter.

"You can identify this Jakob Klaus?" Toscano asked.

"Absolutely," she said.

"Then you are coming with us," Toscano said. "But if this is a waste of time, you *will* be placed under arrest for giving false evidence."

"Any chance we can swing by my pension and pick up my bag?"

"Ha," Toscano said.

No change of clothes, no toothbrush. But not a problem. Colleen was still in the game. One way or another she was going to track down Ingrid Richter.

CHAPTER THIRTY

1979

The black Alfa Romeo hurtled out of Rome on the ring road where it met the *Autostrada del Sole*, then proceeded to barrel up north. Around Orvieto, large raindrops hit the windshield in blotches, becoming a torrent that threatened the frantic little wipers. Roads became greasy but did not lighten Agent Albini's lead foot in the slightest. Toscano, in the front passenger seat, did not seem bothered either. Meanwhile Colleen clutched the grab handle in the back.

The town of Lindenhof in the South Tyrol province of Italy was normally a seven-hour drive from Rome, but Colleen knew that Agent Albini—Pimpi—would improve on that considerably, despite the weather. That meant they should reach Lindenhof late tonight.

*   *   *

At Pension Sylvia in Rome, a matte-black Ducati GTS motorcycle pulled up by the old double front door with the small inner door. Two men were aboard the bike, both clad in black leather and motorcycle helmets. The tiny street reverberated with the noise of the powerful 900 cc engine.

The driver shut it off and there was comparative silence.

The man on the back dismounted and pulled off his helmet. He was in his thirties, grizzled, with short dark receding hair, and a sneer to prepare him for the task at hand.

Early evening, the inner front door to the building was already locked.

The rider rang the bell for Pension Sylvia.

The intercom crackled. "*Sì?*"

He asked for a room.

The signora told him they were full.

"Ai," he said. "I should have known better than to come to Roma so late without a reservation. Do you know of any other places nearby that might possibly have an inexpensive room, Signora?"

She told him she did not, but that there was always the youth hostel.

"A good idea, Signora. Thank you. I wonder if I might leave my rucksack here for the night. You know those hostels. I'm happy to pay the storage fee. I can pick it up tomorrow."

She said that would be fine.

The door unlocked. He pushed it, turned to the driver.

"Be ready to leave."

The driver, a tall lean man in a cracked helmet, nodded.

Upstairs at the door to the pension, the rider slipped his helmet back on and gave a light rap on the door, pulling a Beretta 92S from his shoulder holster.

Inside, Sylvia wiped her hands on a dishtowel, unlatched the door.

There was a man in black, wearing a motorcycle helmet, pointing a pistol at her.

She jumped as a heart valve twisted.

"No noise, please, Signora," he said quietly, putting a finger up to the mouth guard of his helmet. He came into the hall guiding her gently with the gun.

Hyperventilating, she said: "I'll get the cash. It's not much. Please don't harm the guests."

"I don't want to rob anyone, Signora, least of all you." He shut the door quietly behind him.

She blinked in confusion, her chest hammering. "What *do* you want, then?"

"The Americana? Colleen Hayes? She's a guest here?"

"She hasn't returned yet."

He nodded. "Show me her room, please."

Sylvia pointed down the hall.

"Is that the dining room?" He nodded at the room along the hallway, on the way to Colleen's room.

She said that it was.

He gestured with the pistol. "Shut the door to the dining room, please, Signora. We don't want to disturb your guests."

"No." Shaking, Sylvia took a key off the wall by the tiny front desk, led him back past the dining room where she pulled the door shut on laughter and lively conversation.

She led the man with the gun to a room, unlocked the door with trembling fingers.

The man motioned her into the small room with his gun, flipping on the light.

"Stand over there, Signora. Please stop shaking. I won't harm you." He signaled her into the corner of the room. "I will soon be out of your way."

She saw the tattoo on the back of his hand as he motioned with the gun: a fist gripping a hammer over a Z on its side, half of a zigzag swastika. *Terza Posizione:* Third Position. A fascist organization that had killed several in the last few years. They had been on the news.

She shook even more.

"I implore you, Signora," he said, "please don't be afraid. When do you expect the Americana to return?"

"I don't know," Sylvia said in deep breaths. "I don't know."

"Did she come in at all tonight? Say where she might be going?"

"I haven't seen her since this afternoon." Then, "She's a nice woman. She's just a tourist."

"Of course." He moved around the room, gun up. "Please don't move." He rummaged through the red flight bag on the straight-back chair. He pulled the small drawer open on the nightstand. Some pamphlets on tours of Rome the pension provided. He looked under the mattress.

"Where is her passport, Signora? Do you have it at reception?"

"The *Polizia* came and took it this afternoon."

The man nodded. "*Bene.*" He noticed the big bag of trash by the wastepaper basket. "So much trash." He spotted the paperback book on the nightstand. He picked it up, shook it.

A slip of uncrumpled paper escaped from the pages, fluttered to the floor.

He picked up the scrap of paper.

Lindenhof. Today's date. A phone number in northern Italy.

An interesting bookmark.

He slipped the paper in his pocket.

"We're finished here, Signora," he said. "I am sorry if I alarmed you in any way. I leave you to your guests now. Your cooking smells delicious by the way. You can show me out. Oh, and no mention of this visit to anyone, of course. Not the Americana. Or your guests. And especially not to the police."

"No," she said, still shaking. "No."

They left the room. The man led Sylvia up to the front door, past the dining room where people were laughing at some story a guest was telling.

*   *   *

Shortly after, the Ducati pulled over by the Teatro Marcello. The rider climbed off again, removed his helmet, used the payphone in a bar, dumping in change to call the long distance number on the wrinkled paper in his hand.

Finally, a man answered: "Castello di Lindenhof."

So it was the Lindenhof. He hung up, called the other American woman, this one staying across town: Doris Pender. He had trouble with the names. *Doris Pender. Colleen Hayes.* None of them rolled off the tongue.

"Yes?" Doris Pender said in English when she answered, not even bothering with an attempt at the language.

He explained who he was in English.

"What have you got for me?" she said.

"Castello di Lindenhof," he said. "That is where Ingrid Richter is most likely headed." *Ingrid Richter*—another mouthful. "And Colleen Hayes."

"'Most likely'?" Doris Pender said.

He said it was *very* likely based on the address he found in Colleen Hayes' pension.

"Did that note say anything about Jakob Klaus?"

"No. But . . ."

"What is Lindenhof?"

"Castello di Lindenhof. It's a hotel in the Alps—northern Italy."

There was a pause.

"Get your amigos ready," she said. "We're heading up there now."

Amigos. He shook his head. Americans.

*   *   *

Windshield wipers did double duty outside of Arezzo as the wind buffeted the boxy Alfa into another lane. Agent Albini jerked the car back into position, stepped on the gas.

Colleen asked Toscano why the Guardia di Finanza was interested in Ingrid Richter.

"First Trust Bank of Zurich is involved in money laundering," Toscano said from the front seat. Taillights smeared by as Agent Albini passed everything in sight. "But the executives rarely come to Italy, our jurisdiction. So this is our chance."

"Is Ingrid Richter suspected of laundering?"

"We know Signora Richter is connected. And she has a history that goes back to the Second World War."

"And the Nazis."

He turned in his seat. "How much do you know about Signora Richter?"

"I know she was a prisoner in Sachsenhausen concentration camp as a teenager. Her father was shot by the Nazis and she was arrested."

"Then you are more informed than most."

"Unfortunately," Colleen said, "my information stops at Barracks 19. Some special project the Nazis kept secret."

Toscano nodded as the car skipped over a pool of water in the middle of the freeway that made Colleen's heart skip all by itself.

"Barracks 19 was the heart of Operation Bernhard," he said.

"Operation Bernhard?"

"The Nazi counterfeiting effort intended to ruin the British economy. Ingrid Richter was one of the early team members recruited and the only woman. The Nazis assembled a crack team of counterfeiters from camps and prisons all over the Reich. The prisoners were given special treatment: civilian clothes, extra rations, cigarettes. The major in charge of the operation provided them with proper beds, a recreation room, newspapers, a radio." Toscano shrugged. "All in the middle of a concentration camp surrounded by death."

"What became of the prisoners?"

"They were supposed to be executed. But a fluke allowed most of them to live. Most are gone by now. But Signora Richter—it's rumored she became the—*ah*—*padrona* of the major."

Padrona. Mistress.

"She *was* a teenager," Colleen said. "In fear of her life, I suspect."

Toscano shrugged again as the car shot around a truck. "That doesn't make her any less of a criminal."

"And Castello di Lindenhof?"

"The plan to dump counterfeit currency over Great Britain was abandoned by the Reich," Toscano said. "But the forgeries were used to fund operations for the Nazis. They paid off spies, and financed all manner of projects. The German mark was worthless on the international market during the war and the British pound was the world's settlement currency. There were more pounds in circulation outside of the UK than inside the country. It was the prefect ruse. Needless to say, many people got rich too. It's rumored that the major and his *assistant* Ingrid left Sachsenhausen, took over the currency distribution for the Reich, from their new base at Castello di Lindenhof. They had the top floor. A commission was made on every single pound that went through the major's hands. We are talking about millions."

"What does a judge at the Vatican have to do with all of this? Where Ingrid Richter got the address?"

"The Vatican has a long history of supporting the Nazis. They backed the Reich and provided many escape routes towards the end of the war, when war criminals were fleeing Germany. *Ratlines.* Rome was a center for their operations. Former Nazis were given new identities and papers—often Red Cross passports—and funds to begin a new life elsewhere—frequently South America. It's no surprise that this Judge Pibiri might be connected."

As they passed cars that seemed to be standing still, Colleen recalled the Gestapo ID she had seen in Jakob Klaus's air vent in the Hotel Metro in San Francisco.

"That major," she said. "In charge of Operation Bernhard—was his name Werner Beckmann, by any chance?"

Toscano nodded from the front seat. "Very few people know that."

"He died in a fire," Colleen said. "After the war. In Rome. 1945."

"I'm sure he was planning his escape at the time," Toscano said. "His millions were never found."

Colleen reflected on a teenage girl who might have leveraged a Nazi major and millions of counterfeit pounds to her advantage. Was she an opportunist? Or simply a survivor?

And if Werner Beckmann was already dead, why had he been on Jakob's kill list?

CHAPTER THIRTY-ONE

"Why do I have to leave the castle, Auntie Ingrid?" Jakob said.

Ingrid saw her seven-year-old "nephew" look down at the fine Persian rug of their suite on the top floor of Castello di Lindenhof. No expense had been spared when Werner and Ingrid came here, bringing Jakob as part of the bargain. Paintings "liberated" by the Reich adorned the walls. Her very own Matisse, museum quality, hung in her bedroom.

"Because you're going to school," Ingrid said. "A proper school. One of the best in Europe."

With sadness pulling at her, Ingrid crouched and straightened the collar of Jakob's Stachus jacket. The handmade horn buttons contrasted the fine forest green wool, complementing his lederhosen shorts, green knee socks, polished shoes. She popped his Tyrolian hat on his head and set it at a tilt. "So handsome!" Jakob's features might be more eastern European than most German boys, but his garb more than made up for it. Suitable for a Hitler Youth recruiting poster. That, along with a governess who could have doubled as Eva Braun, and the preparations that had been made, and the money that had changed hands, Jakob would be safe—as safe as anyone could be in this time.

Jakob stared back, serious, never one to smile. A year in Sachsenhausen, even at a special youth barracks, had exposed him to more death and suffering than hardened men five times his age. His grand-mother and mother were both now dead. Thank God Ingrid had managed to save Jakob before he *went up the chimney*. But even so, death had seeped into his life like wet fog dripping from a dead tree into desolate earth.

But he *had* survived.

Ingrid would make sure he kept doing so.

"Will I have to speak French?" Jakob said.

"*Bien sur*," she said. "And English. And Latin." She pulled gently on one of his earlobes. "Paris is a wonderful place. You are a lucky boy."

"But I want to stay *here*," Jakob said. "With *you*."

"And I would like nothing else, Jakob. But I have work to do here with your Onkel Werner."

"He's *not* my uncle. I don't even like him."

She shook Jakob's lapel gently in admonishment. Dropped her voice. "You must never say that. He's been very good to us."

Jakob looked up. "Do you like him, Auntie?"

A perceptive little boy. She stared back.

"I like him just fine. Because he likes you, hmm?"

"I'm not so sure."

"He's been very good to you." *Saved you from the train to Auschwitz. Saved you from starvation and death. Medical experiments.* Werner was not like other SS officers. Werner protected his "Jews" and the other artisans who made Operation Bernhard in Barracks 19 a success, saving him from the Russian front, of course, and the rest of them from certain death. But it all ultimately came down to the money, the false money, the fake British fivers. Once the operation came to an end—and it was coming to an end—Werner's benevolence, well, it would come to an end, too. It would *have* to. Self-preservation reigned supreme.

Just as it did for her.

And a Nazi was a Nazi, even one like Werner, who wasn't even a party member, who made jokes about Hitler and his goose steppers and said he would rather eat turnip soup with his Jews in the print shop at Sachsenhausen than drink schnapps with the stuffed shirts in the officers' mess.

But he would ultimately turn.

She was no fool.

She was no different.

"It's better where you are going, Jakob. Why, this time next week you'll be sailing model boats in the Luxembourg Gardens in Paris." She remembered doing the same with her father, long before the war, when she was a girl. When the world was different.

"When are you going to come, Auntie?"

She gave a melancholy smile. How she hated to lie to him. "Soon."

"And Werner too?"

"*Onkel* Werner."

"Onkel Werner," Jakob said dutifully. "Must he come too?"

"Don't say 'must.'"

Jakob sighed. "*Will* he come too?"

"I don't know."

A half-smile formed on his face, hopeful. "You're not going to marry him, then?"

She took a deep breath. "I'm too young to get married. And you, young man, are far too young to be asking such questions."

Outside in front of the grand hotel that had been appropriated for Operation Bernhard they heard the Mercedes crunch up the driveway. An authoritative tap of the horn sounded.

"Here's your car to Paris, Jakob."

"I don't want to go.'"

"All I can say is that one day you will understand."

"I don't think I will ever understand."

"Yes, you will. Now, time to say goodbye. To say *au revoir.*"

Down in front of the hotel, the roses were in bloom. The sun broke through the clouds over the hillside, highlighting the lavender of the trees. Compared to where Ingrid and Jakob had recently come from, a KZ full of death, it was day and night. But it still didn't mean it felt right.

The driver loaded the trunks into the back of the Mercedes.

Hannah, Jakob's governess, stood by, hands clasped in front of her. Her blond hair was pulled into a severe bun. Good to ward off the dangers on the road to Paris.

"*Come now, Jakob,*" she said in French with a German accent, "you'll be late. Kiss your auntie good bye."

Ingrid steeled herself for one last kiss and Jakob pecked her cheek, and she knew it would have to last her. She would treasure it for as long as she lived.

She had done a good thing.

She stood up, in a royal blue Mainbocher gown, the latest from Paris. Her raven hair had grown back and touched her collar again.

She handed Hannah the transit documents. All signed off at the highest level. Along with an envelope stuffed with lira, marks—worthless as they were—and counterfeit British currency. Counterfeits so good German agents had opened Swiss bank accounts with them. She should know. She had perfected many of the notes herself.

"Any problems, Hannah—contact me."

Hannah took the envelope and returned a reassuring smile. "There will be no problems, madam. You worry about yourself."

Hannah knew it was coming to an end soon as well. Even the most resolute Germans knew.

"Come, Jakob," Hannah said, hand on the boy's shoulder. "We can't stand around all day."

"Yes, Hannah," Jakob said, climbing into the Mercedes.

And Ingrid waved one last time, hiding her wet eyes, ostensibly from the sun. The car set off, little Jakob looking at her from the back. A solitary wave back.

Ingrid waved, let out a sigh, and turned back to the grand entrance, weighed down by sorrow. The guards on the door in their black Panzer uniforms, bereft of SS emblems, swastikas, and distinctive Stahlhelm helmets—low profile in a clandestine location—saluted her.

In the lobby she found Graf, the former camp officer, dressed in a tweed business suit and smart shoes. She was as perfectly put together as her days in uniform.

"Is Herr Beckmann still out riding?" Ingrid asked.

Graf bowed. "He's in the storeroom waiting for you, madam."

Eighteen years old and being called "madam." By the very woman that could have easily sent her to the execution trench in Sachsenhausen a year ago.

Ingrid took the stone stairwell down to the wine cellar where the temperature drop chilled her, despite her long-sleeved dress. Two more guards stood outside an oak door as thick as a man's fist, emblazoned with decorative hinges centuries old. One guard, a brute with a blank face, opened the door for her. The door gave a heavy creak as he let her in and shut it behind her.

Inside the huge cellar with its coved brick ceiling, the bare overhead bulb was surprisingly bright. Wine casks had been doubled up along one side to make room for a row of pallets from Sachsenhausen. The half dozen pallets lined one wall and were stacked with military crates, all labeled as combat rations and ammunition.

Werner was sitting at a rough table, going over figures in a ledger. When Ingrid entered, he put down his pencil and looked up, beaming. He stood, in jodhpurs and riding boots and a Trachten riding jacket with elaborate embroidery on the pockets. His blond hair was out of place, fresh from his morning ride.

"Inga," he said. "Now the sun shines, even down in this cellar."

She didn't care for the nickname, but there were a few things about Werner she didn't care for.

"You didn't come to see Jakob off," she said.

Werner came around the desk.

"It's not that I forgot," he said. "I wanted you to have the time with him alone."

"It would have been a show of support. He's taking a big step in his life."

Werner came a few inches closer, and she could tell he wanted to come closer still and touch her, but she radiated coldness to match the cellar.

He broke into a frown. "The boy doesn't care for me, Inga. Why pretend?"

"Because it would have helped settle his worries," she said.

"After all I've done for him, I should think a simple 'thank you' now and then might be fitting. All he does is scowl at me."

"His mother and grandmother were executed by Nazis. What do you expect?"

"Does he ever thank you for saving his life, Inga? Does he?"

He didn't. But he was a boy. "In his own way he does."

"Which means he doesn't."

"Never mind," Ingrid said. "Where are we with our plans?"

"Wait until you see!" Werner sprang over to a pallet of crates the size of small travel trunks. He pulled the lid back on one and peeled back two layers of heavy brown wax paper covering.

Rows and rows of stacks of white five-pound notes were lined up, multiple Britannias staring back. Some of the hardest work she had ever done.

"Courtesy of Ingrid Richter, prisoner 32715." He plucked a note from a stack, held it up. "Oh, Inga's a master with the eyes. Even Alexei said so, that crafty old Jew. 'She's really very good, Major Beckmann.' I knew he was trying to save your skin but I couldn't disagree. I mean, look at this. How many Britannias did you save? How many Brit fivers?"

"The eyes are the key. Just like with people, the eyes give away the lie."

Werner flicked the bill with a fingernail, generating a satisfying *pick* sound, the result of months of work with the local paper mill near Sachsenhausen to copy the paper used by the Bank of England. "Will you listen to that? It wants to buy you a drink."

"It's good work."

"Good? *Good?*" He tossed the bill into the air, let it flutter to the floor. "Even the Reichsbank was fooled."

Even so, there had been mistakes that had gotten through. "But for how much longer, Werner?"

His face grew serious for a moment, before he broke into a broad smile. "Months? A year? Ultimately everyone knows the war is lost."

"And then so are we. We're living in the eye of a hurricane."

"There are the commissions."

In Swiss banks. In Werner's name. Not hers.

"And what if that money is impounded, Werner? When the Allies swoop in?"

"That's why you must trust me, Inga."

Trust a Nazi. Even one who had never been a good Nazi. What would her father have thought of her new life? Would he have understood?

"So serious for such a young woman," Werner said. "Come, Inga." He took her hand, led her to the end of the row where a packing crate was nailed shut. Stamped with the Nazi Eagle and marked: *Sarin*

Nervengas. Skulls and crossbones. A person would be a fool to open that box of death.

Werner picked up the crowbar that lay on top and pried the crate open carefully, the nails squealing in response. Ingrid tensed up.

Inside, a layer of heavy brown paper. He pulled it back. A layer of wax paper. That too. Lines of fivers.

"What is your point, Werner?"

He turned to Inga and pointed at the other pallets, full of crates that came and went. "Those are for our 'customers.' But this one" —he indicated the Sarin gas crate—"is our spare parachute. Yours and mine."

She looked at it again. Millions? Perhaps.

"Should we move it somewhere?"

He raised a finger. "Absolutely."

"Then we should do it soon."

"There's still time."

"Soon," she said again.

"As you wish, Inga."

"I will take care of it."

His face grew dark.

"Don't you trust me, Werner?" she said.

There was a pause.

"Of course, Inga."

Did he? She would have to prepare her own escape. "And we will do it soon."

CHAPTER THIRTY-TWO

It was close to midnight when the Hotel Castello di Lindenhof finally came into view, rising out of wet mountain fog, a German-style chateau replete with turrets and high peaked roofs. The Italian Alps loomed beyond. Agent Albini shifted the Alfa down on the deserted mountain road. They were still technically on Italian soil, but it felt much farther north.

The only light in the grand *schloss* glowed through leaded windows by the hotel's scalloped entrance. The upper three stories were dark. None of the accent lights on the roads or paths were lit.

Agent Albini stopped the car at a large wooden sign in front of the approach road. Underneath the hotel name, established in 1384, was another sign: *Chiuso.*

Random raindrops pattered the windshield and car.

"Closed for the season," Colleen said. "So if Ingrid Richter is here, she's a special guest." From the back seat she saw, through the trees, several vehicles parked in front of the hotel. A van. A 1960s Land Rover. A late model white Fiat 128, square and generic. "I wonder if one of those vehicles out front is hers."

Toscano got out a pair of binoculars, focused. He discussed license plates with Agent Albini. Colleen was finding it easier to understand the language. The van and the Land Rover were older vehicles and had local plates, as designated by BZ—Bolzano, the nearest city. The Fiat had a *Roma* designation. That was a candidate for a visitor's vehicle—possibly Ingrid Richter's.

Agent Albini got on the radio while Toscano read off the plate number. They waited while the radio crackled.

The operator came back. The Fiat was a rental car.

"Any way of telling who it's rented to?" Colleen asked.

Agent Albini put the radio mic to her mouth, asked. The clerk on the other end said he could call the rental agency, but it might not be until morning before they got hold of somebody.

Toscano said it was good enough. Agent Albini hung up the radio. He looked at his watch.

"If we ask for Signora Richter at this hour," he said, "we give ourselves away. I want to know where she's going, who she's planning to meet. We'll watch the hotel until morning."

"We can't stay here," Agent Albini said. "We're too easy to spot." She put the Alfa into gear, spun around in a tight turn, motored back down the hill to a dirt road leading to a farm, where she backed the car in behind a hedge. They could see most of the hotel and spot anyone coming or going.

Toscano said: "It's been a long day. We'll watch the hotel in turns: an hour each."

"I'll take first watch," Colleen said.

Toscano handed her the binoculars over the seat. She took them, focused. She couldn't see the lower part of the schloss in the distance. She opened the car door, got out.

"I'll be able to see better from up there," she said, nodding at the trees in front of the hotel. It was spitting rain. All she had was her blue pantsuit. "Do you have anything like a poncho?"

Toscano instructed Albini to help Colleen out.

"*Sì*," Agent Albini said, climbing out of the car, going to the trunk. Colleen followed. Agent Albini opened the trunk, rummaged around. Colleen couldn't help but notice an olive drab combat shotgun clipped to the bottom of the trunk lid. It had a folding stock with a large metal hook carrying handle that doubled as a firing brace, a military-looking heat shield, and long magazine extension that resembled a second barrel.

Agent Albini shook out a blue windbreaker with a hood. On the back were the letters *GdF* in white. *Guardia di Finanza.*

Subtle, Colleen thought, taking it, slipping it on. It smelled of mildew. "Flashlight?" she said in Spanish.

Agent Albini dug around, found one, tested it inside the trunk, lighting up the interior for a moment, turned it off, handed it to Colleen.

Colleen noted a small black collapsible baton, about the length of a flashlight, but not nearly as thick. That might come in handy.

"Any chance of a pistol?" she asked in Spanish, knowing full well what the answer would be.

Agent Albini sighed, went around to the front of the car, had a quiet discussion with Toscano. *Now she wants a gun,* Colleen heard her say.

Colleen helped herself to the collapsible baton, slipping it in her back pocket.

Toscano rolled down the window, leaned out.

"No weapon," he said to Colleen. "If you see anything, you will notify us immediately."

"Observe and report," Colleen said. "Got it."

Albini returned to the rear of the car and shut the trunk lid quietly. Then she got into the car. Toscano rolled the window up, adjusted his suit coat, pulled the collar up, tilted his head back. Albini did the same with the collar of her leather jacket, propping her head against her window. She had to be exhausted driving all night from Rome, most of it in wind and rain.

Colleen was still living on jet lag. And knowing that she was so close to finding out what the hell was going on with Ingrid Richter was keeping her wide awake.

She headed up to the turnoff to the hotel, passed the sign, marched through the trees to a secluded view of the doorway in a spot shielded from the wind and rain. She squatted on her haunches, back against the tree, checked the hotel through the binoculars. She turned to the road. No traffic. The rain had let up but remnants of it dripped through the branches.

Time passed slowly, the wind rushing up the mountain road and rustling the trees. But, after a decade in prison, waiting was one thing she knew how to do.

Then she saw a light go on in one of the upstairs rooms. She lifted the binoculars but couldn't see through the curtains. A shadow moved.

The light went off.

A minute or two later the front door opened inside the scalloped entryway. A figure appeared, wearing a light-colored windbreaker, one Colleen recognized from following it through Rome that morning. The hood was up but Colleen got a glimpse of Ingrid's squarish face. She wore trousers and hiking boots. A daypack was slung over her shoulder.

It was her; no doubt about it.

CHAPTER THIRTY-THREE

1979

Hidden below the spread-out branches of a linden tree, Colleen focused her binoculars on Ingrid Richter. The woman was leaving the hotel grounds, heading across the gravel access road to a field in the direction of the mountains. Going out for a hike in the middle of a wet rainy night? Right.

Colleen considered going back to the car, alerting Toscano and Albini, but held off. She might lose Ingrid Richter if the woman got too far ahead of her.

She set off after Ingrid alone, keeping her distance.

Across the field, Ingrid hopped a small gulley and began to ascend a trail up the mountain. Colleen kept after her, her eyes adjusting to the darkness. It had stopped raining and a hint of moonlight glowed through the clouds.

She followed Ingrid for a good fifteen minutes.

The path up the mountain would not have been difficult during the day, but on a wet night with the possibility of being discovered, it was a different story. Ingrid obviously knew where she was going and Colleen did not. Colleen's stylish ankle boots were no match for Ingrid's hiking boots and were muddy and slippery.

After ascending a narrow path that wrapped itself around the base of the mountain, Colleen saw a flashlight beam break the darkness up ahead where the path rose. Her guess would have been about a hundred yards away. The light flickered in the misty night. Colleen dropped into a crouch, pulse racing. Had she been spotted? Then the flashlight was extinguished and Ingrid vanished from sight. Colleen looked, listened. Nothing.

She continued up the path.

A way up the mountain, she reached the ledge where Ingrid's flashlight had seemingly switched off.

She stood at a slanted opening to a granite cave. There was a significant drop-off to one side where the wind howled. The cave entrance was no more than a few feet across. Colleen cocked an ear, heard water dripping deep within. She couldn't turn on her own flashlight, and she couldn't afford to make a sound. She stood at the mouth of the cave, listening.

She heard footsteps approach, slow and measured. One person taking their time. The flickering of a flashlight broke the darkness, about thirty yards in, coming from around a corner.

Colleen moved to the other side of the cave entrance, found cover squatting behind a large rock jutting out. A blast of wind rushed up from behind her and she turned to see a chasm that plunged two stories or more. She took a deep breath to steady her nerves.

Ingrid Richter's profile appeared, broken by minimal moonlight through clouds. Colleen blinked away the shadows. Ingrid no longer had her pack. She turned away, headed back down the path towards the hotel.

She must have left the pack in the cave.

Colleen waited until Ingrid's footsteps faded off, gave it a couple more minutes, then got up, entered the cave herself, using her flashlight when she was well inside. The cave was wider once she entered, the walls fashioned by Mother Nature with crags of gray and blue granite, high and angular in places, lower in others. The floor descended slightly, and was strewn with more alpine rock. The air was sharp and cold, much colder than outside, and she shivered in her light suit and thin GdF windbreaker. The smell was thick, damp, and earthy, like a tomb, she imagined. The cavern reverberated with the dripping of water.

She directed her flashlight down the shaft, about the length of her apartment in San Francisco. A wall of fallen rock made it seem inaccessible after that.

But Ingrid seemed to have gone farther, judging by her flashlight and footsteps.

Colleen tread warily in her street shoes, careful not to slip.

Body tense, she reached the rock slide, which blocked most of the way. Who knew how long it had been there? She peered around the edge of it with the aid of the flashlight, saw more cave beyond.

The cave continued, more narrow, the walls glassy in places where ice had formed.

Colleen had to hunch down and squeeze to clear the minimal clearance around the pile of loose rock. Claustrophobia clinched her as she wedged herself through.

She got past the rock collapse. Her flashlight exposed a square shape of some sort off to the side. Not a natural shape.

She stood up, saw an old brown tarp over something large and square. The canvas was filmed with cracked ice. It looked recently broken.

Colleen walked over, pulled the tarp back, ice splintering. Her flashlight beam settled on a wooden case with a Nazi Eagle stamped on the lid, and a warning in German. Ingrid's daypack sat on the ground next to the crate.

The words *Sarin Nervengas* appeared over a skull and crossbones on the crate.

She'd heard of sarin gas.

A little voice said no way was she going near this crate. But crouching, she shined the flashlight on the lid and saw that a gap existed between it and the crate. This crate had been opened before. The wood was damaged where it had been jimmied open and hammered back down.

She pulled the collapsible baton from her back pocket, shook it out to its two-foot length. She jammed the narrow tip into the gap between lid and crate, began to pry the lid open, nails squealing in the cave. She stopped, turned her head to listen, make sure she was alone. She set the flashlight on a rock to light her work area and went to work with her hands.

It took a minute or two, the rough pine on freezing cold fingers. Screeches of wood and nails echoed through the cave. She stopped from time to time, listening for unwanted visitors.

When she was done she picked up the flashlight, looked inside the case.

A layer of heavy dark brown protective paper covered the contents. It was stained with the years and wrinkled where it had been opened before.

She peeled it back. Another layer of paper. Also previously opened. She pulled that back too and pointed her flashlight at the contents.

Row upon row, stack upon stack, of old British five-pound and one-pound notes.

A sudden realization struck her.

Jakob Klaus' half of a five-pound note. Jasia Salak's other half.

Colleen pulled an inch of crisp fivers, cold to the touch, flipped through them. A faint scent of ink and linen wafted up. A new money smell, albeit decades old.

Some of the serial numbers were consecutive. Repeats.

Forgeries.

All the notes were dated 1936.

The same year as Jakob's and Jasia Salak's.

Flashlight in hand, she rifled through a stack that seemed to have been disturbed at some point. A few might have even been removed.

She saw one recurring serial number that triggered her memory.

57903.

The same number as the one she had already encountered in San Francisco. She selected a bill, studied Britannia in the upper left-hand corner, sitting regally on her throne. Colleen rubbed her thumb across the face. It had the ruffled texture of fine bond but was otherwise smooth. She tried several more until she found one where an eye felt slightly pinpricked, like the half she had seen in Owens' motel room, the one that had been found on Jasia Salak. She examined it closely under the flashlight. If you weren't looking for it, you wouldn't notice. But the tiny hole, almost imperceptible, was there. Possibly touched up with ink.

And then she knew what Ingrid Richter had done.

CHAPTER THIRTY-FOUR

1979

Colleen kept two counterfeit fivers, put the rest of the stack back, smoothed the layers of paper into place, pushed the lid down with a squeak. Threw the tarp back over the case, grabbed the daypack. Squatting, she opened it, pointed the flashlight in.

Two envelopes. One clearly money. Dollars. Pounds. Bills of all denominations.

The other, documents wrapped in a rubber band.

A British passport. She opened it.

George Caplin, 52 Rosemary Avenue, London, N3. She examined the photo.

George Caplin was Jakob Klaus. Ingrid Richter's "nephew." In San Francisco he had been Erich Hahn.

And then it hit her.

Ingrid wasn't gunning for Jakob Klaus after all.

Just the opposite.

Colleen's mind did a 180 as she quickly reassessed the woman she had initially seen as an ex-Nazi hunting down Nazi hunters.

Who was she?

Colleen kept the passport, realizing Jakob Klaus might show at any time to retrieve his escape package. She didn't need a confrontation with an assassin in the middle of the night in a cave on some god-forsaken mountainside. But she didn't want him having an easy way out of Italy either.

She pocketed the passport. No passport, no exit.

She squeezed out past the fallen rock, and negotiated her way out of the cave.

It was easier getting back down the mountain, even in darkness. She knew the way.

Back at the hotel, the white Fiat was still parked out front. The second-floor window that had lit up briefly before Ingrid Richter had left for her trip up the mountain was lit up once again. Ingrid was back in her room.

Back at the Alfa, still tucked away by the side of the road, the windows were down and cigarette smoke drifted out.

Toscano was more than a little displeased.

"Where the hell do you think you've been?" he said to Colleen, getting out of the car, flicking ash angrily into the air.

"I can explain," Colleen said.

*   *   *

"You're saying you saw Signora Richter come back to the hotel?" Toscano said. "After she left a backpack in that cave?"

"She's in that room," Colleen said, indicating the only lit window on the second floor. "Her reason for coming here wasn't to hunt down Jakob Klaus. She's his accomplice." Colleen didn't mention the passport yet but described the case in the cave, under the tarp. "It's full of wartime counterfeit money."

"They found several cases of Operation Bernhard forgeries at the bottom of a lake in Switzerland in the 1950s," Toscano said. "The Nazis tried to hide the evidence when the Allies invaded."

"Ingrid Richter must have concealed her own private stash here," Colleen said.

"Well, it's worthless now—not that it was technically worth anything then." Toscano got on the radio, asked to be put through to headquarters. He relayed the information that Colleen had told him, and asked for backup. He was told a team would have to be assembled in Bolzano.

"But why here?" Colleen asked, nodding at the hotel. "Why would Ingrid Richter keep her wartime secrets here?"

"She lived here during the war. Castello di Lindenhof was a Nazi retreat," Toscano said. "Close to Austria, Switzerland, France."

Colleen saw the light go out in Ingrid Richter's room.

"She thinks her work is done," Colleen said. "She's taking off."

A moment later the front door opened and Ingrid Richter appeared again, carrying a small suitcase.

"And there she is," Colleen said.

Toscano instructed Agent Albini to move. She fired up the Alfa and tossed it into gear, swerving onto the narrow mountain road and up to the turnoff, taking a sharp right towards the hotel. Churning up the gravel access road, she pulled up behind the white Fiat, blocking it.

The three of them got out.

Suitcase in hand, Ingrid Richter looked at them in surprise. She wore a clear plastic rain scarf.

"Signora Richter?" Toscano said, as polite as when he had stopped Colleen in the Piazza Mattei.

"What is this all about?" she replied. Putting on the innocent act.

Toscano flashed his badge. "A few questions."

"Am I under arrest?"

"Let's start with questions and see where it goes from there, shall we?" Toscano said. Agent Albini stood by, hands on her wide hips, her right hand close to her holstered pistol. She eyed Ingrid Richter, ready to make a move.

"But I must leave for Rome," Ingrid Richter said haughtily. "I have a flight tonight."

"There will still be time," Toscano said, "if you do indeed make it to Rome."

Ingrid Richter's eyes met with Colleen's, and Colleen saw a look of recognition as she realized who Colleen was. Then Ingrid resumed her poker face.

"I want a lawyer," she said.

"Questions first," Toscano said.

Ingrid Richter exhaled a hard sigh.

Toscano indicated the hotel. "Let's go inside. It's cold out here. But first . . ." He gave Agent Albini a nod, followed by one indicating Ingrid Richter.

Albini moved in, took Ingrid Richter's bag, set it down, gave Ingrid a pat-down amidst protests, flipped her around against the car, continued. Then Albini took the bag, slapped it on the hood of the Fiat, went through it. Satisfied, she shoved clothes and toiletries back into the bag haphazardly, jammed it shut.

"Am I under arrest?" Ingrid Richter asked again.

"Not yet," Toscano said.

Albini picked up the suitcase, rang the bell, several times in quick succession, even though it was the middle of the night. Lights went on. Shouts of "*momento, momento!*" echoed through the hotel. An older man in wire-rimmed glasses and a robe answered the door.

Badges were flashed. Holding Ingrid by the arm, Agent Albini led her inside. Toscano and Colleen followed.

The hotelier wasn't pleased with the surprise visit. Toscano didn't seem to care.

The large dining room at the front of the hotel was dark and cold. Gold-framed mirrors reflected ambient light. Agent Albini set Ingrid Richter's suitcase down, flicked on a light in one corner by a serving counter, and Toscano had Ingrid sit at a table, along with Colleen. He stood, instructed Agent Albini to give the hotel the once-over. She left. When the manager protested, Toscano said, "I'll deal with you in a moment, and let's just hope you haven't been complicit in the commission of a crime. In the meantime, you can make us some coffee."

The manager huffed off behind the counter and went to work.

Toscano lit a cigarette and straightened the pocket flap of his suit coat. It was looking decidedly rumpled, along with his shirt and tie. His five o'clock shadow was well past midnight and he was starting to resemble someone he might be questioning.

Agent Albini came down the stairwell in the hallway into the dining room. She gave Toscano a thumbs-up and came back and stood against the wall, crossing her arms while she watched the table.

"Why did you come here?" Toscano asked Ingrid Richter as he smoked. "Who did you plan to meet?"

Ingrid Richter looked at Toscano, then Colleen. Agent Albini stood behind her.

"I want a lawyer."

"Fine," Toscano said. "You may call one when we take you into custody. In Rome. Or you can answer a few questions."

Ingrid Richter seemed to think that over.

"I had a business meeting in Bolzano," she said.

"Why didn't you stay there?" Toscano said. "Surely, if you needed to return to Rome tonight, it would be much more convenient to stay in Bolzano."

"I was planning to stay here longer and enjoy the mountains," Ingrid Richter said. "But the weather didn't agree."

"So you leave in the middle of the night? Why not at least wait until daytime? When the roads are safer?"

"I received an emergency call to return to work. Berlin."

"Ah. Where did you receive your call? Here at the hotel?"

Ingrid Richter frowned. "I called before I came here. In Bolzano."

"I see," Toscano said icily, walking as he smoked. "I will need the time and location of where you made that telephone call. But we'll return to that. You made the airline reservation after that?"

"Yes."

Toscano stopped. "And how does your trip up the mountain factor into all of this?"

"I already explained that. I came up here earlier this evening."

"No," Toscano said. "I mean your night trek up to the cave not two hours ago."

Ingrid Richter's face turned to stone. "I want a lawyer."

Toscano took a final puff on his cigarette, smashed it out in an ashtray on another table. "As you wish. We will be taking you in."

Ingrid Richter sat back, crossed her arms. "Then I have nothing further to say."

The manager smacked a glass carafe of coffee on the counter, gathered some cups together noisily. Service with a smile. He turned to go back into the kitchen.

"You!" Toscano snapped after him. "Stay out here where I can keep an eye on you."

The manager turned back around, obviously taken aback. Toscano shot him a hot look, then spoke to Albini, telling her to take down the manager's particulars. Agent Albini went over and got started.

Colleen reached into her pocket, came out with George Caplin's British passport. She held it up, showed it to Ingrid Richter, along with raised eyebrows.

"Are you sure you have nothing further to say?" she said.

Ingrid Richter was clearly surprised. But once again, she recovered quickly.

"Your 'nephew' isn't going to get far," Colleen said. "Not without this. He's not leaving Italy anyway."

Ingrid Richter took a deep breath. "I have no idea what that is. It looks like a passport of some sort. British, is it?"

"Odd you don't recognize it," Colleen said. "I found it in the backpack you left in the cave."

Ingrid Richter's face resumed its forced composure.

"Someone better tell me what this is about," Toscano said, obviously peeved. He came over to Colleen and took the passport, flipped through it.

"Ingrid Richter left that for Jakob Klaus," Colleen said. "He couldn't very well use his previous one. Not after he stabbed that priest in Anguillara."

"This is Jakob Klaus?" Toscano said.

"He gets a new one with each hit he makes for Black Cross," Colleen said. "Along with money and instructions. Courtesy of his 'aunt.' It's part of his assassination protocol. One, no doubt, for the priest in Anguillara the other day. The week before, it was Werner Beckmann—although that was abandoned and a woman was stabbed on SF Muni, a hit woman sent after Jakob Klaus. The week before it was the concentration camp guard in Buenos Aires."

"But Werner Beckmann has been dead since 1945," Toscano said, turning the passport sideways to study it. "This is excellent work."

"It should be," Colleen said. "Ms. Richter learned her trade from the best—almost forty years ago—at Sachsenhausen concentration camp."

Toscano looked at Ingrid. "It makes sense."

"What didn't make sense to me before," Colleen said, "was that Ms. Richter seemed to be gunning for Jakob Klaus. She hired me to find him in San Francisco with some story about a missed family visit. I thought she was trying to intercept him, working with Aryan Alliance, a neo-Nazi group in SF. But I had it reversed. When she learned that neo-Nazis were onto Jakob, she wanted to warn him, protect him. Let him know that their operation had somehow been compromised."

Ingrid gave Colleen a slit-eyed stare.

"Because someone had blown the whistle on Jakob," Colleen said, "someone in Black Cross is my bet. And after I found Jakob, who was in hiding, whoever wanted him stopped sent Jasia Salak—a former kapo at Sachsenhausen concentration camp—posing as a member of Black Cross. Salak planned to kill Jakob, but he beat her to the punch, stabbed her to death on SF Muni, left her corpse to ride the train all day. I thought Ms. Richter was the one who had sent Salak. It all fit. She had me locate Jakob Klaus, then all of a sudden, his potential assassin appears. But I had it backwards."

She turned to Ingrid. "You left Salak a bad token in the San Francisco drop box—her half of the five-pound note she needed to authenticate with Jakob. You left her a dud. One Jakob would identify as such. He knew your handiwork. If Jakob didn't recognize Salak when she contacted him at the Metro Hotel—and why should he—he was a boy when he last saw her—then he'd see her half of the fiver was a mismatch for his—even though it had the same serial number. And, of course, you had matching serial numbers. You had access to the old banknotes—up in that cave." Colleen reached into her pocket, came out with two fivers. She showed them to Toscano. "Take a look at the eyes on the second one."

Toscano took the half notes, rubbed his thumb over the one.

"It seems you have unearthed a missing link to the Nazi's Operation Bernhard," he said, setting the notes down on the table. He strolled over to the counter, poured himself a cup of coffee, took a gulp. He made a face, came back, sat down.

"I'm afraid you won't be making your flight tonight in Rome, Signora Richter."

Ingrid Richter stared daggers at Colleen.

"I hope you're proud of yourself," she said.

"Go to hell. You played me for a fool. Your little games led to one death in San Francisco and the subsequent attack on my daughter by neo-Nazi thugs. You had me chase you here thinking you were some ex-Nazi bent on assassinating Jakob Klaus when in fact you were his protector. Working for Black Cross. Murdering people all over the globe with impunity."

"Versus the deaths of six million Jews?" Ingrid Richter said. "Over a million gypsies? Millions of Soviet prisoners? Hundreds of thousands of political prisoners, homosexuals, disabled persons? The list goes on. And yet you choose to waste your time on *me*."

"Tell me how killing a former kapo in cold blood resolves anything. Killing ex-Nazis in bars in Argentina? In churches in Italian villages?"

"You would never understand."

"I know something about revenge," Colleen said, recalling the night over a decade ago when she put an end to her husband in the kitchen with a screwdriver to the neck. "There are ways to deal with it. Not by using the same methods as the criminals."

Ingrid Richter shook her head. "Closure. For the millions."

"Closure is a myth," Colleen said.

"Perhaps to you."

Colleen stood. "If you want justice, you do it through the system."

Ingrid Richter crossed her arms, sat back again. She spoke to Toscano. "The lawyers at First Trust of Zurich take up an entire floor of the building. We'll see what they have to say in my defense."

Colleen went over to the counter, poured herself a cup of warm coffee. Drank it in the shadow of the lights. It was better than no coffee. Barely.

She could see Ingrid's point. There was no evil like that which the Nazis had perpetuated.

But bloodthirsty vengeance had to stop.

She went back to the table. Spoke to Toscano.

"I need to talk to you—in private."

Toscano looked at Colleen, someone who had been sitting in an interrogation room not long ago herself. He instructed Agent Albini to keep an eye on Ingrid Richter while he and Colleen went outside. A cold wind whipped through the trees in front of the hotel, sweeping down out of the mountains.

Toscano lit up another cigarette, sucked in smoke, blew it out.

"Let her go," Colleen said.

Toscano eyed Colleen with amusement. "Signora Richter can lead us to the officers of her bank involved in money laundering. A case I've had on my plate for years." He took another drag, exhaled. Smoke was pulled away by the wind. "And you say 'let her go.'"

"Look at what you've got," Colleen said. "The final chapter to Operation Bernhard—up in that cave. The answer to murders Interpol has been tracking all over the world. A recent murder right here in your own country. Feathers in your cap to spare. Ingrid Richter isn't the one you want. It's her 'nephew': Jakob Klaus."

Toscano drew a puff. "But I don't have him, do I?"

"You will soon enough. When he comes for his passport. And you better be ready."

Toscano nodded. "It's possible."

"And when he does," she said, "let her go." Colleen added, "Do it for all the reasons she said in there."

Toscano smoked, blinking in thought as he looked at the mountains.

CHAPTER THIRTY-FIVE

1979

Back in the hotel, Toscano used the phone to call Bolzano and ask about his reinforcements, who had not shown up. Agent Albini was posted out front. The manager sat at another table in semi-darkness in his robe, seemingly brooding his fate. Colleen and Ingrid Richter were at their table under the lamp, silent.

It was dark, just past four in the morning.

"What happens now?" Ingrid Richter said with an air of defiance.

"We're waiting for your nephew," Colleen said. "Or whoever he might be."

Ingrid Richter gave Colleen a guarded look.

"You met Jakob Klaus in Sachsenhausen," Colleen said. "Along with Jasia Salak."

Ingrid Richter took a deep breath, let it out. "Jakob, his mother, and grandmother were on the same truck as I into Sachsenhausen. I had just been arrested. I was seventeen. My father had been shot by the Nazis. They unloaded us in the middle of the night. It was raining. The kapo—Salak—"

"—the one Jakob killed in San Francisco," Colleen said.

Ingrid Richter nodded. "Salak was on duty that night at Sachsenhausen to 'greet' us. With her club. Always with her club. It was the middle of the night. Raining, so cold. After unloading the truck she promptly clubbed Jakob's grandmother to death as a show of strength, to let us know what we could expect as prisoners of the Reich."

She said it so matter-of-factly, Colleen couldn't help but flinch.

"Jakob was six years old at the time," Ingrid Richter said. "And although I saw the effect it had on him, I also saw him steel himself in a way a grown man might not under the circumstances. Well, if he could do it, so could I. And if I could live, so could he. Saving him was my justification for doing what I did in Barracks 19."

Toscano was listening intently, standing in the shadows, smoking another cigarette.

"They killed Jakob's mother as well," Ingrid Richter said. "After she had walked eleven hours a day in boots the local shoe factory made for the troops, a factory that utilized the camp's slave labor. Boots too big for her, without socks. With a pack on her back. Round and round the gravel track. Until she collapsed of exhaustion. Then she was shot."

"The guard who shot her," Colleen said, "was the one killed in Buenos Aires."

Ingrid Richter didn't acknowledge that.

"You were recruited for Operation Bernhard," Colleen said.

"I was one of the lucky ones," Ingrid said. "I had skills the Nazis wanted. Yes, I was assigned to Operation Bernhard. The alternative options weren't promising."

"You assisted the Nazis," Toscano said.

"And what did *you* do during the war?" Ingrid Richter shot back. "When Mussolini and his fascists took over your country? Rounded up Jews? Yes, I wanted to live. But in exchange for my dirty work, I was able to ensure that Jakob Klaus, along with a few others, were spared. All Jews who would have gone *up the chimney*. I did what I could to even the score."

"And what became of Werner Beckmann?" Colleen asked.

Ingrid Richter started at first, then regained her composure.

"We know he ran Operation Bernhard at Sachsenhausen," Colleen said. "Where is he?"

"Major Beckmann died in a fire in Rome. Hotel Damasio. 1945. Trying to escape the Allies." Ingrid shook her head. "He had just gotten his Red Cross passport. Had the hotel fire not taken his life, he would've been on his way to South America."

By the tone of Ingrid's voice, Colleen understood she had been close to Werner Beckmann. But who was Colleen to question a young woman who wanted to stay alive?

"And the two of you lived here for a time," Toscano said. "Linden-hof. While you distributed the counterfeit currency."

"The irony was that the grand plan to destroy the British economy," Ingrid Richter said, "—drop bills over the British Isles—was abandoned before we even started."

Toscano said: "That counterfeit currency was used to pay spies for the Reich. To fund illegal projects. It was used to enrich all of you."

"Rich?" Ingrid Richter gave a bitter laugh. "I work for a living. Any money I had is up in that cave—worthless now."

"Then why did you run?" he said.

"After Werner died," Ingrid said and Colleen noted the use of the man's first name, "I had to go into hiding myself. Yes, I was a former prisoner. But in the eyes of the Allies I was a collaborator. I went to Damascus, where the Nazis had many contacts."

"How did you get away?"

"The Vatican issued me a Red Cross passport as well."

"But you came back," Colleen said. "To Germany."

"Once the furor over punishing Nazis and collaborators died down, and several former prisoners at Sachsenhausen gave evidence of my efforts to save them, I was issued a pardon. I came back. Germany is, after all, my country."

"Something doesn't add up," Colleen said. "Werner Beckmann died in a fire. 1945. How did he wind up on Black Cross's hit list?"

"Black Cross doesn't always get their information right. So many records were destroyed during the war. They work with what they have. Sometimes it's the faded memory of a former prisoner, and sometimes it's wrong."

"Another reason you wanted to stop Jakob," Colleen said. "You knew he was on the wrong track with Werner Beckmann."

"I was working in San Francisco for a client, attending the conference, and I learned that a local neo-Nazi group had infiltrated Black Cross."

"Aryan Alliance," Colleen said.

"Yes," Ingrid Richter said. "Aryan Alliance."

"Doris Pender."

"I don't know the names." Ingrid Richter wasn't going to divulge more than she had to. "There was a threat to Jakob. That's all I knew."

It was coming together. "There's more to it, though," Colleen said. "You penetrated Aryan Alliance yourself, posing as a Nazi. But you're really a member of Black Cross. You knew Jakob had been dispatched. And when you saw Jasia Salak involved in an operation to kill a man who was already dead, you knew something wasn't right. You knew Salak. She might have been a former victim in a sense, but she was a cold-blooded murderer willing to kill for the Nazis. You knew she was after Jakob. So you warned him. By making sure Salak's half of the five-pound note didn't match his half. A signal he'd easily spot."

Ingrid looked at Colleen circumspectly and Colleen thought she might actually come clean. But Ingrid's truth had its own rules. She wasn't going to expose Jakob, or herself, more than she had to.

"I'm not a member of anything," Ingrid Richter finally said. "I watch out for those that mean something to me. You weren't there. I don't expect you to understand."

Colleen understood more than Ingrid gave her credit for. "How did Jakob become involved with Black Cross?"

"A better question might be: how could Jakob *not* become involved? After what the Nazis did to his grandmother? His mother? He will always be a prisoner in Sachsenhausen. Always." She yielded a sigh. "And now, I think I'm done talking. Until I have my lawyer."

Colleen's view of Ingrid Richter had changed from the one she held only a few hours ago. Ingrid was no Nazi. She did what was necessary to survive. Cooperate with the Nazis during the war, and save whoever she could along the way. Work for Black Cross, keep an eye on her so-called nephew. In Ingrid's world loyalties shifted. It was the difference between being a survivor and not being one.

They waited. Jakob Klaus would make his appearance. Colleen knew. He was the reason Ingrid had come here.

It was still dark when the grandfather clock in the hall of Castello di Lindenhof chimed five bells. The sound of the vehicles coming up the mountain road approached outside the hotel.

The front door opened. Agent Albini came in, the military shotgun slung over her shoulder.

They all looked up. Toscano, Ingrid Richter, Colleen. Even the manager who sat in the shadows at the other table.

"Someone's coming," Agent Albini said in Italian to Toscano. "Two vehicles."

"The police reinforcements I requested," Toscano said. "About time."

"No." Albini shook her head. "I don't think so." A sense of wariness darkened her voice.

CHAPTER THIRTY-SIX

1979

Toscano went to the front door, came back into the semi-dark dining room. His face was compressed in a grimace.

"Two unmarked vehicles," he said to Albini. He rubbed his eyes with a finger and thumb. "Not good." He reached inside his coat, pulled an automatic pistol. He motioned for Agent Albini to join him by the front door. Albini caught his eye, nodded at Ingrid Richter and the manager and spoke to Toscano in Italian, along the lines of "what do we do with these two?"

"I'll watch them," Colleen said.

Toscano pursed his lips as he looked at Colleen, blinking in thought.

"Ms. Richter isn't going anywhere," Colleen said. "Not until she sees Jakob. He's the reason she came here in the first place. And you've got his passport." The manager didn't seem to be an issue. He was on his feet, too, peering out a leaded glass window, looking fretful.

Toscano returned to the front door. Colleen stood up, went to one of the dining room windows, looked out a leaded pane. A big beige Citroen that looked like a spacecraft glided up in the gravel. Another vehicle, a dark van, pulled up behind it.

Car doors opened, back and front.

Several men got out of the Citroen, half a dozen from the van. Shotguns and rifles stuck out in morning shadow. Balaclavas covered two faces and there was a preponderance of buzz cuts and shaved heads. The men were young for the most part, although one middle-aged man had slicked-back hair like a '50s rocker.

Last to appear, from the passenger side of the Citroen, was a tall thin woman, one Colleen knew.

Doris Pender.

In denims, boots, and a dark coat, she didn't seem fazed by the fact that Agent Albini and Toscano were standing at the door with weapons drawn.

Colleen joined Albini and Toscano.

"That's Doris Pender," she said to Toscano. "Number two at Aryan Alliance, the neo-Nazi group in San Francisco."

Toscano nodded.

"What do you want?" he said to Doris Pender in English.

Doris Pender stood, hands in the pockets of her coat, as if chilly.

"She knows what I want," Doris said in her nasal accent, nodding at Colleen. Colleen felt vulnerable without a weapon.

"Jakob Klaus," Colleen said. "The reason you told me where I could find Ingrid Richter. You knew she'd be on Jakob's trail. You wanted me to hunt him down for you."

"And you took the bait," Doris Pender said. "So, where is he?"

"Gone," Colleen said.

"Gone where?"

"Good question." Colleen moved out front. "Bottom line is that you're too late."

Doris rubbed her pointed chin. The crowd of men watched from the predawn shadows. A cigarette glowed by the van.

Doris Pender spoke: "I think we'll just come inside and make sure."

Toscano replied: "You have precisely one minute to get in your vehicles and leave." Agent Albini fingered the shotgun by her side. The stock had been unfolded and the hook braced her arm so she could fire with one hand.

"That doesn't work," Doris Pender said. "I need to come in with my men and search the place."

"I have reinforcements on the way," Toscano said, pistol by his side.

Doris Pender turned to the men gathered, gave them a nod. They dispersed, spreading out, some heading around the side of the hotel.

"Inside!" Toscano said tightly to Albini and Colleen. "Now!"

Toscano, Agent Albini, and Colleen quickly moved inside; Toscano slammed the door, locked it. Albini, the shotgun ready, peered out the glass panes in the top of the door. In the dining room Ingrid Richter was still sitting at the table, resigned. The manager stood by, still in his robe, fretting.

"Two of them are going around the back of the hotel," Albini said in Italian.

Colleen caught Toscano's attention.

"It looks like you might need some help," she said.

He nodded in agreement, spoke to Agent Albini who unholstered her pistol, handed it butt first to Colleen.

A black Beretta 92S, similar to a Colt 45, which Colleen saw was already racked and decocked. Ready to fire. Agent Albini preferred expediency over safety.

"You two," Colleen said to Ingrid Richter and the manager in the dining room, "find somewhere safe to hide."

Ingrid was already heading out to the hallway where she appeared to know the layout of the place. She opened a door and took a stairwell down to a basement or a cellar. The manager followed.

Toscano covered the front door of the building, Agent Albini the back. Colleen stayed where she was, midway in the long hallway full of dark paintings.

A grandfather clock ticked.

Out front, Doris shouted, in English: "Last chance to open up." Despite the volume, her voice was calm.

"No one is letting you in," Toscano replied.

"You were warned."

A whistle blew out front, piercing the air.

Men's voices broke by the back of the hotel.

Suddenly, a window in back shattered, followed by another one in the dining room. Two thumps pounded the floor and Colleen saw an oblong object tumbling into the hall from the back door, whitish smoke billowing from its tail.

A cutting stench filled the air as smoke mushroomed.

Tear gas.

Colleen tore into the dining room where another canister was spinning like a top on the floor, shooting blossoms of smoky gas in a spiral. She snatched a cloth napkin from a stack on the counter, set her pistol down while she fastened a makeshift bandana around her face. Her eyes were already smarting and nausea was close behind. Shouts echoed as Colleen's senses started to boom between her ears.

More shouting came from the hallway. She heard Albini's shotgun blast and the chatter of small arms in response.

Colleen ran over, grabbed the dining room canister, and hurled it back out the shattered window. Coughing and spluttering, she dashed back into the big hallway. Men were shouting and smashing the front door with some kind of battering ram. The big old door was heavy but even so rocked on its hinges.

She seized the second canister off the floor, ran to the front door, hurled it through the smashed window. Shots ensued, making her duck. She turned, spun, flinched when she saw Agent Albini on the floor by the back door, faceup, motionless. The shotgun was extended from one hand.

Colleen fired into the back door with the Beretta, using both hands, the Beretta jumping, her hands buzzing as she emptied the gun. A man screamed. She ran over to Agent Albini, crouched down. The woman's neck was bubbling blood from her heart. She'd been hit in the chest too. Her eyes were open, but staring up at nothing. She was in shock. She was dying.

Colleen wrestled the shotgun from Agent Albini's hand, which soon went limp. But the hook was caught around her arm. It sickened Colleen even more as chemicals and smoke hung in the air. Her skin burned and itched.

Spluttering, eyes streaming and stinging, Colleen freed the weapon from Albini's dead hand and whirled back to the front door. The heavy gun, over ten pounds, swayed slightly.

Toscano was manning the front door, which had been loosened from its hinges by the battering ram, firing shots, but having problems with the effects of the tear gas, wiping his eyes with the sleeve of his free hand and coughing violently. Colleen knew Ingrid and the manager, hiding downstairs, wouldn't be safe for long. Especially when Doris's men entered, which seemed imminent.

"Upstairs!" she shouted at Toscano, pointing up the stairwell where they could hopefully escape the gas. Toscano turned, saw Colleen, and, pistol in hand, staggered over to the stairwell, gripping the banister to steady himself.

Colleen heaved open the cellar door.

"They're using tear gas!" she shouted downstairs. "Grab something to cover your faces and follow us upstairs!"

Moments later, Ingrid and the manager appeared, Ingrid holding her jacket over her mouth, the manager a rag over his. Colleen led them to the staircase where Toscano waited, swaying. He fired off a couple of wild shots at the front door, generating more shouts outside.

Colleen leveled the shotgun at the front door and let off a blast, which took out the rest of the glass. An empty shell ejected and pinged off the wall. Outside, men shouted to take cover. Colleen grabbed Toscano's arm, led him upstairs.

"Top floor!" the manager yelled.

It seemed to take forever, but somehow they managed to get themselves to the fourth floor.

"This way!" The manager led them into a grand suite and shut the door. In a bathroom Colleen grabbed a hand towel, soaked it in the sink, tied it around Toscano's mouth and nose. His eyes were bloodshot and streaming tears. Likewise, Colleen's eyes were on fire, her vision smeared with tears. Her entire body itched unbearably.

"We aren't good for much longer," she coughed. "Especially if they fire more tear gas." Ingrid and the manager were lining wet bath towels along the bottom of the door.

"Those . . . reinforcements," Toscano wheezed, sitting on the floor, resting back against a bed, holding his forehead.

And then, relative silence fell over the schloss.

They heard Doris Pender shout from out front. "Come on out or you'll get more gas!" Her voice, even from a distance, sounded muffled.

Colleen and Toscano looked at each other. If they responded in any way, they'd give their position upstairs away.

"We'll wait for reinforcements," Colleen said, going over to the window, peering down at the Citroen and the van. She couldn't see the front door below from where she stood, but two men hovered by the van. Both wore gas masks. *Damn.* They could enter with ease. And there were others, out of sight.

Out front, downstairs, they heard Doris Pender again.

"Last chance!" she yelled.

CHAPTER THIRTY-SEVEN

1979

Down by the front door, Doris Pender stood with the rest of her men, all in green canvas gas masks with round eye holes, Doris included. She had already lost one man, around the back.

"We're going in," she said. "Two of you around the back." Her voice was muted through the mask and she had to speak up.

"Okay . . ." the older one with the pompadour began.

Suddenly his head exploded in front of her, making her jump with shock. The echo of a rifle shot reverberated through the canyon as he tumbled at her feet, his lifeless head smacking the brick steps of the entrance.

She hyperventilated; one lens of her mask splattered with his blood.

The other men spread out, one fleeing for the van.

Another shot cracked and that man plunged into the gravel, his weapon twisted under him. He came to a dead stop.

Heart jumping, Doris wiped her mask with the back of her hand and ran for a hedge along the front of the hotel. Crouching, she drew her pistol, raking her neck out, trying to make sense of things. Her body throbbed with adrenaline.

Another shot. Then another, zinging off the building.

Someone was picking them off.

Jakob Klaus.

She saw her men, brave when it suited them, when the fight was on their side, slink off into the trees and bushes.

Doris squatted, her own fear starting to take hold. But she wasn't about to let it. She just had to regroup her men, snake around the back of the hotel, go in the back way. They had more tear gas. It was too late to turn back. She wanted Ingrid and Jakob both. Ingrid was in the hotel.

And with Ingrid she had Jakob.

And that damned Hayes woman wasn't going to live either.

"Come on!" she bellowed to the men hiding. "Around the back."

*   *   *

"Someone's shooting at them," Colleen said, peering out the fourth-floor window.

Toscano fought himself off the floor, staggered over. "Who?" He looked out. His eyes were red and his cheeks were wet.

"It's Jakob," they heard Ingrid Richter say matter-of-factly.

Colleen and Toscano turned to look at her, sitting calmly in a chair by the fireplace, wiping her eyes.

"He just saved your lives," she said. "Are you sure you still want to arrest him?" A mocking tone in her voice underscored her words.

"Your life, too, don't forget," Colleen said. "You're the reason he's here—and his passport."

Toscano wobbled over to the bathroom where he held onto the doorframe for a moment to steady himself, then went in. He shut the door. They heard him get violently sick to his stomach.

Downstairs, the crashing of the back door by the main hallway echoed.

"They're coming in." Colleen tightened her impromptu mask around her mouth, readied the shotgun, ventured out into the hallway.

Stood at the top of the stairs of this grand old building, off to the side.

She heard voices downstairs. One of them was higher, albeit muffled. Doris Pender.

Let them come up? No, they might fire another one of those tear gas canisters and then it would all be over.

Colleen had to hold them off.

She headed down the stairs quietly, the shotgun ready.

On the second-floor landing, she saw a stag's head on the far wall staring impassively at her. She stepped out, peered down the stairwell. She heard two voices, saw a big man coming up, green gas mask over his face. The bristles of his crew cut protruded around the straps stretching over his skull. He was holding a short black grenade gun in both hands.

More of that damn gas.

A lanky figure lurked behind him on the stairwell. Female. Doris Pender.

Colleen raised the shotgun, pointed it at the big man.

"*Drop it.*" She repeated her command in Spanish, as close to Italian as she could get.

He raised the weapon anyway.

Aiming for his legs, she pulled the trigger, the boom of the shotgun deafening in the stairway. The kick of the gun rocked her back onto her butt on a stair as the man took flight, the blast throwing him back down to the landing. An empty shell pinged off the wall. The man twisted as he landed on the Persian rug, legs splayed. The cream paint of the stairway splattered pink where he had stood a second before.

Colleen heard Doris Pender pounding down the stairs to the ground floor.

Heart thumping, Colleen scrambled to her feet, headed down, the shotgun gripped tightly in her hands. She hoped the gun had been fully loaded when deployed, which would mean she had four or five shots left.

On the landing she saw her gunman still breathing but his legs twisted under him, motionless. She kicked his grenade gun out of the way.

Colleen went over to the gunman, pulled off her towel mask, tried to wrestle the gas mask off his face. Frantic, he tried just as hard to hold onto it.

She raised the shotgun, rammed the butt end into his face, the metal hook brace doing damage she did her best to ignore. Amidst the crunch of nose and screams, he relinquished the mask. She fought the mask off his face, slipped it on her own. It was hot and slimy inside and smelled of his stale breath. One eye was obscured by blood.

He rolled on the landing, clutching at his smashed face. He vomited a splash onto the hardwood floor beyond the runner.

Slowly Colleen headed down to the ground floor, trying to see from one smudged eyepiece.

"It's over, Doris," Colleen shouted, her own voice muted by the mask. She fired the shotgun down the stairwell. The boom was followed by plaster dust and wood splinters flying.

Slowly, slowly, she stepped down.

She got to the hallway.

Partially covered by the back door, now smashed off its hinges, was Doris Pender. Agent Albini's body still lay faceup in front of the door, frozen.

Doris fired her pistol and Colleen ducked back up the stairwell as a shot blew through the hallway. Her heart responded in thick beats.

Shotgun up, Colleen recovered, taking calm breaths. Peeked out. Doris was gone.

She heard another shot—not Doris. A rifle shot, followed by a woman's muted scream.

She headed out back. A man lay dead at the foot of the few stairs up to the door, mouth open to the dark sky. Killed during the first wave, when she was trying to rescue Agent Albini. She recalled a scream.

Further away, Doris Pender was sprawled on the ground, writhing, clutching her hip. Her pants leg glistened with blood. Her gun was gone.

Then she saw, in the faint predawn light, a short man in a heavy wool coat and watch cap approach with a long-scoped rifle in his hands. She knew from the catlike movement that it was Jakob Klaus.

He approached Doris Pender on the ground, rifle by his side.

Doris looked up at him.

He reached down, ripped the mask off her face, tossed it, stood back.

"Your turn to die," he said in a dark voice. He spoke English with a German accent.

"Go to hell, Jew," she seethed. "There are ten more to replace me."

"Then I kill ten more." He raised the rifle in both hands, taking aim at her head.

"Stop right there," Colleen said, bringing up her shotgun.

Startled, Jakob looked at Colleen.

With her free hand, Colleen pulled off her own gas mask, the shotgun fixed on Jakob. Now she could see better, despite the residual tears in her eyes.

"It stops," she said, tossing the mask. She gripped the shotgun in both hands. "It stops now."

Jakob eyed her, the barrel of his rifle still trained on Doris Pender's head.

"Whose side are you on?" he said. "She was going to kill you. And the others."

Colleen recalled killing her husband in a fit of rage, over a decade ago. It had seemed so warranted. Until the very moment it was done.

"Not hers," Colleen said. "And not yours. There are ways to administer justice. This isn't one of them."

Behind her, Colleen heard footsteps, staggering through the hotel lobby.

Toscano appeared, his towel mask around his face, pistol in hand. He took in the proceedings. He raised his gun, pointed it at Jakob Klaus.

"If you don't drop your weapon," he said to Jakob, "then you give me no choice but to shoot."

They stood there for a moment while the wind rushed down the mountain, blowing through the trees.

"My death doesn't bother me," Jakob said. "I died years ago. But her . . ."—he shrugged at Doris— "I can't let the cycle of hate keep renewing."

Colleen's limbs smarted with tension as she held the heavy shotgun on Jakob. Despite what he had just said, he was hesitating.

"There's someone here you should talk to first," Colleen said to Jakob. "She's the reason you're here."

Jakob's eyes narrowed. On the ground, Doris Pender clutched herself, groaning. She was in agony but would live.

Colleen spoke to Toscano. "Go get Signora Richter, please. Hopefully she can put an end to this."

"Yes," Toscano said, relaxing his gun arm. "Yes." He went back into the hotel.

He returned with Ingrid Richter.

She started when she saw the standoff.

"Jakob."

Jakob looked at her with plaintive eyes, the rifle barrel still pointed at Doris Pender, his finger on the trigger. For her own part, Colleen's arms were aching as she kept the shotgun on Jakob.

"You're alive," Jakob said to Ingrid with obvious relief.

"Yes," she said, edging closer. "And you must *not* pull that trigger, Jakob. Not with the police here . . ." She waved a hand at Toscano, who had his pistol up, pointed at Jakob. "It will be a murder charge."

"And what has it been all these years?" he said.

"Justice," she said. "But this, shooting her in cold blood when she is down . . . you won't have a chance."

"She's right, Jakob," Toscano said. "If you stop now, you have a like-lihood for leniency. My partner was shot and killed on Doris Pender's orders. You stopped them. You saved Signora Richter." He let that sink in. "You saved all of us. But it must end now. Drop your weapon and turn yourself in. I will see you get all the clemency that is available."

Jakob frowned, thinking it over.

"There's no death penalty in Italy," Toscano added. "You have a chance for a compassionate sentence. People will understand."

Colleen could see the same tension that was eating at her rivet Jakob's face.

"Under one condition," he said.

"And what is that?" Toscano said.

"Let my aunt go," he said.

Toscano recoiled. "Signora Richter?" He shook his head. "No, I don't think so."

"Do it," Colleen said to Toscano. "You've got her." Colleen nodded at Doris Pender. "You've got a cave full of counterfeit money that puts a Nazi financial crime to rest. And you get Jakob Klaus into the bargain—alive. You get a lot."

"I lost my partner," Toscano said. "Signora Richter is wanted in connection with money laundering."

Colleen replied, "With Jakob Klaus alive, think how many ex-Nazis law enforcement might lay their hands on. But with him dead, the trail grows cold."

She could see Toscano blinking in thought.

Finally, he said, "Very well."

Jakob moved his rifle barrel away from Doris Pender. Then he lay the weapon down on the grass and put his hands up halfway. Doris Pender breathed a sigh of relief.

"It's over," Colleen said to Ingrid Richter.

She gave a sad shake of the head. "No. It will always be 1942. Sachsenhausen."

"Where is Beckmann now?" Colleen said.

"I told you. He died. 1945. In a fire in Rome."

Jakob interrupted. "Then why did Kontrol leave me his ID in the San Francisco drop box?"

"A mole, Jakob. Within Black Cross. Salak. But I found out. Warned you."

"The banknote," Jakob said in realization. "Her half didn't match."

"Precisely," Ingrid said.

"She pretended," Colleen said. "Pretended to be a Nazi. Helping Aryan Alliance. She pretended to be one of them. Just like she did all those years ago—in Barracks 19."

"That's twice you saved me, Auntie," Jakob said in a hollow voice. "Sachsenhausen and San Francisco."

Ingrid Richter had played both sides. All her life, Colleen suspected. Allegiances to this group or that group didn't matter. But survival, and the survival of those close to you, did.

"And now, Jakob," Ingrid said. "It's time to close the book on revenge."

"Why didn't you ever come back for the money?" Colleen said to Ingrid. "In the cave? All those years ago?"

"It was worthless sooner than we thought," Ingrid said. "The Bank of England changed their notes, recalled the old ones. Ours became nothing but collector's items."

"Very well," Toscano said to Ingrid. "You have twenty-four hours to leave Italy before I file my report."

Ingrid gave a nod. She went over to Jakob. "A hug for my adopted nephew? Who knows how long this one will have to last me? I remember sending you off to Paris, a mere boy."

He lowered his arms. "I didn't want to go, Auntie."

"I know," she said. "I know." They met in an embrace.

"One last hug to the woman who saved me," he said.

"You are going to get the best representation possible, Jakob. This isn't over."

"It's never over, Auntie," Jakob said, holding her. "It's never over." Colleen's chest welled with emotion.

In the distance, from the road, they heard vehicles. They approached the front. Doors squealed open. Men leapt out, shouting.

Toscano's reinforcements.

"Better late than never," Toscano said, holstering his pistol under his arm. Then he spoke to Ingrid Richter.

"On your way, Signora Richter," he said, "Quickly now."

Ingrid Richter let Jakob go, stood back at arm's length.

"Yes," she said, then set off, disappearing into the trees behind the hotel, heading to the mountain.

Jakob raised his arms in surrender. "I'm ready," he said.

CHAPTER THIRTY-EIGHT

"Doris Pender is facing some serious charges in Italy," Owens said.

Colleen and Owens were in one of the meeting rooms on the fourth floor of 850 Bryant, wrapping up the details of her trip, Colleen jet-lagged one more time. She could almost say she was getting used to it. She had gone home after landing at SFO, showered, changed into her soft-as-chamois flared jeans and a light blue and white muslin shirt. She sipped from a cardboard cup of coffee out of the vending machine, the kind with a partial poker hand on it. The last card was printed on the bottom. So far she had two pairs: eights and aces. A dead man's hand. One that could go either way.

"Felony homicide," Owens continued. He wore his blue suit, tie knotted up to the collar. "With the murder of an Italian police officer, and the other extenuating circumstances, including organizing a terrorist cell, she won't be going anywhere for years to come. Although the U.S. wants her extradited." Owens tapped his no. 2 pencil on a yellow-lined pad containing several pages of neatly-written notes. Next to the pad was a thick file folder and next to that, the murder book on the case file, which now had a name: Jasia Salak.

"Jakob Klaus awaits trial, too," he said. "Although there will likely be leniency, seeing as he gave himself up."

In exchange for letting his faux auntie leave Italy.

"Who knows how many he's killed over the years," Colleen said. An ex-Nazi priest north of Rome. Members of Terza Posizione in the defense of his aunt—and the rest of them. A former camp guard in Buenos Aires. Jasia Salak.

"After eight years in prison, he'll be eligible to work a day job outside, returning to prison at night."

"Jakob might be a cold-blooded killer, but I still can't help but hope he catches a break," Colleen said, sipping coffee. "His life pretty much started in a concentration camp and another prison is what he gets for trying to even the score. But bottom line, I had it wrong. I thought Ingrid Richter was one of *them*. But she was looking out for her 'nephew,' whom she 'adopted' when she was in a position to do so at Sachsenhausen."

"And Werner Beckmann?" Owens said.

"Werner and Ingrid had a relationship. Which she parlayed into advantages—the biggest one being Jakob. When Beckmann died in a fire, she moved on."

"That explains her standing as an ex-Nazi."

Colleen shook her head. "I think Ingrid Richter is on Ingrid Richter's side. No surprise given her history. She's a survivor. One who wasn't going to let her 'nephew' walk into his own assassination."

"Maybe she shouldn't have gone free."

"She may have helped counterfeit money for the Nazis as a seventeen-year-old to save her life. But along the way she managed to save a number of people destined for the gas chamber."

"Then how did Black Cross screw things up with Beckmann?" Owens said. "Sending out a hit man for a dead man?"

Colleen frowned as she drank terrible coffee. That very thing was still bothering the hell out of her.

"I don't know," she said. "Maybe it was a ruse to lure Jakob Klaus."

Owens tapped his pencil. "I still don't think she's the saint you do."

"I know you don't."

"But this is the end of this case as far as you're concerned." He raised his eyebrows. "You were supposed to observe and report in Italy. And you did more. A *lot* more."

"I would have thought the chief would have been just a little bit pleased," she said. "He got an awful lot out of some free airline miles."

"The chief isn't too displeased—put it like that. But Toscano gets all the glory. The juicy stuff happened on his turf."

"It's amazing what you can get done when you don't care who gets the credit," she said. And then she thought of Agent Albini, Pimpi, who gave her life. In part to protect Colleen. What credit would she get? Who would raise her bambino?

"I'd like to meet him," she said.

"The chief?" Owens shook his head. "Confidential Informants are like women on the side. Kept in the shadows. No one wants to know about them—even if everyone knows they exist."

"I'd love a good word to my parole officer if nothing else," she said. "My lawyer is trying to make my PI license happen."

"An ex-felon? Be honest, Colleen—that's a stretch. If I were you, I'd learn how to type and take shorthand."

"And cook casseroles for some breadwinner? I tried that. It cost me ten years in prison."

"I'll pass your concerns along to the chief."

Owens took a measured breath, looked at her thoughtfully. "Between you and me, you knocked it out of the park, even if no one else knows. Continue to help us. In the meantime, it's back to keeping your nose clean."

"I was actually thinking of spending one more day wrapping up this case," she said.

Owens blinked in exasperation. "Wrapping up what, exactly?"

"That banking conference is still going on at the Fairmont."

He sat up. "Do you really think Ingrid Richter will show her face? Whatever she is, she's lucky to be breathing. Aryan Alliance are bound to be gunning for her."

"I know," she said.

"So leave it at that," Owens said. "That's an order. This is the end of this gig. Go work on one of your divorce cases. They must be backing up. And I hear they actually pay."

"It beats typing and cooking casseroles." Colleen stood up. "Are we done here?"

"For now." Owens scribbled a note on his yellow pad. "Be available to answer any more questions. Don't go to the Fairmont." He eyed her. "Repeat: *Don't go to the Fairmont.*"

She still wasn't satisfied. Why *was* a hit planned on a dead man?

There was a knock on the door.

"Come in," Owens said.

The door opened. There stood Matt Dwight.

"Care to tell me what the hell is going on, Colleen?"

CHAPTER THIRTY-NINE

"Well, Colleen?"

Matt Dwight stood in the doorway of the interrogation room, dressed in his narrow-waisted check blazer, big tie, and big collar. His hair was recently blow-dried. He radiated a scent of freshly applied Brut. He'd just come into work. Other officers and detectives were doing the same, moving along the narrow hallway.

Matt clearly wasn't happy.

"Debriefing Owens," Colleen said.

Matt stuck his head in the door. Owens looked up from his yellow pad, gave Matt an informal salute with his pencil.

"You pleased with yourself?" Matt said to Owens. "Interfering with a federal case?"

Owens stared. "You've still got Dr. Lange. Aryan Alliance. Nothing's changed."

"Not Doris Pender anymore—key to the case. And what did you get out of it? Your dead Jane Doe on Muni solved? Some ex-camp guard? Versus the leader of an up-and-coming neo-Nazi group?"

"*All are equal before the law,*" Owens said.

"Thanks for the civics lesson," Matt said.

"Maybe you need one, Matt," Owens said. "I'm just doing my job. What about you? Lange is still out there."

"I'm not going to forget this."

So it was going to get personal. Colleen stood up, put herself in between Matt and Owens, pulling the door shut behind her on the conference room. "That's enough, Matt."

Matt stood in the hallway, hands on his hips, nostrils flaring. "Why didn't you tell me you were going to Rome?"

"Last time I checked," she said, "you weren't interested."

"No," Matt said. "I think what I said was 'stay away from my case.'"

"*Your* case," she said. "Not SFPD's. Got it."

He shook his head. "You misled me with some story about a road trip with Pam. Do you know how much work I've put into this? Over a year."

"And, like Owens said, nothing changes. If you stop being territorial for one minute, you'll see how much ground has been covered. Jakob Klaus, in jail, awaiting trial. Doris Pender, accomplice to murder of a police officer, same. An Italian neo-Nazi group, *Third Position*, decimated. Anyone else going after Lange might be pleased with the outcome. All for a standby ticket and a couple hundred bucks."

"You CIs," he said. "You do work cheap."

Colleen stared daggers at Matt.

"Fuck you," she said quietly.

She turned, headed for the elevator lobby.

CHAPTER FORTY

1979

International Banking Conference
Today, 9–11 a.m.
Conference Room C
The Pitfalls of International Exchange Rates in a Time of Economic
Uncertainty
Johan Hummel, President, First Trust Bank of Zurich.

The sign in the lobby of the Fairmont was clear enough.

Colleen checked her watch. The lecture had begun about ninety minutes ago.

The company the speaker was from rang a familiar bell—First Trust Bank of Zurich—the same bank Ingrid Richter worked for.

Had Ingrid returned to work? If so, would she have the audacity to come back to the U.S? This conference? Colleen wouldn't put it past her. Yes, Colleen wasn't supposed to be here, but there was nothing like someone calling her cheap to make her less than compliant.

She headed to Conference Room C. A man in a suit stood by the door, hands behind his back, smiling pleasantly.

"Conference pass, ma'am?"

She flashed her beat-up leather ID holder with its genuine Arizona State Chauffeur's badge, remarkably close to what law enforcement carried. It had gotten her through a few doors.

A good hundred conference-goers were sitting in rows of chairs listening to a lecture on exchange rates given by a middle-aged German man with sculpted white hair wearing an expensive suit. Colleen walked around the room, ostensibly looking for a seat, but primarily searching for Ms. Richter. She didn't spot her.

"Ma'am?" another hotel employee whispered, leaning over. "Would you kindly take a seat?"

She didn't want to but she did, at the end of the second row. Maybe there was coffee and pastries at the break. She'd missed breakfast.

"Another interesting pattern we see is the classic inverted yield curve between short-term and long-term rates . . ." the speaker said in a Germanic monotone. He tapped a chart with a pointer.

Colleen kept looking around the room.

And there, by the door, was a familiar face. A big, heavyset man in a beige raincoat, with a flop of black comb-over hanging in his morose, fleshy face. It took her a moment to recognize him. He was out of context.

Nathan. The same sad sack who hung around the Hotel Metro south of Market, where Jakob Klaus had stayed, a veritable economic world away. She had given him seemingly endless twenty-dollar bills to let her into Erich Hahn's—Jakob Klaus's—room. What was he doing here? A fan of international economics? He did have a conference ID hanging around his neck. He was watching the speaker intently. Colleen's nerves tingled.

"Notice how the yen drops dramatically around USD two twenty-four . . ."

Colleen turned to look at the speaker again.

And then she saw him for who he really was.

The same man in the SS ID she had seen in the air vent of Jakob Klaus's hotel room.

SS Sturmbannführer Werner Beckmann.

The shock of seeing him here, now, made Colleen sit up straight.

The years had been relatively kind to Beckmann, adding a corpulence to his jowls and neck, but it was the same man. No doubt.

He'd been right under her nose. Not dead at all. Very much alive. The man Jakob Klaus had come to kill.

And now? Colleen turned in her chair casually and saw Nathan watching the major intently.

And then she got it. Nathan was taking over where Jakob had left off.

Nathan was Black Cross.

Colleen consulted her watch. Ten thirty-five.

Nathan would wait until the conference was over. It was the MO Black Cross seemed to favor: kill the target after the event.

She stood up, exited the conference, found a pay phone in the lobby. Called Owens at work. He wasn't at his desk. She left a message with the duty officer, for Owens to get to the Fairmont, Conference Room C, ASAP.

"Werner Beckmann is the guest speaker," she said. "Under an alias: Johan Hummel. And there's a guy here angling to kill him, I'm sure." She described Nathan. "I'm just not sure when."

Next, she called Matt Dwight. He, likewise, was out. She left the same message.

She went to the front desk, asked for the shift security manager. Nicolas Carr, her contact at the Fairmont, was filling in. He was downstairs in the employee locker room, getting changed for work. Colleen left a note where she'd be, then returned to the conference room, took her seat, watching Nathan watching Werner Beckmann.

Not long after, Nicolas Carr entered the conference room discreetly. He was tall, with neat reddish hair, and freckles. He wore gray polyester slacks and a blue blazer with a white shirt and clip-on tie. Basic low-key security outfit, one step up from movie usher. He saw Colleen, came over, sat next to her. In whispers she explained the situation while he stole glances at Nathan, then the speaker, without giving himself away.

"I'll go check on SFPD," he said. "I'll stay outside for now. I don't want to keep coming and going and alert this guy."

"Good idea."

As he got up to leave, his belt radio crackled. "Unit 1, this is Unit 2."

Damn. He quickly turned the volume down, exited the conference room.

Colleen saw Nathan looking her way. Squinting. Getting suspicious?

At ten to eleven, the speaker, Johan Hummel, stopped to take questions. Neither Owens nor Matt Dwight had shown up.

Nathan left the room. Was he getting ready?

Colleen exited the conference room as well. Nicolas Carr was waiting by the front desk, leaning over, talking to one of the desk clerks, but looking around. Keeping watch.

Colleen approached. "What gives?"

Carr nodded at the elevator. "No SFPD yet. Your buddy Nathan just went upstairs."

"What room is Hummel in?"

"Room 1118. In the tower. Eleventh floor."

"I bet that's where Nathan's headed. He's waiting for Hummel to go to his room, hit him there."

He nodded. "Seems like a distinct possibility. I'll go up, scope it out."

"You guys aren't armed," she said. She wasn't either. "But you can bet Nathan is. And you're in uniform. If he spots you, he might take off." Or even worse. "Let SFPD handle it when they get here."

"Copy that." Carr got on his radio. "Unit 1 to unit 2. 10-19 to the main lobby. ASAP."

"10-4."

The double conference room doors opened and a slew of people filed out, Johan Hummel amongst them, talking to a woman.

A young Filipino guard appeared, moving briskly across the lobby to join Colleen and Carr. His name was Vasquez. Carr explained the situation to him. He checked his watch.

"Still no SFPD," Carr said to Vasquez and Colleen. "I'm going up, see if the 10-66 is hanging out near Hummel's room. You keep Hummel down here."

A 10-66 was a suspicious person.

"Still not a good idea," Colleen said to Carr. She'd seen how Black Cross reacted to threats. Jakob Klaus and Jasia Salak on SF Muni came to mind. "Give me one of your radios. I'll go up, report back. One of you keep Hummel busy down here, the other wait outside for SFPD."

"But doesn't this Nathan character know who you are?" Carr said.

"He saw me once, a while back. He's not expecting me. I'm good. Better than you guys in your uniforms." Even so she pulled her light sunglasses from her coat, slipped them on, pulled her hair back and fastened it with a spare hair band she carried.

Carr was looking tense. Most security personnel were invisible and the job was 99 percent tedium broken up by 1 percent pure adrenaline. Every guard knew the possibility of such every start of every shift. Meanwhile they had to stay cool and fade into the wallpaper, frequently without a weapon. This could easily become a 1 percent situation.

"It might be overkill," Colleen said. "But we don't want Hummel to bolt either. He's been hiding for thirty-seven years."

Carr went to the desk, got the replacement radio—unit 3—gave it to Colleen. He instructed Vasquez to go outside and wait for SFPD. Colleen headed over to the elevators, holding the bulky black radio down by her side as Carr approached Johan Hummel, spoke to him quietly, giving him some BS to keep him in place. Hummel was listening intently.

Colleen got in an elevator, hit 11. There were several other conference-goers and half the floor buttons were also lit. Crap.

Finally, she got off on 11. Checked the floor, both ways. Empty. She headed down to 1118. The floor was deserted.

She got on the radio. "Unit 1—this is unit 3. It's looking like a false alarm."

A moment later, Carr responded. "10-4."

She sauntered by room 1118.

Something told her the room wasn't empty.

She went a few doors down, pulled a fire extinguisher from the wall sconce, set the radio down, readied the extinguisher.

Went back to 1118.

Knocked.

"Housekeeping," she said in a Spanish accent, to mask her voice in case Nathan was in there, recognized her voice. The fire extinguisher was heavy in her hands.

"No need," a man's voice said. "Thank you."

She knew that somber voice. It *was* Nathan.

She couldn't let him get away. Black Cross had to be stopped. Beckmann had to pay for his crimes.

She went back down the hall a couple of doors, retrieved her radio.

"Units 1 and 2. 10-66 in 1118. It's who we thought."

There was a pause.

"10-4," Carr said. "Unit 2: 10-19 to 1118. Unit 3, stand by."

"10-4," Vasquez said.

She clicked off.

Breathing evenly to steady her nerves, she set her radio down, headed back to 1118, gripping her extinguisher.

Her better judgement told her to go wait by the elevator. The guards would show.

Unarmed.

SFPD would show.

Eventually.

Better judgement didn't always win over.

She knocked.

"Housekeeping," she said again.

"It's not necessary!" Nathan snapped.

"I need to tally and stock the minibar, sir."

"Just go away!"

Heart pounding, she tried the door. Locked.

She knocked on the door one more time. "I'm going to have to let myself in, sir."

"Go away!"

"I'm just doing my job, sir! There's no need to be rude! I'm coming in!" She rattled the door handle, stood to one side of the door, flattening herself against the wall, out of view from anyone opening the door. She held the fire extinguisher up, unhooked the nozzle, ready. She pulled the pin.

A moment later, the door opened. There was a pause before Nathan stuck his head out, obviously wondering what the hell was going on.

He turned her way and she blasted him in the face, giving him the full load. Clouds of white foam made him look like he was melting.

He stumbled out into the hallway, bringing a gun up and she swooped in and cracked him across the skull with the base of the empty extinguisher. He went down, gripping his head, dropping the gun. It bounced across the hallway floor. Within seconds it was in her hand. Slippery. But hers.

She recognized it. A Hungarian FEG. She had seen it in Jakob's air vent.

Down the hall she heard the elevator doors ding and the two security guards charging out, their feet thumping, pounding down the hall toward her.

Carr landed on Nathan as he struggled to get up, pinning him down. Vasquez followed suit.

EPILOGUE

"It seems Ingrid was one of them, after all," Professor Fisher said, sitting in the Depot at SF State, a pile of term papers stacked on the small table in front of him. "An ex-Nazi." The college bar was uncharacteristically quiet in between classes. The music on the radio was sedate as if in harmony: "Time Passages" by Al Stewart.

"I'm not so sure," Colleen said, sipping a cappuccino, nothing like the ones you could get at the La Tazza café in Rome. One day, she'd go back. For pleasure.

But she couldn't deny that after all these years, the myth of Werner Beckmann dying in a Rome hotel fire in 1945 had been just that—a myth.

One Ingrid Richter had perpetuated.

"I'm still leaning towards the good guys," Colleen said.

"You still subscribe to that concept?" Professor Fisher said with a shake of the head. He pushed his glasses back up into place.

Colleen set her cup down on its saucer. "Ingrid played along with the Nazis out of self-preservation and later with the neo-Nazis to protect Jakob. But when push came to shove, she opted for working with Black Cross, saving her 'nephew.'"

"While she covered for Werner Beckmann. She ended up working with him long after she had to, at First Trust Bank of Zurich. Hiding his identity all these years. What does that make her?"

"Call it 'love,'" Colleen said. "Or a reasonable facsimile thereof. Her fortune had been rendered worthless. He was her boss."

It wasn't the most outlandish thing to happen. Ultimately Ingrid wasn't going to let her nephew be killed. Or Beckmann, Colleen had to admit. But who knew what kind of hold he had on her?

"I'm not sure I can classify it," she said.

"Well, I can."

"Beckmann was not your textbook Nazi. When he 'died,' more than a few of his former prisoners testified to his leniency."

Fisher gave her a sardonic look. "And Adolf Hitler loved dogs. It doesn't make him any less than what he was—a monster. Despite what his 'Jews' might have said about him, Beckmann helped the Nazis achieve their goals by financing their evil and perpetuating their reign of terror. As did Ingrid. He ran, faked his death rather than answer to his crimes. Crimes which will now land him in prison for the rest of his life—and rightfully so. And Ingrid covered for him until her 'nephew' found out where Beckmann was. Almost four decades later."

Colleen wasn't going to get anywhere with this argument. She was still wrestling with the impression of a woman she had met, who had navigated from seventeen-year-old concentration camp inmate to pariah. To a man with Professor Fisher's history and background, who had lost his family to the horrors of the Holocaust, there would never be anything redeemable about Ingrid Richter, no matter her reasons, or the fact that she'd saved a few destined for the gas chamber. But Colleen's world wasn't his. Or Ingrid's. She would never truly understand what Fisher, and millions, had gone through.

In the end, Ingrid Richter had protected both men.

Colleen stood up.

"Well," she said. "I just wanted to thank you in person. We never could have gotten to the bottom of this without your help."

"'*The truth will make you free*,'" Fisher said, standing himself. "And you're far too modest. It was much more 'you' than 'we.'"

They shook and said their goodbyes. Colleen headed upstairs, leaving the student union, walking across the foggy campus. Universities felt foreign to her, intimidating, and she was a little bit envious of the students chatting comfortably as laughter drifted across the green grass. Her education had been an associate's degree earned while in prison. She owed it to herself to continue.

But she still couldn't shake the feeling that Ingrid was an uncertainty.

*   *   *

A few days later, midmorning, the phone rang in her office on Pier 26. It was Owens.

"Peninsula Bank and Security," he said.

"Erich Hahn's safe deposit box," Colleen said, recalling the letter that had been opened in Jakob's flop hotel.

"Several names are on the list of approved users," Owens said. "Angelica Czarny included."

"Jasia Salak's alter ego," Colleen said. "Muni Jane Doe. The mole within Black Cross."

"Not to mention Natan Nowak."

"Who would be Nathan," she said. The man she'd stopped from shooting Beckmann.

"Turns out he's Polish, too. We found the safe deposit box key on him when we arrested him. The safe deposit box is essentially a drop-off messaging point for Black Cross. It's how they communicate their hits."

"Command central," she said. "Keeping the cells separated. So you've spoken to Peninsula Bank and Security?"

"Not with their immediate consent. But a search warrant changed their minds."

Colleen sat up. "You finally got a search warrant for the safe deposit box?"

"After we arrested Natan Nowak and brought Beckmann in, the judge decided we could look for information pertinent to Black Cross. With the developments in Italy, we were able to make a case for another possible hit. It seems Johan Hummel—aka Werner Beckmann—is wanted in connection with international money laundering charges."

The case that Toscano was originally working.

"Then you know what my next question is," Colleen said.

"Since you're the one who covered Natan Nowak head to toe in fire retardant foam and brought him down, and solved the Jakob Klaus case, it only seems fair you should get to see the safe deposit box opened," Owens said. "But you have to get to Peninsula Bank in the next ten minutes."

"I'm there," she said, standing up, hanging up the phone. She had her black leather coat on and office door locked in less than thirty seconds.

Peninsula Bank and Security was a brisk walk from the Embarcadero. More like a sprint. But that was fine. The sun was fighting to get through the low summer fog that wasn't going to lift today.

She found Owens at the corner of Market and Montgomery, the financial district. He was waiting for her outside the bank in a gray sports coat and black slacks.

The bank officers met them with grimaces when Owens presented the search warrant.

In a small room lined with safe deposit boxes, the financial officer pulled the box noted on the warrant: 1781.

He set it on a plain oak table, stood by.

"I can take it from here," Owens said to him.

"With a warrant," the bank officer said, "we need to be here, too."

"Suit yourself," Owens said. He turned to Colleen, still flushed from her jog. Handed her a small key. "Would you care to do the honors, madam?"

She stood over the safe deposit box. Inserted the key.

Opened the latch.

The box wasn't empty.

Inside was another pistol with the serial numbers filed off.

Owens had an evidence bag ready.

"Looks like they were setting up their next hit," he said, slipping on plastic gloves. He picked up the pistol by the heel, dropped it into the evidence bag.

Colleen saw a slip of yellowed paper in the bottom of the safe deposit box.

She picked it up. The paper was old, cracked. Something was stapled to it. She flipped it over.

Häftlings-Personal-Karte.

Prisoner papers.

Sachsenhausen. 1942.

Attached was a faded black-and-white mug shot of a seventeen-year-old woman. Her head shaved. Looking terrified. A number below her face.

But underneath the fear, a look of resolve. A survivor.

Ingrid Richter.

A shock wave rolled through Colleen.

"She was next," Owens said in disbelief. "Ingrid Richter was next on their list."

Colleen couldn't quite believe it either.

But then she could.

"Looks like you might have just saved her life," Owens said.

When Colleen thought about it, saving Ingrid didn't bother her at all. Wherever she might be. Whoever might be hunting her.

Because there was a line. A line of darkness, where the truth blurred. Some crossed that line willingly. Others had little choice. Those were the ones who never returned. They remained on the other side, lost in shadow.

HISTORICAL NOTE

Although *Line of Darkness* is a work of fiction, the WWII plot is rooted in history. Barracks 19 did indeed exist at Sachsenhausen concentration camp and Operation Bernhard was a reality, a top-secret project in which the Nazis forged millions of pounds' worth of British currency in the hope of destroying the British economy. The plan never came to fruition, but much of the counterfeit cash was used for myriad purposes by the Nazis. Major Bernhard Krüger, who ran Operation Bernhard (named after him), was known for his leniency with his "Jews" and was ultimately pardoned after the war. Ironically, he then went to work for the same paper company that produced the bond used for the operation's currency, so good it fooled Swiss banks. At its peak, Operation Bernhard "employed" a hundred and forty prisoners from all over the Reich's concentration camps and prisons, experts Major Krüger handpicked for their respective talents in counterfeiting, printing, engraving, and such. There were no women, however. The prisoners, by sheer luck, managed to escape execution when the clandestine project was quickly shut down toward the end of the war. More than a few testified on Major Krüger's behalf during his trial.

A fascinating book for the reader who wants to know more is *The Devil's Workshop: A Memoir of the Nazi Counterfeiting Operation* by Adolf Burger, the lead forger on the project, a man who lived well into his nineties near Berlin.

ACKNOWLEDGMENTS
AND THANKS

Thanks, as always, are due my stalwart writing group. They are, in no particular order: Barbara McHugh, Dot Edwards, Heather King, Eric Seder, and Jan Gurley, all talented writers whose patient and insightful feedback is invaluable in shaking out my drafts. Where would I be without you?

Thanks as well to Graham Cowley, former investigator with the SF Medical Examiner's Office, for insight into how the job was done back when Colleen was doing her thing, and to Adam Chin, filmmaker, whose documentary *Graham's Tales* details much of what that era was like.

But most of all, thank you, dear reader, for reading *Line of Darkness*. It was a pleasure to write and I hope you enjoyed it. You are the reason I do this.

Max Tomlinson
maxtomlinson.wordpress.com

PUBLISHER'S NOTE

We hope that you enjoyed *Line of Darkness*, the fourth in Max Tomlinson's Colleen Hayes Mystery Series.

While the other three novels stand on their own and can be read in any order, the publication sequence is as follows:

VANISHING IN THE HAIGHT

It's 1978 and Colleen Hayes sets off to solve the decade-old murder of a wealthy man's daughter. She is an ex-con, recently out of prison after nine years for killing her abusive husband, now trying to make ends meet as an unofficial PI. She has little to go on in this case, but fearlessly searches the underbelly of San Francisco for a link to that brutal murder of a young woman ten years ago at Golden Gate Park.

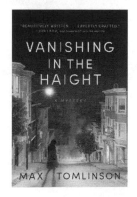

"*Vanishing in the Haight* makes for a classic detective tale: a postmodern noir featuring period perfect San Francisco settings that wondrously carve a slice out of time. Max Tomlinson's new series launch takes us into the waning days of the counter culture where private eye Colleen Hayes picks up the trail of a decade-old murder."

—Jon Land, *USA Today* best-selling author

TIE DIE

Colleen Hayes is hired by a 1960s rock star to find his kidnapped teenaged daughter. This search takes her to 1970s London, where she discovers a thread that traces to the death of a forgotten fan, connected not only to a music industry rife with corruption and crime, but to the missing teen.

"Tomlinson deepens the character of his multi-layered lead, Colleen Hayes, an unlicensed PI and ex-con who's still on parole. Readers will want to learn more about this surprising and pragmatic woman."

—*Publishers Weekly* (Starred Review)

BAD SCENE

San Francisco, 1978. While investigating a suspected plot to kill the mayor, PI and ex-con Colleen Hayes learns that her runaway daughter has joined a shadowy church. The cult is now building a settlement in South America near a volcano about to erupt. Death is the path to perfection—and the day is fast approaching for her daughter and hundreds of others.

"The fast-paced action, colorful setting, and realistic mother-daughter dynamic help make this entry a winner. Readers will look forward to Colleen's further exploits."

—*Publishers Weekly*

We hope that you will read the entire Colleen Hayes Mystery Series and will look forward to more to come.

For more information, please visit the author's website: maxtomlinson.wordpress.com.

Happy Reading,
Oceanview Publishing